Pride and
Pleasure

Also by Sylvia Day

Pride and Pleasure

SYLVIA DAY

KENSINGTON PUBLISHING CORP.
http://www.kensingtonbooks.com

KENSINGTON BOOKS are published by

Kensington Publishing Corp.
119 West 40th Street
New York, NY 10018

All Kensington Titles, Imprints, and Distributed Lines are available at special quantity discounts for bulk purchases for sales promotions, premiums, fund-raising, and educational or institutional use. Special book excerpts or customized printings can also be created to fit specific needs. For details, write or phone the office of the Kensington special sales manager: Kensington Publishing Corp., 119 West 40th Street, New York, NY 10018, attn: Special Sales Department, Phone: 1-800-221-2647.

KENSINGTON and the K logo are Reg. U.S. Pat. & TM Off.

ISBN-13: 978-0-7582-3173-4
ISBN-10: 0-7582-3173-3
First Kensington Trade Edition: May 2013
First Kensington Mass Market Edition: August 2014

eISBN-13: 978-0-7582-9065-6
eISBN-10: 0-7582-9065-9
Kensington Electronic Edition: August 2014

10 9 8 7 6 5 4 3 2 1

Printed in the United States of America

This one is for Kate Duffy, friend and mentor, for her countless contributions to my writing, career, and general well-being. She was incomparable. I miss her fiercely.

ACKNOWLEDGMENTS

Huge thanks to my editor, Alicia Condon. Her edits to this book were invaluable, and her willingness to learn/work with my process is deeply appreciated.

There aren't words to describe my appreciation for my agent extraordinaire, Robin Rue. If I listed all the ways she facilitated the writing of this book, it would fill as many pages as the story. Suffice it to say—she rocks!

I owe a huge debt of gratitude to cover goddess Kristine Mills-Noble, who knocked it out of the park with the cover for this book. She's been giving me great covers for years, but this one is definitely my favorite so far.

Hugs to my BFFs Karin Tabke and Shayla Black, who know how close this book came to killing me. Their support kept me going when I didn't think I could take another step.

And major love to all the readers who waited a few years for me to release another historical. I hope you love Jasper and Eliza's story.

Chapter 1

As a thief-taker, Jasper Bond had been consulted in a number of unusual locations, but today was the first in a church. Some of his clients were at home in the rookeries his crew haunted. Others were most comfortable in the palace. This particular prospective client appeared to be one of strong faith since he'd designated St. George's as the location of their assignation. Jasper suspected it was considered a "safe" place, which told him this person was ill at ease with retaining an individual of dubious morality. That suited him fine. He would probably be paid well and kept at a distance: his favorite sort of commission.

Alighting from his carriage, Jasper paused to better appreciate the impressive portico and Corinthian columns of the church's façade. Muted singing flowed outward from the building, a lovely contrast to the frustrated shouts of coachmen and the clatter of horses' hooves behind him. His cane hit the street with a thud, his gloved palm wrapped loosely around the eagle's-head top. With hat in hand, he waved his driver away.

Today's appointment had been arranged by Mr. Thomas Lynd, a man who shared Jasper's trade and confidence for many reasons, not the least of which was his mentorship of Jasper in the profession. Jasper would never presume to call himself a moral man, but he did function under the code of ethics Lynd had taught him—help those in actual need of it. He did not extort protection money as other thief-takers did. He did not steal goods with one hand in order to charge for their return with the other. He simply found what was lost and protected those who wanted security, which begged the question of why Lynd was passing on this post. With such similar principles, either of them should have been as good as the other.

Because Jasper had an inordinate fondness for puzzles and mysteries, he was too intrigued by Lynd's motives to do anything besides follow through. This, despite the location being one that necessitated his handling the inquiry personally, which was something he rarely did. He preferred to work through trusted employees to retain the anonymity necessary to his greater personal plans.

Mounting the steps, he entered St. George's and paused to absorb the wave of music that rolled over him. Near the front on the right side was the raised canopied pulpit; on the left, the bi-level reading desk. The many box pews were empty of the faithful. Only the choir occupied the space, their voices raised in musical praise.

Jasper withdrew his pocket watch and checked the time. It was directly on the hour. In his profession, he found it highly useful to be a slave to punctuality. He moved to the stairs that would take him up to the right-side gallery for his appointment.

When he reached the landing, he paused. His gaze was drawn to and held by wild tufts of white hair defying gravity. One hopelessly overworked black ribbon failed to tame the mass into anything but a messy, lopsided queue. As he watched, the unfortunate owner of the horrendous coiffure reached up and scratched it into further disarray.

So fascinated was Jasper with the monstrosity of that hair, it took him a moment to register the petite form beside its owner. Once he did, however, his interest was snared. In complete opposition to her companion, the woman was blessed with glossy tresses of a reddish-blond hue so rare it was arresting. They were the only two people in the gallery, yet neither had the tense expectation inherent in those who were awaiting an individual or event. Instead they were singularly focused on the choir below.

Where was the individual he was scheduled to meet?

Sensing she was the object of perusal, the woman turned her head and met Jasper's weighted gaze. She was attractive. Not in the exceptionally remarkable way of her hair but pleasing all the same. Deep blue eyes stared at him from beneath thick lashes. She had an assertive nose and high cheekbones. When she bit her lower lip, she displayed neat white teeth, and when her lips pursed, she revealed a tiny dimple. It was a charming face rather than beautiful, and notable for her seeming displeasure at the sight of him.

"Mr. Bond," she said, after a slight delay. "I did not hear you approach."

One could blame the choir's singing for that. However, the truth of it was that he walked silently. He'd learned the skill long ago. It had saved his life then and continued to do so in recent years.

Standing, she moved toward him with a determined stride and thrust out her hand. As if cued, the singers below ended their hymn, leaving a sudden silence into which she said, "I am Eliza Martin."

Her voice surprised him. Soft as a summer breeze, but threaded with steel. The sound of it lingered, stirring his imagination to travel in directions it shouldn't.

He shifted his cane to his other hand and accepted her greeting. "Miss Martin."

"I appreciate your courtesy in meeting with me. However, you are exactly what I feared you would be."

"Oh?" Taken aback by her direct approach, he found himself becoming more intrigued. "In what way?"

"In every way, sir. I contacted Mr. Lynd because we require a certain type of individual. I regret the need to say you are not he."

"Would you object to my request for elaboration?"

"The points are too numerous," she pronounced.

"Nevertheless, a man in my position seeks predictability in others but fears it in himself. Since you state I am the epitome of what you did *not* want, I feel I must request an accounting of the criteria upon which you based your judgment."

Miss Martin seemed to ponder his response for a moment. In the brief time of introspection, Jasper collected what his instincts had recognized upon first sight: Eliza Martin was intensely aware of him. Without her cognizance, her baser senses were reacting to him much the way his were to her: her delicate nostrils flared, her breathing quickened, her body swayed with the undercurrent of agitation . . . a doe sensing the hunter nearby.

"Yes," she said, with a catch in her voice. "I can see why that would be true."

"Of course it's true. I never lie to clients." He never bedded them either, but that was about to change.

"You have not been engaged," she reminded, "so I am not a client."

The man with the frightening hair intruded. "Eliza, marry Montague and be done with this farce."

With the voicing of that one name, Jasper knew why he'd received the referral and how little chance Eliza Martin had of dismissing him.

"I will not be bullied, my lord," she said firmly.

"Invite Mr. Bond to sit, then."

"That won't be necessary."

Skirting her, Jasper settled into the pew behind the one they occupied.

"Mr. Bond . . ." Miss Martin gave a resigned exhalation. "My lord, may I present Mr. Jasper Bond? Mr. Bond, this is my uncle, the Earl of Melville."

"Lord Melville." Jasper greeted the earl with a slight bow of his head. He knew of Melville as the head of the Tremaine family, a lot renowned for their eccentricities. "I believe you will find me to be highly suitable for any task in want of a thief-taker to manage it."

Miss Martin's blue eyes narrowed on him in silent reproach for attempting to circumvent her. "Sir, I am certain you are capable in most circumstances. However—"

"About the many points . . . ?" he interjected, circling back. He disliked proceeding when there were still matters left unaddressed.

"You are overly tenacious." She remained standing, as if prepared to show him out.

"An excellent trait to have in my profession."

"Yes, but that doesn't mitigate the rest."

"What rest?"

The earl's gaze darted back and forth between them.

She shook her head. "Can we not simply leave it at that, Mr. Bond?"

"I would rather we didn't." He set his hat on the seat beside him. "I have always taken pride in my ability to manage any situation put before me. How will I provide exemplary service if I can no longer make that claim?"

"Really, sir," Miss Martin protested. "I did not say you are unsuitable for your trade as a whole, only in regards to our situation—"

"Which is . . . ?"

"A matter of some delicacy."

"I cannot assist you if I am ignorant of the details," he pointed out.

"I do not want your assistance, Mr. Bond. You fail to collect that."

"Because you refuse to explain yourself. Mr. Lynd thought I was suitable and you trusted his judgment enough to arrange this meeting." Jasper would pay Lynd handsomely for the referral. It had been far too long since he'd felt this level of interest in anything beyond his need for vengeance.

"Mr. Lynd does not have the same considerations I do."

"Which are . . . ?"

"Sir, you are exasperating."

And she was fascinating. Her eyes sparkled with irritation, her right foot tapped against the floor, and her fisted hands moved often as if to rest on her hips. But she resisted the urge. He found her resistance most appealing. What would it take to break it and see her unrestrained? He couldn't wait to find out.

"I will compensate you for your time today," she said, "so all is not a complete loss to you. There is no need to continue this discussion."

"You overlook the possibility that I might have intended to assign a member of my crew to you, Miss Martin. I would, however, need to know what your situation is so I can determine whose skills would best suit your requirements." He intended to service her himself, but he wasn't above a little subterfuge when the prize was this delicious.

"Oh." She bit her lower lip again. "I hadn't considered that."

"So I noted."

Miss Martin finally sank back onto the pew in a movement of eminent grace. "Just so we are clear you won't do."

"It isn't clear." He set his cane between his legs and placed his hands atop it, one over the other. "At least, not to me."

She glanced at his lordship, then—reluctantly—back to Jasper. "You force me to say what I would rather not, Mr. Bond. Frankly, you are too handsome for the task."

He was stunned into momentary silence. Then, he relished an inner smile. How delightful she was, even when cross.

"Mr. Lynd was less conspicuous than you," she continued. "You are quite large and, as I said, far too comely."

Lynd was a score of years older and average in height, features, and build. Jasper looked to the earl and found the man staring at his niece with confusion. "I fail to see what bearing my face has on my investigative skills."

"In addition—" her voice grew stronger as she warmed to the topic of his faults, "—it would be impossible to disguise the air about you which distinguishes you."

"Pray tell me what that is." He was beginning to find it difficult to hide his growing enjoyment of the conversation.

"You are a predator, Mr. Bond. You have the appearance of one, and you carry yourself like one.

To be blunt, you are clearly capable of being a dangerous man."

"I see." Fascination deepened into captivation. Perhaps she wasn't so innocent, after all. He spent obscene amounts of coin on his attire, deliberately crafting an appearance so polished very few saw past it to the rough edges underneath.

"I doubt you would be effective at your profession if you were not possessed of both predatory and dangerous qualities," she qualified in a conciliatory tone.

"And many others," he offered.

Miss Martin nodded. "Yes, I suspect the trade requires you to be well versed in a multitude of skills."

"It certainly helps."

"However, your masculine beauty negates all of that."

Jasper was ready to move forward. "Would you get to the point, Miss Martin? What—exactly—did you intend to hire me to accomplish?"

"Quite a bit, actually. Protection, investigation, and . . . to act as my suitor."

"I beg your pardon?" Bond's voice rumbled through the air between them.

Eliza was flustered and out of sorts, and her state was entirely his fault. She had not anticipated that he would be so persistent or so curious. And she had certainly not expected a man of his appearance. Not only was he the handsomest man she had ever seen, but he was dressed in garments fit for a peer and he carried his large frame with a sleek, predaceous grace.

He also regarded her in a manner that would only lead to trouble.

To receive such an examination from a man who looked like Jasper Bond was highly disconcerting. Men such as he usually dismissed women of average appearance the moment they saw them. That was why she took such pains to be as unobtrusive in her attire selections as possible. Why encourage responses she was ill-equipped to deal with?

Perhaps his interest was engaged by the color of her hair? Her mother had posited that some men had a peculiar preference for specific parts of the female body and for tresses of a certain hue.

"Repeat yourself, please, Miss Martin," Bond said, watching her with those dark and intense eyes.

It was her curse to feel compelled to gaze directly at the person with whom she was speaking. She found it difficult to think quickly when awed by Jasper Bond's perfection. Stunning as he was from the shoulders down, he was more so from the shoulders up. His hair was as thick and dark as her favorite ink, and blessed with a similar sheen. The length—slightly overlong—was perfect for framing his features: the distinguished nose, the deep-set eyes, the stern yet sensual mouth. It was a testament to the way he carried himself that he could be so formidable with such a pretty face. He was very clearly not a man one wished to cross.

"I need protection—" she said again.

"Yes."

"Investigation—"

"I heard that part."

"And—" her chin went up, "—a suitor."

He nodded as if that were a mundane request, but the glitter in his eyes was anticipatory. "That's what I thought you said."

"Eliza . . ." The earl stared at his clasped hands and shook his head.

"My lord," Bond began in a casual tone. "Were you aware of the nature of Miss Martin's inquiry?"

"Trying times these are," Lord Melville muttered. "Trying times."

Bond's precise gaze moved back to Eliza. Her brow lifted.

"Is he daft?" Bond queried.

"His brain is so advanced, it stumbles over mediocrity."

"Or perhaps it's tangled by your reasoning in this endeavor?"

Her shoulders went back. "My reasoning is sound. And sarcasm is unproductive, Mr. Bond. Please refrain from it."

"Oh?" His tone took on a dangerous quality. "And what is it you hope to produce by procuring a suitor?"

"I am not in want of stud service, sir. Only a depraved mind would leap to that conclusion."

"Stud service . . ."

"Is that not what you are thinking?"

A wicked smile came to his lips. Eliza was certain her heart skipped a beat at the sight of it. "It wasn't, no."

Wanting to conclude this meeting as swiftly as possible, she rushed forward. "Do you have someone who can assist me or not?"

Bond snorted softly, but the derisive sound seemed to be directed inward and not at her. "From the beginning, if you would please, Miss Martin. Why do you need protection?"

"I have recently found myself to be a repeated victim of various unfortunate—and suspicious— events."

Eliza expected him to laugh or perhaps give her a doubtful look. He did neither. Instead, she watched a transformation sweep over him. As fiercely focused as he'd been since his arrival, he became more so when presented with the problem. She found herself appreciating him for more than his good looks.

He leaned slightly forward. "What manner of events?"

"I was pushed into the Serpentine. My saddle was tampered with. A snake was loosed in my bedroom—"

"I understand it was a Runner who referred you to Mr. Lynd, who in turn referred you to me."

"Yes. I hired a Runner for a month, but Mr. Bell discovered nothing. No attacks occurred while he was engaged."

"Who would want to injure you, and why?"

She offered him a slight smile, a small show of gratitude for the gravity he was displaying. Anthony Bell had come highly recommended, but he'd never taken her seriously. In fact, he had been amused by her tales and she'd never felt he was dedicated to the task of discovery. "Truthfully,

I am not certain whether they intend bodily harm, or if they simply want to goad me into marriage as a way to establish some permanent security. I see no reason to any of it."

"Are you wealthy, Miss Martin? Or certain to be?"

"Yes. Which is why I doubt they sincerely aim to cause me grievous injury—I am worth more alive. But there are some who believe it isn't safe for me in my uncle's household. They claim he is an insufficient guardian, that he is touched and ready for Bedlam. As if any individual capable of compassion would put a stray dog in such a place, let alone a beloved relative."

"Poppycock," the earl scoffed. "I am fit as a fiddle, in mind and body."

"You are, my lord," Eliza agreed, smiling fondly at him. "I have made it clear to all and sundry that Lord Melville will likely live to be one hundred years of age."

"And you hope that adding me to your stable of suitors will accomplish what, precisely?" Bond asked. "Deter the culprit?"

"I hope that by adding *one of your associates,*" she corrected, "I can avoid further incidents over the next six weeks of the Season. In addition, if my new suitor is perceived to be a threat, perhaps the scoundrel will turn his malicious attentions toward him. Then, perhaps, we can catch the fiend. Truly, I should like to know by what methods of deduction he formulated this plan and what he hoped to gain by it."

Bond settled back into his seat and appeared deep in thought.

"I would never suggest such a hazardous role for someone untrained," she said quickly. "But a thief-taker, a man accustomed to associating with criminals and other unfortunates . . . I should think those who engage in your profession would be more than a match for a nefarious fortune hunter."

"I see."

Beside her, her uncle murmured to himself, working out puzzles and equations in his mind. Like herself, he was most comfortable with events and reactions that could be quantified or predicted with some surety. Dealing with issues defying reason was too taxing.

"What type of individual would you consider ideal to play this role of suitor, protector, and investigator?" Bond asked finally.

"He should be quiet, even-tempered, and a proficient dancer."

Scowling, he queried, "How do dullness and the ability to dance signify in catching a possible murderer?"

"I did not say 'dull,' Mr. Bond. Kindly do not attribute words to me that I have not spoken. In order to be acknowledged as a true rival for my attentions, he should be someone whom everyone will believe I would be attracted to."

"You are not attracted to handsome men?"

"Mr. Bond, I dislike being rude. However, you leave me no recourse. The fact is, you clearly are not the sort of man whose temperament is compatible with matrimony."

"I am quite relieved to hear a female recognize that," he drawled.

"How could anyone doubt it?" She made a sweeping gesture with her hand. "I can more easily picture you in a swordfight or fisticuffs than I can see you enjoying an afternoon of croquet, after-dinner chess, or a quiet evening at home with family and friends. I am an intellectual, sir. And while I don't mean to imply a lack of mental acuity, you are obviously built for more physically strenuous pursuits."

"I see."

"Why, one has only to look at you to ascertain you aren't like the others at all! It would be evident straightaway that I would never consider a man such as you with even remote seriousness. It is quite obvious you and I do not suit in the most fundamental of ways, and everyone knows I am too observant to fail to see that. Quite frankly, sir, you are not my type of male."

The look he gave her was wry but without the smugness that would have made it irritating. He conveyed solid self-confidence free of conceit. She was dismayed to find herself strongly attracted to the quality.

He would be troublesome. Eliza did not like trouble overmuch.

He glanced at the earl. "Please forgive me, my lord, but I must speak bluntly in regard to this subject. Most especially because this is a matter concerning Miss Martin's physical well-being."

"Quite right," Melville agreed. "Straight to the point, I always say. Time is too precious to waste on inanities."

"Agreed." Bond's gaze returned to Eliza and he

smiled. "Miss Martin, forgive me, but I must point out that your inexperience is limiting your understanding of the situation."

"Inexperience with what?"

"Men. More precisely, fortune-hunting men."

"I would have you know," she retorted, "that over the course of six Seasons I have had more than enough experience with gentlemen in want of funds."

"Then why," he drawled, "are you unaware that they are successful for reasons far removed from social suitability?"

Eliza blinked. "I beg your pardon?"

"Women do not marry fortune hunters because they can dance and sit quietly. They marry them for their appearance and physical prowess—two attributes you have already established I have."

"I do not see—"

"Evidently, you do not, so I shall explain." His smile continued to grow. "Fortune hunters who flourish do not strive to satisfy a woman's intellectual needs. Those can be met through friends and acquaintances. They do not seek to provide the type of companionship one enjoys in social settings or with a game table between them. Again, there are others who can do so."

"Mr. Bond—"

"No, they strive to satisfy in the only position that is theirs alone, a position some men make no effort to excel in. So rare is this particular skill that many a woman will disregard other considerations in favor of it."

"Please, say no—"

"Fornication," his lordship muttered, before returning to his conversation with himself.

Eliza shot to her feet. "My lord!"

As courtesy dictated, both her uncle and Mr. Bond rose along with her.

"I prefer to call it 'seduction,' " Bond said, his eyes laughing.

"I call it ridiculous," she rejoined, hands on her hips. "In the grand scheme of life, do you collect how little time a person spends abed when compared to other activities?"

His gaze dropped to her hips. The smile became a full-blown grin. "That truly depends on who else is occupying said bed."

"Dear heavens." Eliza shivered at the look Jasper Bond was giving her. It was . . . expectant. By some unknown, godforsaken means she had managed to prod the man's damnable masculine pride into action.

"Give me a sennight," he suggested. "One week to prove both my point and my competency. If, at the end, you are not swayed by one or the other, I will accept no payment for services rendered."

"Excellent proposition," his lordship said. "No possibility of loss."

"Not true," Eliza contended. "How will I explain Mr. Bond's speedy departure?"

"Let us make it a fortnight, then," Bond amended.

"You fail to understand the problem. I am not an actor, sir. It will be evident to one and all that I am far from 'seduced.' "

The tone of his grin changed, aided by a hot flicker in his dark eyes. "Leave that aspect of the plan to me. After all, that's what I am being paid for."

"And if you fail? Once you resign, not only will I be forced to make excuses for you, I will have to bring in another thief-taker to act in your stead. The whole affair will be entirely too suspicious."

"Have you had the same pool of suitors for six years, Miss Martin?"

"That isn't—"

"Did you not just state the many reasons why you feel I am not an appropriate suitor for you? Can you not simply reiterate those points in response to any inquiries regarding my departure?"

"You are overly persistent, Mr. Bond."

"Quite," he nodded, "which is why I will discover who is responsible for the unfortunate events besetting you and what they'd hoped to gain."

She crossed her arms. "I am not convinced."

"Trust me. It is fortuitous, indeed, that Mr. Lynd brought us together. If I do not apprehend the culprit, I daresay he cannot be caught." His hand fisted around the top of his cane. "Client satisfaction is a point of pride, Miss Martin. By the time I am done, I guarantee you will be eminently gratified by my performance."

Chapter 2

"There are times when I impress myself with my own brilliance," Thomas Lynd crowed when entering Jasper's study with hat in hand.

One could always trust Lynd to eschew the services of a formal butler. He preferred lackeys over servants whose training in deportment exceeded his own.

Jasper settled back in his chair with a smile of welcome. "You've outdone yourself this time."

As usual, Lynd's garments were overdone in style and underwhelming in fit. The result of a poor tailor provided with expensive material yet lacking the knowledge of how best to utilize it. Regardless, Lynd presented a decidedly more refined appearance than others of their profession. He walked a fine line, one that enabled him to remain respected and welcomed by the lower classes, while presenting himself in a way the peerage found non-threatening.

Lynd dropped into one of the two seats set in front of the desk. "The moment she mentioned Montague, I had no doubt."

Although he visited Jasper's home with regularity, he surveyed the room as if seeing it for the first time. His gaze lingered on the mahogany bookshelves lining the far wall and the sapphire-hued velvet drapes framing the windows opposite. "Besides, she wanted a bloody lapdog, and none of our acquaintances can boast your pedigree."

"Bastardy is no advantage in any situation." Jasper straddled the line Lynd traversed so well, which worked—surprisingly—to Jasper's benefit. He was often hired by those who wanted his services to go unnoticed and were capable of paying the added expense such stealth required. That proclivity enabled him to work with Eliza Martin, because his face was not well known.

"It is in this one." Lynd ran a hand through brown hair as yet unaffected by the graying of age. "It takes breeding to tolerate the sorts of pompous asses Melville's niece expects you to rub along with, and you will be far less noticeable in the venues she will expect you to attend than anyone else I could think of."

Standing, Jasper moved to the console table by the window where decanters of liquors and crystal tumblers waited. Lynd was one of very few individuals who were aware of Jasper's lineage. He had Jasper's confidence because he'd once shown Jasper's mother a kindness when she desperately needed it.

As Jasper poured two rations of Armagnac, his

gaze took in the two disreputable-looking lackeys who waited out on the street. Lynd's men.

It had taken Jasper some time to locate a respectable neighborhood that would accommodate his activities without undue strain. His neighbors tolerated the endless comings and goings of his crew because they found his presence useful in minimizing footpad crimes in the immediate vicinity. He considered his services to the community a small price to pay to avoid residing in the areas surrounding Fleet Street and the Strand, where Lynd and many other thief-takers lived. It was nigh impossible to abide the stench from the sewer ditch, which was an inescapable odor embedded into the very walls of the surrounding buildings.

Returning to his seat, Jasper set Lynd's glass at the edge of the desk. "I have an appointment with Miss Martin this afternoon. I'll learn then how serious Montague is about winning her hand. Perhaps he has grown desperate enough to become foolish."

"Preposterous," Lynd scoffed. "The whole affair. If someone is so determined to marry the chit, he should ask her outright. But then, I suppose the entire lot of hopefuls is daft or desperate beyond reason to mix their lineage with the Tremaines'. She should be grateful her late father's fortune has attracted suitors to her. She would have a devil of a time enticing a man without it."

Jasper's brow went up. He'd been enticed the moment she first opened her mouth.

"Truly," Lynd went on, "she should just pick a poor fellow and be done with it. Any other woman would. Been allowed to run amok, that one. She took it upon herself to engage a thief-taker to intercede and his lordship is too preoccupied with the maze of his mind to rein her in. Melville's participation in my interview was only with himself."

"Do you have a point to this disparagement of my client?"

"Six weeks will seem a lifetime, I vow. No compensation can restitute the loss of your sanity. She is contrary in the extreme. Unnatural in a female. She had the gall to look down her nose at me—a feat, I must say, since I'm taller—and tell me I would do well to hire a decent tailor. No polish to her at all. I could barely tolerate her for the length of the interview. Made my teeth grind."

"Good of you to decline the post, then," Jasper drawled. "Clearly you would not have made a convincing suitor."

"If you manage to be, I'd say you missed your true calling as a man of the stage."

"So long as Montague fails to acquire the funds he needs to regain his marker from me, I can do whatever is required." It was a delectable twist that the best way to foil Montague's suit was to woo Eliza Martin himself.

"Revenge has a way of eating at you, my boy, like a cancer. Best to keep that in mind."

Jasper smiled grimly.

Shrugging, Lynd said, "But you'll do as you like, you always have."

The marker Jasper held was for a deed to a parcel of land in Essex that boasted only a modest home and was by far the smallest property Jasper laid claim to. Regardless, its value was priceless. It represented years of meticulous planning and the retribution due him. And in a mere six weeks it would be irrevocably his to destroy or flaunt at his whim.

Jasper withdrew a waiting coin purse from his desk drawer and pushed it to the edge of the desk.

Lynd hesitated before collecting the silken bag. "I wish I could afford not to accept this."

"Nonsense. I owe you more than I could ever repay."

Rounding his desk, Jasper escorted Lynd to the foyer and saw him off. Once his visitor was gone, he shot a quick glance at the clock above the mantel in his office.

He was only a few hours away from paying a call on Miss Eliza Martin. He was anticipating it far more than was seemly. He should not be thinking of her at all, a woman who inferred he was more brawn than intellect. His goals were met by dealing with each challenge at the proper time and with the whole of his attention. Eliza's appointed time was later; there were other items needing to be addressed now. Yet he stood on the threshold of his office where pressing matters awaited him, thinking instead of how he should attire himself to call on her, contemplating whether he should dress to impress or whether mimicking her somber style would better achieve his aim.

Jasper found himself wanting to meet with her approval. It would be hard won, which made it worth the effort.

"The *trone d'amour*," he murmured to himself,

touching his cravat. Decided on a style, Jasper headed to his desk and determined he wouldn't think of his newest employer for at least an hour.

Jasper's foot crossed the threshold of the Melville front door at precisely eleven o'clock. Snapping his pocket watch shut, he waited only a moment while the butler dealt with his hat and cane. But it was a moment he relished for the expectation weighting it. He'd considered the possible reasons why he should be so confoundedly eager to reach this portion of his schedule and come to the conclusion it was Eliza Martin's ability to surprise him that he enjoyed.

The realization came with the sudden understanding that nothing surprised him anymore. He knew precisely what others would say before they said it and how they would respond before they did so. It was the way of the world, the rules of decorum, and his own acute appreciation of human nature. Socializing was like a scripted play, with all the actors aware of what their lines were and when they should be spoken.

Eliza had yet to say anything he expected her to say.

"This way, sir."

Jasper followed the butler to a study and paused on the threshold while he was announced. With his hands clasped at the small of his back, he took in the room, noting how the heavy masculine furniture was offset by flowery pastel drapes and artwork featuring picturesque country landscapes. As if the space had once been a man's domain and was no longer.

"Ah, good morning, Mr. Bond."

The butler bowed and stepped aside, exposing the slender woman who'd been hidden by his tall frame. Eliza sat at a walnut desk so large she appeared dwarfed behind it. Her gaze was downcast, her hair piled high in soft curls, and her shoulders partially hidden by the fine lace decorating a modest bodice.

Jasper entered fully and moved to one of the two carved wooden chairs facing the desk. Before he sat, he glanced down at what occupied her. Ledgers. She worked over them studiously, filling the columns with impressive speed and painfully neat numerals.

"Once again," she murmured, "you are precisely on time."

"Another of my faults?" he asked.

She glanced up at him, studying him beneath the veil of thick auburn lashes. "Would you care for tea?"

"No, thank you."

She set her quill aside and waved the butler away. "The trait of punctuality simply tells me that you value time. It suggests you will value mine as well, which I appreciate."

"What else do you value, Miss Martin?"

"I fail to see how that signifies."

Jasper smiled. "If I am to be a lovelorn swain or even simply a fortune hunter who has set his cap for you, I am expected to know things about you."

"I see." A slight wrinkle marred the space between her brows, then she said, "I value my privacy, solitude, the books in my library, my horse, and my money."

He watched the way her fingertips tapped lightly atop the ledger in front of her. "You keep your own accounts?"

"As my father did before me."

"Why have you not wed?"

Eliza sat back and crossed her arms. "Are you married, Mr. Bond?"

"Jasper," he corrected, wanting to hear his given name spoken in her soft, yet steely voice. "And no, I'm not married."

"Then I ask the same question of you. Why have *you* not wed?"

"The manner in which I live my life doesn't lend itself to matrimony. I keep odd hours and odder company."

"Hmm . . . Well, I have not wed because I've yet to find an individual whose company is worth the expense." She lifted one shoulder in an offhand shrug. "Frankly, marriage for me is an extremely expensive proposition. In addition to the loss of control over my own funds, I'd be agreeing to spend an inordinate amount of time with another person. It makes me odd, I know—or perhaps it just makes me a Tremaine—but I find socializing with others is more exhausting than refreshing. I have to consider everything I want to say, and then filter it through my mind before I speak so what emerges from my mouth doesn't offend with its bluntness."

And there it was, the key to wooing her into

bed: encourage her to be herself. Not a problem for him at all, since he enjoyed her unpolished pronouncements and reasoned judgments. He looked forward to the challenge of unveiling the woman beneath the brain.

"Eliza," he purred, watching her reaction to his uninvited familiarity—the slight dilation of her irises, the unaffected flutter of her lashes, and the quickening tempo of the pulse visible at her throat. "I must confess, I was very much looking forward to our meeting this morning precisely because of what emerges from your mouth."

Which led to thoughts of what else he liked about that particular feature. Such as the full curve of her bottom lip, and the way it pursed lightly when he goaded her. Even the way it moved when she spoke. The things he wanted to do to that mouth shocked even him. He wanted to feel it move over his skin, whispering lewd taunts and pressing soft kisses. Teasing. Suckling. . . .

He inhaled sharply, displeased for the first time in his life with the finely honed instincts he'd long relied on to survive. It was one thing to be sexually aware of a woman—something he found quite stimulating and enjoyable. It was quite another to be physically affected by that awareness.

"It's rare," he continued, forcing his thoughts back to the business at hand, "for a client to be so forthcoming. It makes my efforts far more effective when they are."

Her head tilted to the side, causing two curls to sway beside a delicately shaped ear. She seemed prepared to speak, but then she didn't. Instead, she withdrew a piece of paper from beneath her leather-bound ledger and offered it to him.

He leaned forward and accepted it, turning it around so he could read what was written. As with her bookkeeping, the columns were neat and tidy, yet the way in which she formed her letters was different. Highly slanted as opposed to straight, elongated at the highs and lows, bleeding at the point of ink refill as if she was too hurried to shake off the excess properly. He mulled this over as he read— the care over numerals versus the carelessness over proper names was telling. The list catalogued her suitors by peerage rank—if applicable—as well as length of suit, age, brief but concise physical descriptions, and anomalous traits such as throat clearing and nose twitching. He would easily be able to put a name to a face with the information she provided.

"I'm impressed with the thoroughness of your observation skills," he praised, looking up at her.

A ghost of a smile curved her lips, making him realize he had yet to see her smile in truth. "Thank you. I came to the conclusion last evening that this would be my final Season. I secured an agreement from my uncle long ago that six Seasons would be all he'd ask of me . . . but I was undecided about holding him to the promise. He asks so little of me, after all."

"I see." He should feel no guilt in enjoying her, then. He would not be ruining her if she was seated firmly on the shelf.

"And so I've also decided to utilize your services for the entirety of the six weeks remaining in this

Season, Mr. Bond. If you will advise me of the cost of securing your services for that length of time, I'll see you are paid by the end of the day tomorrow."

Jasper leaned back in his chair, considering. There was something about the way she eyed him that set off a quiet alarm. He appreciated being paid for services rendered—as anyone did—but he wondered if more than the balance of her accounts and a wish to absolve a debt was motivating her. He'd dealt with members of the peerage who felt the act of paying him put him in his place. Once he'd accepted money, he was no longer a businessman but a commodity they had rights and power over. In most instances, he cared not at all what clients told themselves to assuage their pride. In this case, he would not allow Eliza to think she could control him with her money.

"We have an agreement," he said, smiling slightly to soften the rigidity of his position on the matter. "A fortnight without pay. If I have satisfied you at that time, you may make restitution then."

There was a flash of wariness in her blue eyes. Barely there and then gone. "But I do not intend to replace you."

"Excellent. I do not intend to be replaced." He held the list aloft. "Did you, perchance, put these in order of most suspicious to least likely?"

"Yes, of course." She stood and rounded the desk.

He rose quickly, watching in surprise as she settled into the seat beside him. She leaned over the armrest and gestured for him to sit. "If you have any questions, I'm most willing to answer them to the best of my ability."

As Jasper lowered himself back into the chair, he inhaled the rather exotic scent of her perfume, appreciating how different it was from her modest mode of dress. She was a study in contradictions, from her appearance to her voice to her handwriting. "Why is the Earl of Montague so near the bottom?"

Eliza's head tilted so she could better see where he pointed. It was the closest proximity they'd shared yet, affording him the opportunity to note the smattering of light freckles over the bridge of her nose. "Why shouldn't he be within the 'least likely' section? His lordship is handsome and charming and—"

"Desperately in debt." It was by dint of will alone that he managed not to crush the foolscap in his hand. What natural attraction he felt for her was increased by a sense of possessiveness. Damned if Montague would get his hands on Eliza or her money.

"Yes. I know. But so are many of the men on the list. Those who are not in debt are of limited means." She saw his raised brows and another slight smile curved her lips. "I've looked into the circumstances of every gentleman who calls upon me, even the ones whose motives are clear straightaway."

"And how did you manage that?"

"I may not have a bookkeeper, Mr. Bond—"

"Jasper," he corrected, yet again.

Her shoulders went back. "Such familiarity is inappropriate in business dealings."

"Not so." It appeared he was correct about her

wish for distance. "And especially not in this instance. You should be more than a little fond of me. I collect that you find it difficult to contemplate, since I am not your type of male, but the use of given names and time spent in my company will help to alleviate any awkwardness you might feel, creating a more believable presentation."

"You said to leave that aspect of the plan to you."

"Quite right. I will lead, you will follow." He used the tone of voice that never failed to pull others into line. He knew if he gave Eliza the slightest opportunity, she would run roughshod over him. "Now, about how you acquired your information . . . ?"

Her lips pursed. Clearly she was not a woman used to being managed. *Been allowed to run amok, that one,* Lynd had said. Jasper wouldn't change that about her, even if afforded the opportunity, but he also wouldn't be led around by the nose.

"I have a man of affairs," she said, "who makes discreet inquiries for me as necessary. One cannot be too careful."

Jasper leaned back, settling into a comfortable position to better enjoy the conversation. "And what sort of information did you glean from these inquiries? Were you made aware of the full extent of Lord Montague's debts?"

"I know enough to be wary."

"Then why put him in such an elevated position on your list?"

"As I said, he is charming and could certainly secure a better match than me. I think he uses me to make other women jealous. My mother used to say, 'there's nothing so attractive as a man who belongs to another woman.' Montague may be financially troubled, but few know that. He's managed to hide it well. And he is handsome enough to cover many faults in some women's eyes." Her gaze narrowed, and she raked him from head to toe. "In fact, you two are similar in height and coloring. Build, too, although he is not nearly as . . . broad."

It took great effort not to tense and betray his unease at her perceptiveness. "And yet you claimed others would see me and know straightaway I was not like your other suitors at all."

"You have an astonishingly good memory, Mr. Bond."

"Jasper."

She took a deep breath. "Your sharp recollection is laudable . . . Jasper."

"Thank you, Eliza." He held back a satisfied smile at the tiny bit of progress. "I've found the skill quite useful. But I confess, I'm perplexed by your contradictory statements."

"I said there were similarities, but they are not overly evident." She didn't intend for her perusal to be invigorating, but it most definitely was. "He is handsome, yes. As are you. But you are flamboyantly so. It's astonishing really, the way the first sight of you arrests the brain. Whenever I initially catch sight of you, it takes a moment to pull my thoughts together."

"I am gratified you find me appealing." And relieved that the fraternal similarities she'd noted were so quickly dismissed.

"Fustian. I'm certain you must be accustomed to all the attention by now. What is it like, by the way? Having people admire you when you enter a room or pass them by?"

"I don't notice such things."

"Truly?"

"I am usually intent on whatever purpose I have for being in any given location or situation."

"Oh, I see." Eliza nodded. "Yes, you are quite focused. Intensely so. It's another trait distinguishing you."

He swiftly utilized the avenue provided by her curiosity. "Tomorrow, I intend to take you to the Royal Academy of Art. You can see for yourself how others perceive me."

"An outing?" She frowned. Oddly, he liked that as much as her hint of a smile. Her face was so expressive, it took much of the guesswork out of wondering what was on her mind. "I suppose that's the best way to expose me and lure the culprit out."

"I would never use you as bait. It's my intention to become the target instead." He took care to fold the list neatly. "Over the next several weeks, you and I will be spending a great deal of time together. The more you are seen with me, the bigger a threat I will become."

She watched him tuck the folded paper into a pocket of his waistcoat.

"In addition," he went on, "I will need to meet with your man of affairs."

"Why?"

"Some men do not appreciate having their private matters examined, discreetly or not. And I must ask about your investments and Lord Melville's activities."

Her face took on an appearance of great interest. "You suspect another motivation."

"It's a possibility. Malicious intent can be incited by many things: love, money, and vengeance are at the top of the list. You are wealthy, others are not. If any of your investments or ventures has caused an individual to feel wronged, there is motive there. If anyone holds ill-will toward Melville, hurting someone close to him could be motive as well." Jasper held her gaze. "Personally, I can understand why someone would go to great lengths to win you. But to take it to the point of injury against you . . . I cannot wait to learn the identity of our mystery assailant. I anticipate that introduction with great relish."

Eliza did not appear to be alarmed by his fervent hope for violence. "I'm grateful for your attention to the task."

"You would not accept anything less."

She stood, and he stood with her. Her head tilted back to maintain eye contact. "Mr. Lynd and the Runner I hired both seemed to think I was daft. It isn't a pleasant feeling to be treated as mentally inferior. It was a brief glimpse, I suppose, of what Melville bears with terrible frequency."

"Is that one of the reasons why you resist marriage? For your uncle's benefit?"

"No. He's quite capable of caring for himself, at least to the extent that he employs a trustworthy and efficient staff to manage the minutiae he has no patience for." Her gaze moved to the clock on the mantel. "Today I am at home to callers. Will you be one of them?"

"Will it settle your mind if I am?"

Her head gave a slight shake. "Here at home, I feel safe enough."

"Then I shall refrain. I think it will be more effective if I'm not one of the many. Tomorrow will be our first public appearance together, and you will be granting me your undivided attention. That will establish my connection with you in a more prominent way. We'll require a chaperone who gossips. Do you know of someone who will suffice?"

"I'll see to it. What do I say to those who ask about you? What reply can I give to inquiries about your people and situation?"

He breathed in her scent with a deep inhalation, one last delay before revealing a truth no one else knew. "You may tell them I am the nephew of the late Lord Gresham of County Wexford, and our families are old friends from long ago."

"Oh . . ."

Jasper knew little of his mother's relations. Diana Gresham had been disowned after her pregnancy became evident, a circumstance affording her no way out of the hell she'd died in. When Jasper tracked Gresham down years later, the only regret he felt at learning of his lordship's recent passing was that he'd lost the opportunity to repay his uncle in kind.

"You are a conundrum, aren't you?" Eliza said softly. "I should like to figure you out."

"If you have a question, ask me."

"Will you answer?"

That made him smile. When he heard her breath catch, his inner predator licked its lips and purred. For all her protests regarding the suitability of his appearance, it was undeniable that it pleased her. "My past and my future are irrelevant. You have my present. In that, yes, ask away. I will answer."

"I knew you would be troublesome, Mr. Bond."

"Jasper."

"But I believe you will resolve my dilemma, and I find a measure of relief in that." Rounding the desk, she resumed her seat. Her manner changed, became distant. She opened a drawer and withdrew a small book. "Here is a copy of my social calendar for the remainder of the Season as it stands so far. I will keep a list of future invitations I accept."

"Your thoroughness is admirable."

"I think you and I shall work well together. Is there anything else? Or are we finished for today?"

He found himself wanting to linger, knowing it was still early in the day and the most interesting part of it would now be behind him. "These lists are sufficient at present. I'll need to be apprised of the other matters we discussed—your investments, your man of affairs, and anything in Lord Melville's past that might put a loved one at risk."

"An investment pool managed by Lord Collingsworth and rental properties," she answered, with her head already bent and quill in hand. "Both residential and commercial. I can take you to them, if you like."

"I would."

"Will the day after tomorrow be soon enough for a tour and meeting with my man of affairs, Mr. Reynolds?"

"Quite. I will also need a list of your tenants."

She glanced up at him. "Your attention to detail is very impressive."

He bowed. "I do try. I will call on you tomorrow at one."

"I'll be ready."

Turning about, Jasper moved to leave the room. On the threshold, he looked back, finding a small bit of pleasure in catching Eliza staring after him, despite the frown marring her brow. She looked down quickly.

When he reached the foyer, he pulled out his pocket watch and was startled by the time. He'd overstayed his visit by nearly ten minutes, making him late for his next appointment.

Bloody hell. He had completely forgotten the time.

Chapter 3

Eliza was compiling the list of property holdings Jasper had requested when her man of affairs was announced. She looked up at the somberly dressed but friendly-faced man in her study doorway, and gestured for him to take a seat before her desk. "Good morning, Mr. Reynolds."

"An excellent morning, Miss Martin." Terrance Reynolds sat and placed his satchel at his feet.

She shook her head at the butler, who'd been waiting to relay a tea service request to the housekeeper. While she knew she should offer the courtesy, she truly didn't have much to say, and she dreaded the awkwardness that would arise when she couldn't fill the additional time with conversation. Some women possessed a talent for charming but meaningless discourse. Sadly, she was not one of them.

"You will be happy to hear," Reynolds began, "that I've found a shopkeeper for the vacant space on Peony Way. A purveyor of soaps, candles, and such."

"Excellent. You are most efficient, Mr. Reynolds."

"Thank you."

She set her quill aside, noting how much more comfortable she was talking to Reynolds than she was to Mr. Bond . . . *Jasper*. Yet that wasn't to say she preferred the comfort of one over the excitement of the other, which made no sense, considering she'd never been one to enjoy excitation overmuch. Her mother's life had forever been a series of crises and bursts of happiness interspersed with heated arguments and the depths of despair. Eliza had grown so weary of Georgina Tremaine Martin Chilcott's incessant drama that she'd taken great pains to moderate her own life. She preferred private dinners to lavish balls, and the comfort of laying on her boudoir chaise with a book over literary luncheons. There was nothing at all soothing about Jasper Bond, and she was intrigued by the fact that she missed the heightened awareness she felt in his presence.

Eliza returned her attention to the man sitting across from her. "You mentioned last week that your brother's employer had passed on. Is he still in search of employment?"

The males in the Reynolds family were all in trade as men of affairs and bookkeepers. She'd been briefly introduced to another of the siblings, Tobias Reynolds, who was possessed of the same golden locks and green-as-glass eyes as Terrance. She had henceforth inquired about Tobias on occasion—part of a well-meant but surprisingly arduous attempt to be more personable—and she'd learned of his misfortune in the course of those inquiries.

"He's been assisting our father and other brother," Reynolds replied, "but yes, Tobias is without a permanent post at the moment."

"I should like to engage him, if he's so inclined. He will have to travel and leave quickly, but the recompense should be sufficient to mitigate such inconveniences."

Reynolds frowned. "Where would you like him to go?"

"County Wexford. There is a person of interest there I would like to know better. Family, circumstances, community stature. Things of that nature." Eliza ignored the hint of unease that briefly plagued her. Yes, Jasper asserted that his past was irrelevant, and he was not a man one wished to cross. However, she had a right to know if she would be lying on his behalf, or if there was indeed more to her thief-taker than met the eye. "As always, discretion is the rule, but more so in this instance. I don't want Lord Gresham to be aware of my interest. And timeliness will be rewarded.

"Would you prefer me to see to it personally?" he offered.

"No. I need you here. We'll be advancing the monthly tour of my properties to the day after tomorrow."

"As you wish, Miss Martin. I will speak with my brother as soon as I depart."

"If you could also ascertain the extent of the allowance he feels will be sufficient to support the endeavor, I will ensure I have the amount available before he departs."

"Certainly." He didn't query her about the nature of her interest, which was why they worked well together. She did not like to justify her expenses to anyone.

"Thank you." She managed a smile. "That will be all for now, Mr. Reynolds. I appreciate you, as always."

After he left, Eliza glanced at the clock on her desk. Her nose wrinkled. The morning was gone, and the afternoon was rushing by as swiftly. Soon, she would be welcoming guests into her parlor and engaging in conversation so inane she wouldn't remember later what she discussed.

She was disappointed Jasper wouldn't be there. The time would be much more engrossing if he were. When she considered all the amusements used to enliven events that never engaged her—the pianoforte, singing, card games, and chess—she was taken by the realization it was a man best used as a blunt-force instrument who interested her most.

There were some days when Eliza actually enjoyed riding through Hyde Park, despite the torturously slow pace of the congestion and the need for endless smiling that pained her cheeks. Today was one of those good days. The soft breeze and gentle warmth of the sun were refreshing, and the need to prepare quick and appropriate responses to greetings kept her thoughts free of Jasper.

"You seem to be enjoying yourself today, Miss Martin," the Earl of Montague said from his seat beside her. He'd arrived for their agreed-upon outing in a new and clearly expensive curricle. When he first began pursuing her in earnest, she'd wondered why a peer of seemingly substantial wealth would show such dogged interest in her of all people. Then she learned he maintained the appearance of solvency through prudence—and luck—at the gaming tables. It was a clever ruse and one few bothered to delve into.

She looked at him with a frown, slightly chagrined by her inability to navigate the social waters without bumping into things. "Is it so obvious that I usually do not?"

"Not so obvious, no," he said, while deftly handling the ribbons. He maneuvered through the multitude of conveyances on South Carriage Drive with admirable skill. "But I've taken to paying close attention to you, Miss Martin. And I collect that you have little interest in Society as a whole."

"To put it bluntly, my lord."

Montague grinned, his teeth white despite the shadow cast by the brim of his hat. Of all her suitors, she would say he was the most attractive. His dark hair was so thick and glossy she thought it might feel like silk if she touched it, and his eyes were extremely expressive. Similar in color to Jasper's, but nowise near as shuttered.

"I understand," he went on, "that a woman loses a measure of freedom when she takes a husband."

"Most vexing, to be sure."

"And I appreciate your reticence. You see, I've

come to the delayed understanding that people in general perplex you."

Eliza's brows rose. "You have?"

"I realize now I was going about this business of courting you all wrong. Most women want wooing—flowers and tokens of affection, focused attention, and the like."

"The flowers you send weekly are lovely," she said automatically, although she thought it a shame for such beautiful living things to be cut away from their source of nourishment.

"I'm gratified you think so. But I believe you wouldn't miss them if I ceased making the gesture. You would not experience hurt feelings or attribute emotional reasons to my actions based on conjecture."

He offered a genuine smile, and she stared, seeing a charm in it she'd missed previously. It was an aftereffect of Jasper that she was now overly attentive to other males. She wanted to discern why the thief-taker affected her so strongly.

"I am sorely inept at interpreting such things," she agreed, adjusting the angle of her parasol to better shield her face. The slightest touch of sun on her nose would result in more freckles.

"No, you are perfectly reasoned," his lordship argued. "And that's where I erred. I was pandering to your softer nature, when I should have been appealing to your intellect. Therefore, I will not insult your intelligence any further. I'm in need of your fortune, Miss Martin."

Intrigued, she shifted on the seat to better study him. "A novel approach, I must say. Quite bold."

His grin held shades of triumph. "And you like it. For the first time in our acquaintance, I feel as if I have your attention in its entirety."

Montague paused to tip his hat to Lord and Lady Grayson as they passed. When he looked back at Eliza, there was a new gleam in his eye, reminiscent of the way Jasper looked at her. It lacked the ability to make her breath catch, but she recognized it for what it was—the earl was suddenly more intrigued by her as well.

"The best approach to you is so obvious," the earl continued, "that I'm quite put out by my failure to see it before. Whether or not I have elevated feelings for you isn't of enough value to you to equal what you believe you will lose. In the simplest of terms, I haven't shown you that I am a good investment."

Captured by the uniqueness of the conversation, Eliza wished they were not in public so she could fully enjoy the surprise without interruption. "Please, go on."

"First and foremost, the Montague lands are vast and with proper care would yield a tidy return."

"Why isn't the estate supporting you now?"

"My father suffered from a loose hand with coin, an untrustworthy steward, and a greedy mistress. I assure you, however, I am not my father."

"Perhaps not, but you *are* a gamester, my lord. You have managed to do well enough with your winnings." She gestured at his fashionable equipage. "But luck at the tables is a fickle thing, and certainly you would eventually contract mistresses of your own. Perhaps you will become smitten by a paramour who is also afflicted with avarice. I would not take kindly to destitution due to gambling or the waste of *my* funds on another woman who was enjoying the companionship of *my* husband. I expect to own the things I pay for, and I rarely lend them out."

"Ah, so," he said softly, with another warm glance in her direction. "You know, Miss Martin, the more I know of you, the more taken I am."

"Today, I find myself enjoying your company as well. But forgive me, my lord, I have no desire to marry you."

"There are other benefits." Outwardly, nothing changed, but Eliza sensed a new weight of expectation, as if he were debating whether or not to continue with his thought. "Aside from financial considerations, there are other ways in which a man and his wife reach an accord. I want to assure you, you would not find married life to be distasteful. I've no wish for disharmony in my home. I would make every effort to see that you were satisfied in sharing your life with me."

For a moment, she was perplexed by his statement. Did they not have an accord now? Then she recalled the conversation she'd had with Melville and Jasper about the things women wanted from men. Which led her to thinking about the things a peer would want from a woman. . . .

"Are you referring to procreation, my lord?"

Montague visibly jolted. Staring straight ahead, he seemed unable to respond. And then he laughed. It was a full, open-throated sound that drew stares from every quarter. "No wonder you find the usual discourse less than interesting. Speaking one's mind is much more stimulating."

Eliza opened her mouth to reply, then shut it again as her attention was snared by a familiar shade of blue velvet. Montague's carriage continued to move forward, but Eliza's eyes remained riveted to Jasper, who sat astride a black steed just off the Row, watching her with the fiercely intense stare that set butterflies to flight in her stomach. Her response was so strong, it was unnerving. Her palms grew damp, conveying a heat that had nothing to do with the weather. It was rather like spotting a crouched panther in the brush, its rapacious gaze following the prey it intended to pounce upon at any moment.

Without conscious prompting, she straightened in her seat and her hand lifted to the brim of her simple straw hat.

Jasper was such a compelling figure, even the dappled light afforded by an overhanging tree could not diminish his vibrancy. A thrill of awareness moved through her, as did a strong appreciation for the sight of him. How long had he been there? She could have sworn he hadn't been under that tree mere seconds before.

The earl spoke, drawing her thoughts back to him.

She tore her gaze from Jasper. "I beg your pardon, my lord?"

"Wed me," he repeated. "I will give you things you don't yet know you want. I understand you, Miss Martin. We are different in all the best ways. A collaboration between us would be to the advantage of us both."

"I have a better idea. I will find you a more suitable candidate."

Montague's mouth curved. "You intend to play matchmaker?"

"In a fashion." Eliza was keenly aware of Jasper's gaze following her.

"Miss Martin, I want to be clear about my intentions. I've decided you will suit me best of all. I will not be easily dissuaded from my aim of proving I can complement you as well."

"As you wish." She sighed. "Please do not make a nuisance of yourself in the effort, Lord Montague. You've always been one of the more agreeable of my suitors. I should like you to stay that way, if possible."

Montague laughed again and looked at her with sparkling eyes. "You are a delightful surprise. I wish I'd been wiser earlier in the Season."

Eliza looked behind her to where Jasper had been.

He was gone, leaving behind a marked absence.

As Jasper urged his mount away from South Carriage Drive toward the adjacent Rotten Row, the member of his crew assigned to watching Eliza also turned with him.

"She has an eye for you," Aaron White said, gesturing at another crew member further up the Drive who would continue surveillance.

Jasper nodded. He had come without thought.

It wasn't until he'd caught sight of Eliza that he realized why. A vague notion had played in his mind—a budding desire to see her glorious hair in sunlight—and somehow it led him here. Ridiculously sentimental. Completely out of character. Her time in his schedule had passed, and he had other matters to attend to.

"Of course," Aaron continued, "you made certain she saw you."

Jasper could shine in a crowd or hide among it in the space of a breath merely by making minuscule changes in his deportment and posture. He'd been an unnoticed observer until Montague said something to Eliza that snared her attention completely. Jasper had wanted to steal her regard, and he'd done so. "It's best that she not seem too taken with any of her other suitors. Defeats the effectiveness of my plan to secure her safety."

"And your pronounced interest in her has nothing to do with it," Aaron teased, holding his reins loosely in one hand while the other rested atop his thigh. He was a young lad, short and stocky, a hard worker with three small mouths to feed. For that reason, Jasper kept him away from the more hazardous assignments. Watching out for Eliza was perfect.

"Her attractiveness makes the job more agreeable." That was all Jasper intended to say on the matter.

Aaron's gaze followed Montague. "The earl appears to agree. He seems genuinely taken with her."

The sound of Montague's recent laughter lingered in Jasper's mind, and his gloved grip tightened on his reins. "She would be miserable with him. He cares for nothing so much as his own self-interest. I'm doing her a favor."

"That's one way of looking at the ruination of a proper society miss." There was amusement in Aaron's tone, which was understandable considering Jasper's rule against dallying with ladies of quality. It was a rule he was clearly intent on breaking.

"I am not ruining her. She decided long ago she would never wed, and she reiterated that intention to me only hours ago."

"And you'll show her the joys of shagging, so she doesn't die ignorant? Another favor? By God, Bond, you're damn near saintly in your generosity."

Jasper shot the younger man a fulminating glare.

Aaron raised both hands in a gesture of surrender. "You're a shrewd businessman above all. Makes me right curious as to why you plan to stop short of the big prize. Since you're taking her to bed, why not also take her to wife? Add her fortune to the other benefits of the association."

"Wanting and wedding are two very different things. She would be equally miserable with me. I've no notion of how to keep a woman happy outside of the bedroom."

"Don't let her out of bed. Problem solved."

"I am not amused."

"Merely a suggestion." Aaron grinned. "Not sure why I mentioned it, considering I benefit from your remaining just as you are now. If you became obscenely wealthy, you wouldn't work so hard, and I would have fewer opportunities to earn my wages."

Jasper's gaze followed Eliza until Montague's equipage was lost in the crowd. Out of sight, out of mind. He hoped. He withdrew his pocket watch and checked the time. Eliza would return home shortly and begin preparations for the evening.

How would she appear when dressed formally? Not that she would put any effort into it, which he found refreshing. Some women spent excessive amounts of time on their exteriors. Eliza's most attractive qualities weren't the most obvious ones. The hints of stronger passions were so subtle, even she was not aware of them. She was of the introspective sort, quietly curious and sharply intelligent.

Jasper, by contrast, preferred a more hectic pace of living. He kept his hours filled from the time he awoke until he couldn't fight sleep a moment longer. Such preoccupation afforded less time to ruminate on the thorn wedged in his side. Eliza both helped and hindered in that regard. When he was with her, he was so mindful of her there was no room for awareness of anything else. And that was a problem. He could not afford to lose his focus now. Not when he was so close to achieving his aims.

He growled and tugged his hat lower on his brow, hating to be in public while so disconcerted. Over a spinster who thought he was too handsome and too dangerous.

"I shall leave Miss Martin in your capable hands," he said.

"You might consider occupying *your* hands with a visit to the upper floor of Remington's," Aaron suggested. "To take the edge off."

The prod to partake in the more carnal offerings at his favorite gentlemen's club came from keen observation. Although Aaron's observant nature was one of the reasons why Jasper had employed him, it was damned inconvenient when aimed in his direction. "Watch her. Not me."

He turned about in search of another familiar figure. As luck would have it, he didn't have far to look.

The gentleman Jasper sought was en route to him, weaving through the many riders with one hand lifted to his hat brim in perpetual greeting. Gabriel Ashford, ninth Earl of Westfield, was a gazetted rake of prominent family and fortune, which ensured that an inordinate number of female stares were directed his way. Although his exploits were known to include nearly every vice, there were no signs of dissipation marring the features that incited some women to swoon. He looked fit and lean, and his easy smile was on full display.

As Westfield drew near, his countenance changed subtly. The façade he wore so well slipped a little, revealing the true man beneath. A good and kind man whom Jasper had taken into his confidence. A gentleman he considered a friend.

"Good afternoon, Bond."

Jasper tipped his hat. "My lord."

"I saw you eyeing Montague." Westfield drew abreast of Jasper's mount. "Are you worried he'll get his hands on Miss Martin's fortune and settle his debt?"

"Actually, it was Miss Martin who held my interest."

"Ah . . . I failed to collect that elusive bluestockings were to your taste."

"Paying clients are always to my taste."

"Interesting." Westfield's brows rose. "Why does Miss Martin require your services?"

Jasper spurred his horse into motion. The earl followed suit.

"What do you know of her and her kin?" Jasper asked.

"The Tremaine brood is unquestionably an odd lot, which makes them fiendishly easy to gossip about. The males are known to be brilliant to the point of madness, and the females are blessed with that stunningly beautiful shade of hair. Miss Martin seems to have inherited a bit of both traits in addition to her sizeable fortune. As for her parents, Mr. Martin was a man of trade and Lady Georgina was known to be charming and vivacious. Although Miss Martin seems as indifferent to men as her mother was appreciative, I've wondered if a deeper resemblance between them is simply untapped. Intriguing to contemplate."

"Are you saying her mother was indiscriminate?"

"Lady Georgina was known to have a fondness for the social company of men. Does that mean she took many to her bed?" Westfield shrugged. "I cannot say. However, she married Martin immediately following her presentation. She would have had her pick of peers, but instead jumped into matrimony with a commoner. Why, unless it was a love match? And if it was a love match, I doubt she would stray."

"What do you know of Mr. Martin?"

"I know his death was shocking to many. He was said to have a vigorous constitution. He was built like a laborer and often pitched in as one when the opportunity presented itself. A servant found him dead in his office when he failed to appear for supper. A weak heart was blamed."

Jasper decided he would have to dig further back, before Eliza's present-day suitors, to see if the trouble plaguing her had begun long before now.

Westfield inclined his head at a passing acquaintance. "Many have speculated that the vagaries of the family he married into might have hastened him to his grave. His due, so to speak, for his lofty marital aspirations. After his passing, Lady Georgina married again, to another commoner."

A woman of high passions and a lack of prejudice. Did Eliza carry those inclinations? How delicious if she did . . .

Jasper shook off the tangential thought. "Miss Martin has a stepfather?"

"Had. Lady Georgina and Mr. Chilcott were

killed together in a carriage accident before Miss Martin's first Season. The poor girl has been sorely afflicted with tragedy."

Did she grieve? Jasper wondered. Had she always been so detached from others or was that a recently acquired safety mechanism?

"Now tell me," the earl said, "what has Miss Martin engaged you to do?"

"She has cause to fear for her safety."

Westfield's brows rose. "Truly? Who would want to injure her? She's worth more alive than dead."

"She believes someone—perhaps an overzealous suitor—is trying to goad her into marriage as a means of protecting herself. I haven't yet decided if she's correct, but hearing about her parents' untimely demise only incites further concern."

"How diverting," the earl said. "Can I assist you in any way?"

"I was hoping you would ask." Jasper reached into his pocket and withdrew the small book containing Eliza's social calendar. It was an unavoidable fact that there were some doors he needed a peer to open. "I must attend as many of these functions as possible."

The earl flipped through the small bound pages with one hand. "I see I will have to refrain from arranging a liaison tomorrow evening, so I can squire you about."

"I appreciate your sacrifice," Jasper drawled.

"I should hope so." Westfield's tone was droll. In truth, he enjoyed participating in Jasper's work when the circumstances allowed. He was even known to become somewhat of a pest, if Jasper went too long without enlisting him for some task or another. "See you at ten?"

"Perfect."

Eliza had just pulled on a dressing gown and settled in front of her vanity mirror when a knock came to her boudoir door. When bade to enter, a white-capped maid stepped in and curtsied. "His lordship asks for you, miss."

"Thank you."

Frowning, Eliza watched the servant back out of the room. She'd enjoyed tea with her uncle just an hour before, listening fondly as he spoke at length and with great animation about his latest botanical experiments. Once, their solarium had been filled with comfortable chaises and short bookcases. Now, it housed rows of long tables supporting various potted plants. Eliza didn't mind the loss of her former favorite reading spot, appreciating how the experiments in the glass space exposed his lordship to sunlight and fresh air.

What would cause him to ask for her now, at an hour when she was beginning preparations for the evening's social events? Perhaps he had an epiphany of some sort or something of a celebratory nature to share? He once woke her before sunrise because a splicing experiment yielded unexpectedly delightful results.

She stood and pulled a comfortable house gown out of the wardrobe. Then she called for her abigail, Mary, who entered the room from the bathing chamber and assisted Eliza in securing the row of buttons following the length of her spine. Despite skipping her chemise and stays, it took long moments to become presentable. Eliza tied a quick ribbon around her unbound hair and considered herself ready enough.

"What will you wear tonight?" Mary asked.

"Lay out three of your favorites." Eliza opened the door to the gallery. "I'll pick one when I return."

She often left the selection of clothing to her abigail. It didn't matter what Mary chose—Eliza always picked the gown on the farthest right. Her dresses were all impeccable, if unremarkable, having been created by a seamstress who was in high demand for her skill. The *modiste* had originally protested Eliza's selection of colors that, while fashionable, did little to emphasize the hue of her hair. But eventually the hopelessness of the objections became patently clear, and Eliza was spared from hearing them. She felt it was only fair to avoid giving anyone the notion she was attempting to entice or set a lure. Since the most popular shades were pastels and she looked best in darker colors, there was no excuse for her to dress with self-flattery in mind.

She left the room and headed directly to the family parlor on the same floor. The door was ajar. A fire crackled merrily in the grate, and his lordship paced before it in his usual state of dishabille—mussed hair, lopsided cravat, and unevenly buttoned waistcoat sans coat.

Eliza entered with a brisk stride. "My lord?"

He faced her with a distracted smile. "I'm sorry to disturb you, my dear, but you have a visitor."

She glanced down at her hastily composed presentation. "A visitor? Downstairs?"

"Good evening, Miss Martin."

Jasper's voice. A shiver coursed down her spine at the sound. Pivoting, she found him standing behind the door. His gaze was narrowed, his face austere. He was dressed in the same riding garments he had been wearing when she'd seen him in the park, but his cravat was less crisp and the outside of his boots bore traces of scuffing.

As they did every time she saw him, her thoughts skidded to a halt. It took her the length of several heartbeats to remember to speak.

There was no hiding the way her breath hitched when she greeted him. "Mr. Bond."

Chapter 4

"Behave yourself as promised, young man," Melville said, before hurrying from the room. Clearly, he was eager to return to whatever he'd been doing before being interrupted. The door was left open, but Eliza doubted such measures would impede a man like Jasper if he was of a mind to act scandalously.

"You have my word, my lord," Jasper said softly.

There was a pregnant pause after the earl departed. Jasper raked her with a heated gaze, from top to toe and back again. Then he averted his head, exposing a clenched jaw and rapid pulse. Eliza realized he was aware she'd skipped undergarments in her haste. He knew she was unbound and unfettered.

And it was adversely affecting him.

His reaction to her was creating a corresponding reaction to him. The tempo of her heartbeat increased.

Eliza covered her discomposure by moving to the settee and sitting. Smoothing her floral skirts with restless hands, she looked at Jasper's savagely masculine profile and said the first thing that came to mind. "I apologize for not being more presentable."

"How can I accept an apology"—his gaze slowly returned to her face—"for something that brings me such pleasure?"

She swallowed hard, hating that her mouth was so dry. His eyes followed the working of her throat. A thick, hot current of awareness flowed through her. It was difficult to see him there in the private room where only family and close friends gathered. An intimacy was established by his presence. She felt exposed without the stricture of her stays. Vulnerable in a way she'd never known before.

Forcing her hands to be still, she said, "I saw you this afternoon."

She didn't confess that she'd been smitten by the sight of him in his rakishly angled hat.

He nodded. "You should be cautious around Montague."

"I sincerely doubt he is the culprit."

"Why?"

"He is an intelligent man. He must be aware of more productive ways to win my hand. In fact, he said as much to me today. He believes he understands me now and presented himself as a sound investment. He's come to the conclusion that appealing to my reason is far more likely to yield the results he hopes for than attempting to engage my emotions."

Jasper's chest lifted and fell deeply. "The man gambles obsessively."

"Those who lose to him do so by their own choice. His skill is widely lauded. They know what they risk by playing against him."

"Up to this point," he murmured, "I considered you remarkably reasoned."

Eliza's chin lifted. "You are provoking me."

"I'm being frank." He approached, but his gait lacked the seductiveness she'd come to anticipate. Instead, it was determined. "Is Montague your favorite of your suitors?"

"I enjoy his lordship's company," she answered carefully. "However, I enjoy most every gentleman who comes calling. I would avoid anyone whose companionship I didn't find agreeable. In fact, I warned Lord Montague this afternoon to be careful not to become troublesome."

He paused on the opposite side of the low table. "What would prompt you to make such a statement?"

"He has become impatient to wed and claims he is determined to have me. His approach—while unique—did not sway me, but I seem to have become something of a curiosity to him."

"The Quality is ever in pursuit of relief from boredom. After all, it's so tedious to be blessed with the wherewithal to do anything one desires."

There was an undertone to his words that set Eliza on alert. Jasper wasn't simply voicing an offhand observation.

Exhaling harshly, he altered his direction toward

the grate, his boots thudding softly across the well-worn rug. Resting a forearm on the mantel, he stared into the glowing coals. His dark hair gleamed with vitality. The strands sweeping forward to frame his temples and brow were uniquely appealing despite the popularity of the style. Burnished by firelight, Eliza found the lines of his large body to be magnificent. He was exceedingly male, like a glass filled overfull. She wondered how women managed a sip without spilling all over themselves.

Not a poetic thought and definitely an unseemly one, but she chose not to delude herself. She was attracted to him. His mere presence made her highly conscious of her own femininity.

"Why are you here?" she asked, twisting to face his back.

There was a long hesitation, then he said, "Your father's death. Did it come as a surprise to you?"

"Yes." Eliza's fingers linked together in her lap.

Jasper looked at her over his shoulder. "You answered too swiftly. I need you to be honest with me, if I'm to succeed."

The way he stared at her gave her pause.

"Very well," she amended. "I was surprised and not. I knew he was unwell, but I believed he had an affliction of the mind. Not the body."

"Affliction of the mind, you say? Was he lacking reason?"

"He wasn't mad. Although I sometimes thought my mother was determined to drive him to it."

He focused more intently on her. "Explain."

"He was unhappy, which contributed to an excessive fondness for strong spirits, but I did not collect how sick he'd become until it was too late. Why do you ask?"

"You lost both of your parents too early. I must be certain their fate isn't linked to your present situation in some way. Are you quite confident your father's death was natural in cause?"

"It was expected," she qualified. "I wouldn't call it natural. As you said, he died before his time."

"And your mother's death? Are you confident it was an accident?"

"The only surprise about her demise was how long it took to happen," she said sharply.

"Eliza . . ." Jasper came to sit beside her.

The air around her became charged with his energy.

I never feel so alive as I do when I am the object of a man's desire, her mother had said, while spinning like a giddy girl with her skirts held in each hand. *The blood sings, Eliza. The heart races. It is the most glorious feeling in the world.*

Why did Jasper have to be the man to awaken such reactions in her? Why did he have to prove, just by breathing, that she wasn't immune to needing someone after all? She was so disappointed to realize there were indeed some shades of pleasure that could be colored only by another hand.

His dark eyes were warm with concern. "Please understand, I only wish to be thorough. Your safety is of the utmost importance to me."

She nodded, believing the sincerity in his tone. A lock of her hair was dislodged by the movement, slipping free of her hastily tied ribbon to slide over her shoulder.

He stood. Holding out a hand, he assisted her to her feet. "Turn around."

As Eliza pivoted, she disturbed the air, allowing the primitive scent that clung to him—horses and leather, tobacco and bergamot—to tease her senses. She jumped slightly at the feel of his fingers against her nape. Awareness of him swept outward, flowing across her skin like warm water. He lifted the curl from her shoulder and rubbed it between his fingers.

"Like fine silk," he murmured. He loosened the ribbon securing her hair, returned the errant lock to its former place, and retied the whole more securely.

Her gaze darted around the room, hyperaware of her surroundings. Everything was rendered in brilliant clarity, from the crystals hanging from the many ornate candlesticks to the inlaid mother-of-pearl glimmering from the tops of the end tables.

In the swirling confusion, she grasped the first thought that came to her. "Are you one of those gentlemen who has an unusually strong interest in red hair?"

"I have an unusually strong interest in you." He pressed his lips to the bare skin between her shoulder and throat.

"Jasper," she whispered, shocked by the violent quiver that moved through her. "What are you doing? Why did you come now . . . tonight . . . when I'll be seeing you tomorrow?"

His hands fell to his sides. "I saw the way you looked at Montague. What he said made you see him in a way you haven't before."

Eliza faced him. He was more than a head taller, but his frame curved toward her in a way that made their proximity searingly intimate. As if he was about to twirl her into a waltz.

Her heart beat a little faster. Her breathing quickened. "I don't understand."

He cupped her chin and tilted her face upward. "You looked at him the way you look at me."

"That's impossible." Montague incited none of this turmoil.

"I need you to regard me in the same manner with which I regard you."

She was arrested by the way he looked her over. So intent. With a gaze that was fierce. Fervent. His fingertips followed the path of his perusal. Touching her forehead. Tracing her brows. Following the bridge of her nose.

Eliza, in turn, studied him unabashedly. His features were so perfectly formed, beautiful in their symmetry but masculine in their lines. It was such a pleasure to look upon him; he made her want to stare.

"How do I regard you now?" she queried breathlessly.

"Too aware. Trying to reason your way out of this attraction. Stop thinking," he murmured. Tilting his head, he lowered his mouth toward hers. The approach was slow and deliberate. His grip was loose and without force. "Let yourself feel it."

She stumbled back, panting because she couldn't breathe when he was so close.

Jasper watched her retreat with hooded eyes. She was nearly beyond arm's reach when he growled and caught her back. His lips sealed over hers with a boldness that stole what was left of her air. With one hand at her nape and an arm around her waist, Jasper took her mouth as if he owned it. Undeniably skilled and . . . hungry. A slanting, suckling, ferocious possession that stunned her completely.

Eliza sagged into him, unable to comprehend the ardor with which he kissed her. His body was astonishingly hard, like warm marble. From shoulder to thigh, he pressed unyieldingly against her. Without the barrier of her stays the sensation was . . . Dear God, she couldn't describe the need she had to touch more of him. Her hands clenched and released at her sides, reaching for him, then falling away.

Where should—could—she touch him?

As if he understood, Jasper's hand at her nape followed the length of her arm down to her wrist. His fingers circled it, then lifted her hand to his chest. Between his coat and waistcoat he urged her palm to splay over his heart. His skin burned through the layers of clothing between them. His heartbeat raced with the same recklessness as hers.

Her other hand clenched the hem of his coat. She whimpered, overwhelmed.

Her capitulation gentled him. The press of his lips softened and his grip slackened enough to allow her lungs to expand. Teasing rather than taking, Jasper licked the lower curve of her lip, goading her to taste him back. She did, trembling, uncertain.

At the first flick of her tongue, he captured it with soft suction. Startled, Eliza jerked in his arms, her breasts flattening against his chest. His groan vibrated against her, tumbling across sensitized nerve endings.

"Eliza."

The clock on the mantel began to chime on the half hour, but Eliza was lost to time, focused instead on the luxuriant licks stroking deep into her mouth. Her hand moved across Jasper's torso, feeling the muscles tense beneath her touch. A sound escaped her, a soft plea.

Jasper lifted his head, breathing hard. With heavy-lidded eyes, he studied her face.

"This," he said gruffly, "is how you should look at me, the way you look at no one else. As if you long for me to finish what I've started. As if you ache to feel my mouth on you, my hands on you."

She did ache. And felt unappeased, as if she had an unquenched thirst. Her skin was too sensitive. Her fingers trembled. She was far too hot.

He stepped back and turned away in a motion as elegant as it was powerful. She couldn't help but follow him with her gaze. He was such a large and finely built man, yet he moved with such grace.

"Jasper." Her pulse leaped at the look he shot her. "Tomorrow night . . . I will save the first waltz for you."

She hadn't meant to say that. In retrospect, she wasn't certain she'd had anything to say at all. She simply felt the unaccountable urge to stay him and keep him just a little while longer. And she wanted to dance with him, to stand within the circle of his arms in a place where there was safety in numbers.

He returned. Reaching for her hand, he lifted it and pressed a kiss to the back, giving her fingers a squeeze that only added to the tingling his lips had evoked. "I'm not well versed in dancing. Let me rephrase: I do not know how."

"You don't?" Eliza was astonished by the pronouncement and the lack of education it implied. But he comported himself without fault and was well-spoken.

It would be weeks before Tobias Reynolds returned. How would she bear the wondering about his origins until then?

Jasper's smile chased her ruminations away and curled her toes. "I shall endeavor to please you in other ways. Be assured, I will not rest until you're completely satisfied. Until tomorrow."

He departed the room. It was several minutes later before Eliza felt steady enough to do the same.

It was a beautiful afternoon. A brief spate of rain before the sun rose had cleared the worst of the soot from the air, leaving behind a pale blue sky. It was the kind of day that lightened moods and increased the proliferation of smiles.

But Eliza was nervous.

It was a rarity for her to feel out of sorts. There were very few things that affected her mood in a negative way, because reason so often provided the answers required to accept any given situation. But physical attraction had no reason. It was instinctual and separate from the mind. And she wasn't immune to it, as she'd hoped she would be.

What was she to say to Jasper, who was waiting in the parlor to escort her about town for the day? She sighed and turned away from the cheval mirror. Perhaps it would be best to leave the opening of discussion to him. A man such as Jasper Bond must be familiar with such circumstances.

She descended to the ground-level floor with studiously controlled speed, her hand coasting along the top of the wooden handrail to support less than steady steps. She was still chastising herself for deliberately selecting a pale yellow gown, one of the few pastel colors that suited her. It hadn't been laid out on the far right. What did she hope to gain by encouraging Jasper's interest?

On the other hand, what did she have to lose?

"Mr. Bond," she said as she entered the parlor, steeling herself for the sight of him and finding the effort ineffective. When her brain stopped, her feet followed suit by abruptly halting their forward movement. She stumbled.

In the process of standing, Jasper was agile enough to lunge forward and catch her by the elbows. He steadied her with a frown. "Eliza."

"Thank you." She pulled free and stepped back, needing some distance to catch her breath.

How dangerously handsome he was. The fine cut and quality of his dark green velvet coat and the beautiful silver-threaded embroidery in his pale green waistcoat enticed the eye to linger and admire. His fawn-colored breeches hugged powerful horseman's thighs, a sight that made her feel things she oughtn't. But that was merely the packaging. It was the man inside the trappings who so appealed to her. The magnetism he exuded. The sense that at any moment something extraordinary would happen. The phantom tingling of her lips that brought heated reminiscences of his kiss to mind.

She looked away, seeking the clock to distract herself.

"You're early." She startled herself by feeling . . . *pleased* by that.

"You wreak havoc on a man's schedule," he said with a slight smile to soften the sting.

The tiny warmth in her chest blossomed.

"You look lovely, Eliza." His voice lowered. "I wanted a few moments of your time before I'm restrained by decorum."

"You will be restrained by me, *young man."*

Eliza turned as Regina, Lady Collingsworth, entered the room like a whirlwind. She was a guinea-blond matron with piercing blue eyes and cherry-red cheeks. A sweet and pleasant woman for the most part, she was capable of a great force of will, and she took in Jasper's appearance with a steely glance.

Wagging a closed fan at him, she said, "You are a pretty fellow, Mr. Bond. Accustomed to testing your boundaries and finding little resistance, I bet. But I will not tolerate such nonsense. You'll behave yourself. If you want the right to be naughty, you will have to provide more than charm and a smile."

The top of her ladyship's head barely reached

Jasper's shoulder, but there was no doubt she could manage him.

Eliza quickly introduced them. "Her ladyship and her son, Lord Collingsworth, will be escorting us today."

Jasper sketched a faultlessly elegant bow. "A pleasure, Lady Collingsworth."

"Let us see if you feel the same by the end of the afternoon."

In short order they were on their way, comfortably seated in Lord Collingsworth's barouche with the men on one side, and Eliza and Regina on the other. Eliza studied the two gentlemen from beneath the shade of her wide-brimmed hat, attempting to resolve in her mind why she should be so attracted to one man above all others. Was it because Jasper seemed to be equally attracted to her? If so, perhaps the simplest solution was to discuss it with him and see if he wouldn't be willing to be less overt. He'd given no serious indication that he was doing anything more than being very, very thorough about his work. And she knew she wasn't the sort of female who incited raging passions in men.

The thought had a depressive effect on her sprits.

Determined to be less maudlin, she moved her attention to Lord Collingsworth. The epitome of aristocratic excellence, his lordship was tall and slender with stern lips and an aquiline nose. His hair was as light as his mother's, but he lacked her liveliness. Collingsworth had lost both wife and unborn child a year ago, and the light of joy that once filled him had died along with them. His grief was reflected in the somberness of his clothing and the rarity of his smiles. Eliza was still trying to comprehend why the things that brought him happiness before his marriage were no longer capable of doing so now. Yes, he'd lost what Lady Collingsworth had brought to him, but surely he retained the interests he'd had as a bachelor?

Clearly, she was missing something required to reason out the answer. She was becoming resigned to the notion that she would never be capable of understanding romantic natures.

Jasper's boot tapped against the side of her foot. She met his gaze with raised brows.

Look at me, he mouthed with darkened eyes.

Did he not understand how difficult that was? Of course he didn't. He did not feel overheated and confused when he looked at her. He didn't struggle to understand why the act of pressing their lips together had created overwhelming feelings in other parts of the anatomy.

Frustrated, she crossed her arms and looked at the passing carriages.

The toe of his boot touched her ankle, then slid up along the back of her lower calf.

Eliza froze. Her lungs seized, holding her breath. A shiver moved up her leg to unmentionable places. Wide-eyed, she glanced at him.

Jasper winked. As indignation welled up within her, his tongue traced the curve of his lower lip in a slow, sensual glide. Her breath left her in a rush. Instantly and viscerally she recalled the feel of that talented tongue against her lips and in her mouth, thrusting deep and sure in imitation of a far more intimate act.

Her breasts grew heavy and tender. The beat of her heart quickened and her skin tingled from her head to the place where his boot stroked her. It suddenly struck her that Jasper was deliberately arousing her. In the middle of the day. In the center of town. Seated inches away from two other people.

His hand lifted to an unsecured button on his coat. Strong fingers grasped it, the pad of his thumb rubbing leisurely against the outer curve. She watched, mesmerized, imagining him touching her skin that way. On the curve of her shoulder, perhaps. Or somewhere else.

He would know the best place to focus that caress.

The thought of his skill thrilled her.

Her face heated. She shifted restlessly on the squab, hoping to find a more comfortable position and worsening her predicament instead. She clutched her throat, rubbing it to facilitate her breathing. She felt as if she might pant, as if her stays were too tight and she might soon become dizzy.

Jasper's gaze settled on her gently heaving breasts. She knew she should look away and collect herself, but she could not. Her brain writhed in dismay, horrified that her body would so completely fail to function properly for no other reason than that Jasper Bond was undressing her in his mind. She knew he was remembering her as she'd been last night. Partially dressed. Easily bared.

The barouche slowed to a stop.

"Here we are," Lady Collingsworth said with customary cheerfulness.

Jasper broke the connection first, his head turning toward Somerset House. Eliza looked down, watching as his foot withdrew from beneath her skirts.

How she made the journey from the carriage to the interior of the edifice was a mystery to her. By the time she recovered the full use of her mental and physical faculties, they were entering the Exhibition Hall. Light poured into the large room from the arched windows high above the hall floor. The walls were covered in paintings, the gilded frames butting against each other, occupying every tiny bit of space.

As they neared the center of the room, Jasper slowed their progress to a standstill. Eliza looked at him, surprised to find him staring raptly at the images before him. His head was tilted back to the point that the rear of his hat brim nearly touched his back.

Eliza took stock of the room's other occupants, noting that the nearest individual was a few feet away. She leaned nearer to Jasper and whispered his name.

"Hmm . . . ?"

"Do you remember saying you would answer any question I asked, so long as it pertained to the present?"

"Yes." He did not cease his enthralled perusal of the art. "Ask me anything."

She cleared her throat. "Do you . . . want to . . . mate with me?"

He jolted so violently, the reaction shook her, too. His wide-eyed gaze darted to hers. "Eliza."

"I do not see why you should look so astonished," she said, "after kissing me last night, and considering your actions during the ride here."

His gaze warmed. A smile curved his lips. He relaxed, focusing completely on her. "Forgive me. Your choice of wording combined with our location took me aback."

"I didn't expect to have to discuss such things with you," she muttered. "I apologize if I say things incorrectly. But I must know if you can refrain from provoking me. Does the thoroughness of our presentation have to be established with the tactics you've utilized thus far or—"

"—or do I indeed want to *mate* with you?" Jasper's smile widened. "Is that what you want to know?"

Eliza nodded briskly, feeling anxious even though her question was perfectly sound considering their circumstances.

He squeezed her hand where it rested on his forearm. "You are wondering if I'm manipulating the performance I want out of you, or if my blood is so hot for you I cannot bear for you not to feel similarly?"

She averted her gaze. Described in that way, her query sounded ridiculous. Jasper was a dazzlingly handsome man. Even now, as she looked around the room to avoid his stare, she found a number of women ogling him or casting surreptitious glances in his direction at regular intervals. He could have any woman he wanted. One who was charming and flirtatious. Knowledgeable.

"Miss Martin."

Eliza turned her attention to the man who intruded on their conversation. "Sir Richard," she managed. "How lovely to see you here."

Sir Richard Tolliver was an average man, neither young nor old, neither tall nor short, neither portly nor lean. His hair was a soft brown and his eyes a gentle green. He was quiet and unassuming, one of the least aggressive of her suitors.

"You remember my sister, Miss Amanda Tolliver," he said, with a sidelong glance at Jasper.

"Yes, of course. Good to see you, Miss Tolliver." Eliza made the appropriate introductions offhandedly. But when Jasper bowed over Miss Tolliver's hand and the young lady blushed to the roots of her lovely dark hair, Eliza found her mood altering drastically.

Sir Richard offered a tight smile. "I see now why you declined my invitation to escort you to the exhibition, Miss Martin. I did not understand you had a prior engagement."

Eliza realized with some surprise that he was upset. He felt slighted, although that hadn't been her intent. She'd simply been aware that accepting his offer of escort would lead to spending hours in the company of someone with whom she had nothing in common. She thought it best to spare them both the awkwardness.

That was not, however, the explanation she could give. Conversing in society had little to do with truth. It was more about keeping everyone's feelings as neutral as possible. For many, the truth was not a neutral topic.

She was considering how she could reply in an acceptable manner when Miss Tolliver batted her thick lashes at Jasper. Eliza froze with her mouth partially formed around a word. Suddenly she knew precisely how Tolliver felt, and how little sound reasoning had to do with it.

What a morass the art of courting was.

"Will I see you tonight at the Lansing rout, Sir Richard?" she asked.

"If you will be there, Miss Martin, I will certainly attend."

"If you are obliged, I should like to save the first waltz for you."

Tolliver's sudden grin lit up the room. Eliza was slightly frightened by its fervency.

"What about you, Mr. Bond?" Miss Tolliver asked. "Will you be at the Lansing rout? Shall I save a place on my dance card for you?"

Eliza felt Jasper's forearm tense beneath her fingers. When he said nothing, she realized he didn't know how to reply. The truth he'd shared so readily with her was not one he wished to share with others.

"Mr. Bond was injured yesterday," she lied. "His horse was ill-mannered and stepped quite harshly on his foot. While he can walk, dancing is out of the question for now."

"Oh. I'm so sorry to hear that." Miss Tolliver

did indeed look crestfallen. "I hope you recover quickly, Mr. Bond."

Jasper nodded and bid the siblings farewell. He led Eliza away with a briskness that belied the injury she'd invented for him. He drew to a halt when they reached a corner and glared at the painting in front of him.

His foot tapped against the floor. "The dance you gave to Tolliver was mine."

Eliza was confused. "But you do not dance."

"Moments ago," he said in a low, biting tone, "you were asking if I wanted to be inside you and the next, you're encouraging another man's obvious interest in you."

Astonished by the physical response she had to his choice of phrasing, she stared at the painting he was directing his ire at and tried to piece an explanation together.

"I was not encouraging him," she said carefully. "I was commiserating with him. I collected that he was perturbed and perhaps felt . . . marginalized."

Jasper glanced at her with a sardonically raised brow. "You know how he feels, but not how I feel. Care to explain why?"

"Miss Tolliver is clearly taken with you, and she's lovely and charming. As many times as we've met before, today was the first time I resented those qualities in her."

He grew very still.

Unsure if that was a positive or negative sign, she pressed on. "Sir Richard must feel similarly in regards to you. How can he compete with a man such as yourself? I vow there isn't another male in the world who is as stunning. In the face of what must have been a crushing feeling of inferiority, offering a dance seemed the least I could do."

Jasper's face gave away none of his thoughts. After a torturously long delay, he said, "You have no notion that the room just tilted on its axis, do you?"

Chapter 5

Jasper watched as Eliza's gaze darted around the Exhibition Hall in search of proof to support his claim. A rush of tenderness tightened his chest and prevented him from explaining.

Eliza returned her attention to him. "Lady Collingsworth doesn't look as if something so phenomenal has happened."

"Ah, Eliza," he murmured, warmly amused. "Lynd said you would drive me mad, and he was correct, as usual."

Her pretty mouth pursed into a tight line. "I begin to feel as if I am lacking wits," she groused. "I have been at a loss to understand anything since I woke this morning."

He found her confusion poignantly endearing. He wished he could reply to her in a gentler manner, but he was not a gentle man. As surprising as her use of "mate" had been earlier, he found it brilliantly apt now. His desire for her was at a fever pitch, his blood hot and his patience far too thin. If they'd been alone, he would be fucking her now. *Mating* with her. Pumping his cock so deep into her she would have no doubt that her public performance was the furthest thing from his mind.

Rolling his shoulders back, he tried to ward off the tension building there. He could not talk about sex right now, even to say that he wanted it with her. The words would be too coarse, his vehemence too frightening. And he wasn't yet sure that she wanted it with him. Her body did, yes. Watching her melt for him in the barouche had been singularly the most arousing experience of his life. But she had been overwhelmed and not thinking properly at the time. Eliza needed to be cognizant of her decision to take him to her bed if he was to have her as he wanted.

She watched him now, wary and unsure.

He urged her to walk with him, needing to be in motion. It didn't escape his notice that she had him in this state by speech alone. Not with a look or a touch, but with innocently spoken, artlessly truthful words.

"I want you to teach me how to dance," he said.

"Truly?" The excitement in her voice was its own reward.

"It's the only way to make restitution for giving my dance to someone else." And another way to add a block of time with her to his schedule.

Her smile was a sight to behold. "I must warn you, I am not a very good instructor of anything. I lack patience and become easily frustrated."

"I am a speedy learner," he assured, intending to make the lessons worth her while in many ways.

"Very well, then. I would be happy to try."

Returning his attention to the portraits on the wall, Jasper acknowledged that he enjoyed the exhibition. He had not expected to, as he wasn't fond of crowds. The room was almost full and the hum of conversation was a steady but not-unpleasant drone. He should not have felt comfortable there. He was a mongrel among purebreds, yet Eliza made him feel as if he was right where he should be. At the very least, right where he wanted to be.

"Which is your favorite so far?" she asked.

"I think that one." He pointed to an image of a galloping horse. "I can almost feel the wind when I look at it."

"Mine is this one." She pulled him forward and singled out a portrait of a dancing nymph with flowing hair and ribbons. "The skill involved in turning mere paints into an image that looks as if it can walk right off the canvas . . . I am awed by it."

"I'm glad you came with me and not with Tolliver," he said.

She squeezed his arm. "I am, too."

They continued around the room at a leisurely pace, pausing every few feet to take in the many paintings occupying the soaring walls.

After an hour, Eliza begged to be excused. "Will you be comfortable if I leave you alone for a moment?"

Jasper wanted to say no. "Only a moment."

She moved away. He expected her to speak to

someone she knew or visit with Lady Collingsworth for a time. Instead, she left the room. He moved to follow, wanting to ensure her safety by keeping her in sight.

Lady Collingsworth deftly intercepted him.

"My lady," he said, with a slight inclination of his head.

She wrapped her hand around his forearm and waved him forward with her fan. "I would like to become better acquainted with you, Mr. Bond."

"Oh?" He looked toward the exit in time to see Sir Richard Tolliver and his sister make their egress.

"Eliza's mother and I were dear friends. After Lady Georgina's passing, I took Eliza under my wing. I couldn't love her more if she was my own child."

"She is an exceptional young woman."

"Not so young," she said, eyeing him. "She has had six failed Seasons."

"By her choice. And she is young in more than her years. She has an almost childlike comprehension of emotions."

"You sound as if you know her well, yet I have never heard of you prior to yesterday. Why are you here, Mr. Bond? And when will you return to the place whence you came?"

They rounded a corner of the room and Jasper considered his reply. A hastily spoken falsehood could breach Eliza's privacy. "I am here on business."

"You are in trade?" Her ladyship pulled away

enough to facilitate studying his attire. "Success-fully, it would appear."

Jasper smiled. "Is it a mark in my favor that I am not in pursuit of Miss Martin's fortune?"

"Depends on what else you are in pursuit of. I am not blind. I see the way you look at her."

"I am not blind either."

"Cheeky fellow," she admonished, but there was a twinkle in her eye. "What are your intentions?"

He stared at a painting nigh the size of his cur-ricle and mulled over his reply. In the end, he cir-cumvented the question. "I want her to be safe and happy."

And yet his "intentions," such as they were, might very well put her safety and happiness at risk. For her, there must be some comfort in her ignorance of softer emotions. Already their association had caused her to feel bewildered and to act against sound reasoning.

"Excellent sentiments," Lady Collingsworth said. "I could not agree more. Might I suggest you pay your addresses sooner, rather than later? It would be lovely for her to enjoy a few weeks of the Season as an affianced woman."

The tension in Jasper's shoulders returned, but for a different reason. Speaking carefully, he an-swered, "I am not certain she would be best served with me."

"I see." There was a long moment wherein her ladyship drummed her gloved fingertips into his forearm. "Do you know, Mr. Bond, I can count on my fingers the number of times I have seen Eliza smile in public?"

"She does not smile often," he agreed, feeling more than a little triumph that she'd smiled so brilliantly at him today.

"I would suggest you leave the determination of what makes Eliza feel safe and happy to her. Speculation is necessary in business, but in affairs of the heart, it often leads to poor judgments."

"I will take that under advisement."

Her mouth curved on one side. "I can see what she likes about you, Mr. Bond. You listen. I suspect you don't always act on what you've heard, but you listen in any case."

They returned to the entrance and she released him. Jasper bowed, then ducked out of the room with unseemly haste. But he was stopped once again by Lord Westfield, who was a few feet away from reaching the Exhibition Hall with a delicate-looking blonde on his arm.

"Why, Bond," Westfield called out. "Where are you running off to?"

His lordship leaned down and whispered something to his companion. When his head lifted, she was smiling in a way that promised all sorts of delicious things. She moved into the room without him, leaving him to speak to Jasper.

"Miss Martin left the room some minutes ago," Jasper said.

"And you are following her with notable eagerness."

"I have been waylaid twice now." His glare made it clear who the second delay was.

"Well, then," his lordship said, "the least I can do is show you where the ladies' retiring rooms are, as I would imagine that's where she went. Unless you frightened her into fleeing. I say, your scowl is fearsome even to me."

Jasper growled softly.

Westfield laughed and gave concise directions. Jasper was grateful for the assistance, but was less appreciative of the note of amusement that colored its delivery.

With a quick salute of fingertips to his hat brim, he set off in search of Eliza. Several minutes had passed since she parted from him, an inconsiderable amount of time for many women but slightly too long for a lady who didn't fret about her appearance. He turned the corner and heard Eliza's voice float toward him, but he could not see her. There was a statue of a man between them, in the center of the hallway on a platform of rollers. She was speaking with calm efficiency to the men laboring to move the obstruction, explaining that one of the wheels seemed to be caught by the runner protecting the floor.

Shaking his head, Jasper started forward. How like her to linger and offer engineering advice, even of such a small nature. A fond smile curved his lips. She said he was a man clearly suited to more strenuous pursuits and he would not argue the point. However, it appeared a quick mind was as arousing to him as a naked woman.

"Miss Martin," he called out.

"Mr. Bond." She peeked around the thigh of the statue. "I have been eye level with the backside of this artwork for long moments now. It seems one of the wheels is indisposed to motion."

"Perhaps you should just squeeze around the platform?" he suggested, gauging the space on either side. There wasn't much room, despite the generous size of the hallway. In fact, the piece was so large it towered above them.

He slowed as he neared. "Is there another way around?" he asked, directing his question at the two red-faced men straining to push the piece down a tributary hallway.

"Aye," the larger of the two gasped. Straightening, he pulled a handkerchief from his pocket and mopped his brow.

The smaller man, seemingly unwilling to be delayed by courtesy toward a lady, charged into the base with his shoulder. The jolt dislodged the stuck wheel, causing the platform and statue to lurch forward. The wood creaked in protest. One of the thick lines of rope securing the heavy piece snapped. The resulting noise was like the crack of a whip. Jasper watched in horror as the statue listed away from him.

"Eliza!" he shouted, lunging forward but having no way to reach her.

The platform cracked and the troublesome wheel broke away, tumbling a short ways down the hall.

The rest was over far too quickly. The crash was deafening in the enclosed space. Debris from the shattered art piece billowed into the air in a hazy cloud.

Jasper could not see Eliza among the ruins.

Scrambling over the destruction, he reached the spot where he last saw her standing. The torso of the figure lay there in a solid piece. He was so stunned, he couldn't think. His chest was so tight, he swayed on his feet.

Shouts from other parts of the building grew in volume, competing with the thunderous sound of the blood rushing through his ears.

"Heavens," Eliza said. "What a mess."

Jasper's gaze followed the voice. She stood in a nearby doorway, staring at the disorder.

Dear God . . .

He clambered over wobbling chunks of decimated statue and crushed her to his chest.

"It looked as if the rope might have been cut at least partway through." Jasper held his third glass of brandy and continued to pace before the unlit fireplace in his study. His coat and waistcoat had been tossed over the arm of a wingback chair, yet still he felt too constricted. "But there's no way to be certain. I was only granted a brief look at it."

"You don't believe it was an accident," Westfield queried from his position on the settee, "despite the prominence of the location and the randomness of the event?"

"Miss Martin says the statue was waiting in a secondary hall when she went into the retiring room. Upon her emergence, she found it had been moved into her path."

"Two men were having a devil of a time pushing it," the earl reminded. "A lone individual would have found the task impossible."

"But one wheel was troublesome. Perhaps, not by chance." Jasper downed the contents of his tumbler in one swallow, seeking to warm the spot inside him chilled by the near miss. "Is it possible for one person to be the victim of so much misfortune?"

Setting the glass down on his desktop with a harsh thud, he glanced at the clock. It would be hours before he saw Eliza again at the Lansings' rout. He was certain to be in a state of high agitation until then. Assigning more men to watch the Melville household was small comfort.

Westfield made a noise suspiciously like a snort. "You are positively high-strung about the business, while Miss Martin seemed to take the happenings in stride."

"Because she trusts me to manage everything and keep her safe," Jasper said tightly.

"I trust you will, as well. But you appear less confident in your own abilities."

"The gravity of this 'accident' is also responsible for her lack of anxiety. The irony of that . . . Because this was by far the most dangerous event, she believes it's unrelated to the rest."

"Are you saying she's less concerned because she was almost killed?"

Jasper glanced at the earl and noted the amused interest on his lordship's face. For a brief moment, he was enraged by the entertainment Westfield appeared to be taking from the events of the afternoon. In the earl's privileged, pampered, ennui-afflicted life even the misfortune of others could enliven spirits.

Reining in his temper, Jasper turned away. He kneaded the back of his neck with a firm grip. "I am doing all I can. There is nothing to be done about my concern that I'm not doing enough."

He was meeting with Eliza's man of affairs tomorrow, and together they would be visiting her rental properties. His men were looking into the circumstances of her present tenants and recent ones. He intended to speak with Lord Collingsworth this evening about joining the investment pool Eliza mentioned, and he was waiting on word from Lord Melville regarding a time when they could meet. There were still her two fathers—Mr. Martin and Mr. Chilcott—to delve into, but he would see to those inquiries himself. Eliza's family secrets were not ones he wished anyone else to know about, despite the trust he placed in his crew.

"If it's any consolation," Westfield said, pushing to his feet, "you are engaged in a singularly unique investigation, while playing a role far outside your experience. Feeling as if you might be missing something is to be expected. But I'm here for you, if you need. I have the experience you lack. In fact, if you would like me to assume the courting of Miss Martin while you focus on the investigation, I would be happy to do so."

Jasper bared his teeth in a semblance of a smile. "That's quite all right."

The earl laughed. "The offer stands, if you should change your mind. In the meantime, I must eat and prepare for the evening's festivities. You should have a meal as well, and attempt some moderation in your drinking. Otherwise, you won't be much good to anyone."

Waving Westfield away with an impatient flick of his wrist, Jasper sank heavily into the chair behind his desk and mentally took apart every bit of information he'd gleaned so far, looking for any clue he might have missed.

He could not fail in this. Client satisfaction and point of pride be damned. He was acting on his own behalf, stricken by the memory of those brief moments when he'd feared Eliza had been gravely wounded . . . or worse.

It was not a feeling he intended to experience ever again.

"Bloody hell," Westfield grumbled, snatching two glasses of champagne from a passing servant's tray. He shoved one toward Jasper, causing the wine to slosh precariously up to the lip. "I'd forgotten how unintelligible Lady Lansing becomes when excited. I could not comprehend a word she said. How long were we held captive? Twenty minutes? Half an hour?"

"Ten, my lord. At most." Jasper's gaze searched the ballroom from one end to the other. It was a long and narrow space, with inlaid marble floors and three large chandeliers. Fluted columns surrounded the perimeter, as did the occasional potted fern. The far wall consisted entirely of French doors, most of which were thrown wide to allow the night air to circulate.

"Interminable." Westfield tossed back the contents of his glass. "The things I do for you, Bond."

"You should be flattered. Your illustrious presence single-handedly made Lady Lansing's ball a resounding success."

"I am not appeased."

"I owe you a debt, as well, of course," Jasper murmured, distracted by his inability to find Eliza. "Does that soothe your ire?"

The Lansing's ballroom was neither overly large nor overly filled. There was a respectable showing of guests, but it wasn't yet a crush. Why, then, couldn't he locate her glorious red hair?

Are you one of those gentlemen who have an unusually strong interest in red hair?

He hadn't been. He had considered all women equally endowed. Now, here he was, completely oblivious to every other hue but that novel fiery one.

The earl caught his arm. "Walk this way," Westfield urged, attempting to tug him along. "Someone is approaching whom I'd rather not speak to."

With a rueful smile, Jasper followed. They rounded the perimeter at a torturously slow pace due to the number of attendees who wished to greet the earl. Jasper was about to leave Westfield behind when he finally spotted her.

His step faltered. Westfield bumped into him.

"Damnation, Bond, what the devil are you—" The earl fell silent.

Jasper gave a low, appreciative whistle. Uncouth, to be sure, and an undeniable betrayal of his commonness, but it was sincere. He could find no words.

"Why," Westfield said in a contemplative tone, "I have clearly been remiss in not paying proper attention to Miss Martin."

Eliza stood amid a circle of acquaintances, most of whom were gentlemen. Her glorious hair had been arranged in abundant curls that framed her face and caressed her nape. Her body was clad in sapphire satin, the bold color incongruous amid the paler hues worn by the other women in attendance. There would have been no way to miss her, had she not been shorter than the crowd of salivating males around her.

What in God's name was she wearing?

Unable to help himself, Jasper stared with clenched fists. Riveted. The deep color of her gown showcased the creamy hue of her skin and the richness of her tresses to supreme advantage. The cut of the garment was painfully simple, with minimal detail. The gown's true beauty lay in how it clung to its wearer. How the low bodice hugged full, firm breasts and bared more than a glimpse of cleavage. How the long skirts emphasized the length of her legs. The short puffed sleeves failed to meet the uppermost end of Eliza's long white gloves, revealing a sprinkling of freckles on her upper arms that he found enchanting.

He was struck with fierce longing, like a man gone too long without a meal who doesn't realize he's starving until presented with the sight and smell of food.

An amused masculine voice intruded. "Glad to see I'm not the only man to lose all sense of social grace."

Jasper tore his gaze away from Eliza to see who spoke to him.

"Lord Brimley," Westfield said. "Good to see you again."

As the earl made the appropriate introductions, Jasper studied Baron Brimley with his usual thoroughness. The baron was a head shorter than both himself and Westfield, and far more slender. Although Brimley's hairline was receding with regretful swiftness, Jasper guessed he was younger than he appeared.

"Surprised to see you, Westfield," Brimley said after greeting Jasper. "Did word of Miss Martin's transformation spread so quickly?"

"Actually," the earl drawled, "I simply dropped all of this evening's invitations into a hat and withdrew a few. The 'transformation,' as you call it, is an unexpected boon."

"Mr. Tomlinson is of the mind that Miss Martin finally seeks to throw off the mantle of spinsterhood," Brimley relayed.

"Perhaps," Jasper suggested, feeling proprietary, "she's taken a fancy to someone and hopes to encourage him."

"You don't say?" Brimley's eyes were wide. "Care to guess who it is?"

"I am at a disadvantage, I'm afraid. I have yet to become acquainted with every moth circling her flame."

"Moth to flame, eh? Poetic and apt. Well, I shall take it upon myself to discover his identity."

Westfield clapped him on the shoulder. "You will, of course, be sporting and share your findings."

Brimley's chest puffed up. "Certainly, Westfield."

Jasper gave in to his impatience. With a slight bow, he sidestepped away. "If you will excuse me, my lords."

"Not so fast, Bond," Westfield said quickly. "I shall accompany you in your journey to pay court to the lovely Miss Martin. Excuse us, Brimley. Do keep us apprised of your discoveries."

The tension in Jasper's shoulders increased. Bringing Eliza to Westfield's attention—and the reverse—was not something he should view as threatening, but the feeling was there. He remembered what Eliza had said about her unexpected feelings of animosity toward Miss Tolliver and he admired her candor even more.

She caught sight of him when he was several feet away. Courtesy of her décolletage, he saw her breath catch and a gentle flush spread across her luminous skin. She stared, unblinking, and masculine triumph surged through him. She was clearly smitten by the sight of him, yet he had not provoked that response from her with any effort on his part.

He drew to a halt on the fringes of her circle. A pathway was made for him with obvious reluctance.

"Miss Martin."

She lowered her gaze and curtsied. "Good evening, Mr. Bond."

Jasper obliged Westfield with the necessary introductions, then backed away. For a while, he simply observed her in this new environment, smiling inwardly when she spoke so bluntly those around her momentarily lost their way in the conversation. As dramatic as her change of appearance was, she was still Eliza. While others spoke with great animation about the tale of her mishap at the Royal Academy, she frowned and bit her lower lip, clearly not reconciling the expanded tales with the actual reality. She looked at him often, seeming to take comfort in his proximity. He recalled his earlier thoughts about how at ease she made him feel in situations where he was feeling his way blind.

They were not so different. More than anything, he was drawn to the affinity they shared in unexpected and deeply seated ways.

In order to see him schooled properly, Jasper's mother had paid for his education with her pride and her life. He'd protested the expense, knowing what it would cost her, but she would not be swayed. In the end, he conceded only because he intended to support her, not for the reason she espoused—to impress his sire, a man well-versed in ignoring his many bastard issue.

Jasper blamed opium for his mother's failure to see the hopelessness of her quest. Certainly no one possessed of full mental faculty would hold the dream that a handsome son with a decent education and proper speech would engender fondness and paternal pride in a dissolute reprobate like the late Earl of Montague. Yes, Jasper was well-spoken and possessed of a refined sense of style. He could read and write. He was capable with numbers, although he lacked the fondness for them Eliza had. In short, he should fit in, but he did not. And he knew Eliza felt the same way.

A violin played a few opening notes, signaling an end to the orchestra's short break. Guests began to line up along the center of the parquet floor. Eliza shot him a long, meaningful glance and he knew she was going to be dancing *his* dance.

She took to the floor with Sir Richard Tolliver. Riveted by the elegant grace with which she glided across the room, Jasper could not take his eyes from her. The sapphire gown's skirts were noticeably fuller than those worn by the other females in attendance; he thought the style suited Eliza perfectly. There were more layers to her than most women.

The musicians began the opening notes of a waltz. Eliza stepped nearer to Tolliver and clasped his hand. With an accomplished flourish, he began the requisite series of steps.

Jasper frowned, thinking. There had been two Tollivers at the Exhibition Hall. They'd left the room shortly after Eliza and followed in her direction. On Eliza's list of suitors, Tolliver's name had been placed above Montague's, in part because he had a sister who could use a dowry to secure a more advantageous match.

Turning away, Jasper expected the other sibling would be nearby. He had only to find her.

Chapter 6

"You are a vision this evening, Miss Martin," Sir Richard said, as they circled the dance floor along with the other couples.

"Thank you." Eliza wondered if she should say more than that. What did one say that wouldn't sound awkward? She always considered such praise to be a platitude. She was well aware she was no classic beauty. However, since she'd put effort into looking attractive this evening, it would be disingenuous to assume none of the compliments were sincere. Especially considering she was wearing one of her mother's gowns.

Eliza was still stunned at her decision. Her mother was someone she never wanted to emulate. Lady Georgina had been irrepressible and impetuous. She'd paid little heed to the consequences of her actions and how they might affect others. For years, Eliza had asked herself the question "What would Mother do?" so she could choose the reverse option. But after this afternoon, she wanted to do something nice for Jasper. He'd been so distraught after the unfortunate event at Somerset House. It meant a great deal to her that he cared so much for her well-being. If she were completely honest, she would also say she hoped her attire might goad an answer from him in regards to her earlier question about mating.

Of course, there was also the reasonable explanation for her choice: it signaled to one and all that a drastic change had occurred in her life. She'd known the very day her mother had taken a fancy to Mr. Chilcott. Lady Georgina's blue eyes had been bright, her lips red, and her cheeks flushed. She had hummed to herself and burst out in song at odd moments. Over the following week, she'd smiled incessantly. But most telling of all was the way she altered her mode of dress. She'd begun choosing gowns with conservative adornments and richer colors, as if she knew her smitten glow was accessory enough. Eliza understood that she could not continue to go about looking as ordinary as possible and expect others to believe she was extraordinarily attached to a particular man.

Sir Richard cleared his throat. "I pray you'll forgive me, Miss Martin, but I am concerned for you."

"Concerned?"

"I detest stepping into affairs that are removed from me," he said, sounding anything but reluctant. "However, I fear your laudable discrimination in selecting a spouse has become lax."

Her brows rose. "Lax?"

"I speak of Mr. Bond, of course."

"I see." Although Tolliver had been paying court to her for two Seasons now, this was the first display of condescension she'd witnessed. She did not like his tone at all. It was one a parent or tutor would use with a recalcitrant child.

"There is something about Mr. Bond that doesn't sit well with me. I cannot put my finger on it, but something is not right with him."

She turned her head and located Jasper standing by a fluted column with crossed arms and hooded eyes. Not for the first time, she noted how he didn't look at her as he had on the day they'd met. His stare now was hotter, more aware, and it awakened an answering awareness in her. Warmth blossomed in the pit of her stomach and expanded. They had known each other only a few days, but she was irrevocably changed by his acquaintance, newly cognizant of a baser sensibility previously veiled from her.

As for Tolliver's assertions, although she didn't appreciate the manner of their delivery, she could not fault him for making them. Jasper's attire was the only thing polished about him. Although he appeared innocuous on the surface, those with keen perception would recognize how incongruous he was among the crowd. There was a razor's edge of menace to him and a sleek grace to his movements that was inherently predaceous.

"I see no evidence of unsuitability," she lied. "In truth, I find him quite acceptable."

"Miss Martin, I must say, I am alarmed by your estimation. Who are his people?"

"His father is known to Lord Melville." Eliza followed Sir Richard's lead through an unusually vigorous turn. He was such an accomplished dancer; his uncustomary carelessness was telling.

"I suspect he is in want of funds, and you have them."

"That applies to many gentlemen of my acquaintance, wouldn't you agree? But I'm curious. What led you to the assumption that Mr. Bond is a fortune hunter and more of a hazard than my other suitors? Certainly his appearance refutes such a conclusion."

Jasper looked beyond reproach this evening. Dressed in a dark gray velvet coat and a pale blue waistcoat, he looked accomplished and elegant. The expert tailoring of the whole ensemble displayed the power of his body to advantage. She fully appreciated how strong and capable he was. She felt safe knowing he was nearby. The only person capable of harming her when Jasper was near was Jasper himself.

"Miss Martin." Tolliver looked pained. "I must advise you that it's most disconcerting to dance with a female who spends the duration of the waltz admiring another gentleman."

"I am not admiring him, sir." At least, not verbally. "I am merely requesting that you expound upon the methods of deduction you used to reach your conclusion. You say he is in want of funds, I see no evidence of such. I should like to know what you see that I don't."

"A lady of your refined reasoning is at a disadvantage in this situation." His brown eyes were somber. "I shall explain. He's regarding you in an inappropriate fashion, Miss Martin."

"Are you saying," she asked carefully, "Mr. Bond must be in want of money because he cannot take his eyes off me? I don't understand the logic. Isn't it possible Mr. Bond might find something visually appealing about me? Perhaps my trim figure has garnered his admiration?"

"Your form is attractive," he conceded gruffly.

"Or my hair? Some men are excessively fascinated by certain hues, I'm told."

A flush rose from beneath his cravat to color his cheekbones. "You have lovely hair."

"But my attractive form and lovely tresses are not enough to explain why Mr. Bond regards me so intently? I suppose that's due to his exceedingly comely face and its ability to captivate anyone with unhindered vision. Correct me if I'm wrong, but I understand you to mean that my limited physical charms are no match for his. He can certainly find a far more beautiful female." Eliza wrinkled her nose, as if in deep thought. "Well, then, perhaps it's my brain he finds so interesting."

"I agree you are extremely clever, Miss Martin," he said in a fervent rush, swiftly grasping at the change of topic. "It's why I like you so well, and why I'm certain we will enjoy each other's companionship for an indefinite period of time. However, Mr. Bond obviously lends more attention to cultivating his exterior than his interior. One does not attain that physical size through intellectual exertions. I doubt he's capable of grasping the worth of your brain. In fact, in your position, I would wonder if it was even possible to have meaningful discourse with him."

Eliza nodded. "I understand now. Ruling out my mental and physical attributes would leave only my fortune as an enticement for handsome men. I'm quite enlightened, Sir Richard."

The waltz ended. She retreated the moment the last strains faded away. "Thank you. This discussion has been most informative. However, I seek clarification on one point: If attractive men find only my fortune alluring and you find my brain alluring, does that make you unattractive?"

Tolliver's mouth opened, then closed. Then opened again. Nothing came out.

After an abbreviated curtsy, Eliza spun about and left the dance floor. She intended to go to Jasper, but he was no longer where she last saw him.

Jasper found Miss Tolliver on the dance floor. Shortly afterward, he was himself found by Lord Westfield.

"I'm almost inclined to wed posthaste," his lordship said, "to spare myself further pre-matrimonial torment."

"Because post-matrimonial torment is eminently more bearable," Jasper said dryly.

"I don't have unreasonable qualifications for a spouse," Westfield said with some defensiveness. "So long as she doesn't aggravate me unduly, and I'm not averse to bedding her, I am open to anyone of suitable breeding."

"How progressive of you."

The earl arched a brow. "Your tone leaves something to be desired. Now, tell me there's something to be done here. I'm bored."

"When Miss Tolliver exits the dance floor, I should like her to know my theory regarding today's events."

"Ah, you want to see how she reacts. Personally, I don't see how a woman could have moved that statue. And you cannot tell me Sir Richard helped her. I'm not even certain he could lift his sibling."

"Leave no stone unturned."

When the waltz ended, they made certain to place themselves in Miss Tolliver's path. She greeted Westfield with a charming and studied curtsy.

"Miss Tolliver." Westfield gave an elegant bow. "A pleasure to see you."

"Thank you, my lord." She offered a sympathetic smile to Jasper. "How is your foot this evening, Mr. Bond?"

"Improving, Miss Tolliver. Thank you."

The pretty brunette offered a flirtatious smile. The pale yellow gown she wore was more heavily adorned than the similarly shaded gown Eliza had worn earlier in the day. Such details were not something Jasper was accustomed to noting. What a woman wore or how she styled her hair was inconsequential to him.

But Eliza's appearance tonight was such a contrast to her usual mode of dress he suspected she purposely minimized her beauty before. It made him consider the attire of others with a more discerning eye, part of his careful reflection on the desire he had for her. Only days into their acquaintance and he knew he would not be ready to part from her in the foreseeable future. He also knew he was willing to go to great lengths to have her.

"I heard about the unfortunate incident at the Royal Academy." Miss Tolliver shook her head. "How terrifying for Miss Martin! I am certain I would be bedridden for a sennight after such a shock."

"She is managing extraordinarily well," he agreed.

"Especially considering the circumstances," Westfield said, in a confidential tone.

She frowned. "Circumstances?"

The earl leaned closer. "There is some speculation that the rope securing the statue might have been deliberately cut."

"No!" Her hand went to her throat. "Why would anyone do something so heinous? Especially to Miss Martin."

"I didn't say she was the intended target," he qualified, straightening. "She might simply have been in the wrong place at the wrong time."

"Well, there is some small comfort in that." She exhaled audibly. "Deliberately cut, you say. I wonder why?"

She looked away and worried her lower lip with her teeth.

"I wouldn't dare speculate," Westfield said. "It's rarely good to have one's name associated with such sensational tales."

"True of us all," she said gravely, dipping into another curtsy. Miss Tolliver excused herself, and Jasper followed her with his gaze. She headed directly to a group of women.

"She spreads the tale," Westfield murmured, turning his back to her.

"That's no proof of innocence. In fact, a clever person might assume that bearing the news to others would lighten suspicion. After all, what reasonable person would air their misdeeds to all and sundry?" Jasper intended to have both Tollivers followed for a time. He would not take any chances.

"Excellent point."

"What do you know of the investment pool managed by Lord Collingsworth?"

"I participated for a time, but Collingsworth is too conservative for my taste. You might feel similarly."

How like Eliza to be cautious. Money was vitally important to her, not for what it could buy, but for the measure of freedom and control its possession granted her. "Do you know who the other investors are?"

"A few. Not all. Why?"

"Miss Martin is one of them."

"Truly?" Westfield's brows rose. "Wasn't aware of that. Does that make me a suspect?"

Smiling, Jasper said, "Possibly."

The earl grabbed a glass of champagne from a passing servant. "How delicious."

"Not if you're at fault." Jasper moved forward.

"Was that a threat, Bond?"

"Not if you are at fault," he said again. "In that case, it would be a promise."

"Where are you going?"

"To the card room. Perhaps the scent of desperation will lead me in a new direction."

"You never answered my question about what you'll do once you own Montague's property." Although Westfield was the public face of the wager that secured the property, Jasper hadn't revealed why he wanted it.

However, he had no hesitation in revealing what he would do with it. "I will raze the house, then leave England."

"For parts unknown?"

"Didn't I tell you?" Jasper looked at him. "I've purchased a plantation in the South Seas."

"Good God." The earl choked on his champagne. "Only you would find peace living among savages."

"I think similarly about your life."

A brilliant shade of sapphire blue in the periphery of Jasper's vision caught his interest. He turned his head to catch Eliza moving toward one of three sets of French doors leading outside to a wide veranda.

She shot him a look over her shoulder. It was not the calculated look of a practiced flirt. It was simpler and more sincere, betraying pleasure at seeing him and the hope he might follow.

He smiled and inclined his head in acknowledgment.

"I will go ahead without you," Westfield murmured.

"I'll only be a moment."

"You disappoint me, Bond. When a beautiful woman looks at you in that manner, you should need far more time than that."

* * *

Eliza moved toward the nearest exterior exit with the hope that her dark gown would blend somewhat with the darkness of night and provide her a brief spell of anonymity. She felt Jasper's stare following her and fought the urge to quicken her pace. Not because she wished to avoid him, but because it was instinctive to run when caught in the sights of a hunter.

The anticipation of capture was its own pleasure. The hair on her nape stood on end and gooseflesh covered the parts of her arms exposed above her long gloves. When the warmth of a large hand surrounded her elbow, she couldn't fight the shiver that moved through her.

"Miss Martin." Jasper's deep voice caused a tingling in her stomach. With an easy grip, he led her outdoors to where several guests were paired in quietly voiced conversations. "You might have warned me that you would steal my breath upon sight."

"Thank you." Unlike Tolliver's compliment, Jasper's praise did not make her feel awkward. Instead, she felt warm and slightly giddy.

"Altering your appearance to goad speculation was an excellent plan." He looked down at her with warm appreciation. "In case I've failed to mention it, I love the way you think."

Eliza flushed. "Would you admire my intellect less to know I hoped my presentation would impress you as much as my reasoning?"

"No. I would be deeply flattered."

"I feel silly," she confessed. "Simply knowing you goads me into acting in ways I normally wouldn't."

Jasper smiled, and she found him so handsome it made her chest tighten. "Would it ease your nervousness to know I have second-guessed every aspect of my attire from the knot of my cravat to the shoes on my feet before every meeting I've had with you since the first? I believe it's part of the mating ritual."

He slowed as they stepped outside the circle of light cast by the ballroom chandeliers. There were torches set around the veranda, but they were spaced at wide intervals to provide just enough illumination to delineate where stone gave way to lawn.

"Part of the charade?" she asked.

"I've yet to feign anything with you, Eliza."

Unsure of how to banter flirtatiously, she moved on to safer topics. "How do you know Lord Westfield?"

"Lucian Remington introduced us one evening."

She was momentarily surprised Jasper would boast membership in such an exclusive establishment as Remington's Gentlemen's Club. Then, she recalled that Lucian Remington was the bastard son of the Duke of Glasser. He was known to allow gentlemen of any background to join his club . . . so long as they could afford it. The practice was tolerated by those born of higher station because Remington's was grand on the grandest scale. They were loath to deny themselves such luxury.

"Have you known one another long?"

"Not excessively long, no."

Although he didn't move, she sensed the change in him. The sudden alertness. It was similar to being doused by chilled water. She sometimes forgot she and Jasper Bond hardly knew one another, because her overwhelming physical attraction to him fostered an illusion of intimacy.

Eliza deliberately kept her tone light when she said, "Forgive me for prying into your personal matters. They are none of my concern."

She would do well to follow his example and keep to safer topics in their relations. He worked for her, and an employee was all he would ever be to her. Perhaps it would slow her fascination with him to keep that in mind.

How deeply could one fall when the pool was shallow?

While there was no outward sign of it, Jasper knew Eliza had withdrawn and he'd lost ground with her. Relationships were complications for just that reason—at some point, women expected full disclosure. He found the need mystifying.

But he wasn't willing to cede any of the progress he had made with Eliza, regardless of the points on which he would have to bend.

"I met him two years ago," he elaborated. "He finds the work I do interesting and from that interest, we became . . . friends."

"You say the word 'friends' so strangely."

"It's not one I am accustomed to using."

She nodded and softened toward him, both physically and otherwise. "I understand."

Jasper looked at the stone beneath his feet. Of course she would understand. There was an unusual affinity between them. On the surface, they could not be more wrong for one another. In private moments, however, nothing had ever felt more right.

"Ah, there you are, Miss Martin," a confident and familiar voice called out.

Turning his head, Jasper watched Lord Montague exit the ballroom. Wearing dark emerald velvet and an artful amount of diamond accoutrements, the earl looked solvent and unflappable. It was a feat made more impressive by Jasper's knowledge of the truth. Montague's circumstances could not be shakier. Still, the earl's wide smile and bright eyes made it clear he was genuinely pleased to see Eliza. Or at the very least, the fortune she represented.

Jasper straightened. He'd never resented his younger brother for bearing the title and privileges that came with it—until the present. In the case of Eliza, Montague's advantages now posed the first real threat to Jasper's aims. Jasper could provide only intangibles, such as passion, acceptance, adventure, which were things Eliza had only recently shown an interest in. If she came to the conclusion that she needed matrimony to have sex . . .

There was the possibility that in seducing her, he was pushing her into marriage.

Extending his hand, Jasper waited for Eliza to

set hers atop his palm. He kissed the back, hating the white satin barring his lips from her soft, pale skin. "I shall leave you to your admirer," he murmured, giving her fingers a reassuring squeeze.

As much as he disliked it, the best way to establish the distinction between himself and Montague was to let her experience it firsthand.

He passed the earl with no more than a slight tilt of his head as acknowledgment, feeling more than a little satisfaction that he held the marker to the peer's beloved property and the earl didn't know it.

Jasper moved directly toward the card room. Now was as good a time as any to see which of Eliza's swains was dependent upon the whims of chance. In that enterprise, at least, he had no competition.

"Mr. Bond is an exceptionally fine-looking young man," Lady Collingsworth said from her seat on the opposite squab. The Collingsworth carriage inched its way through the congested streets. While most of the other conveyances squired their passengers from one society event to another, Eliza and her ladyship were retiring to their respective homes.

"You mentioned that earlier." Eliza draped her long gloves over her lap. She'd found the sight of Jasper in finery so pleasant, she would have liked to see him again before the evening ended. Their brief discussion on the veranda had been long enough only to make her wish for more time.

"There are certain types of handsomeness that

are so compelling you tell yourself later you must have exaggerated the appeal in your mind. When you see the man again and he exceeds your embroidery, it's impossible not to remark upon it." Although the lamps were turned down low, there was enough light to see her ladyship's smile.

"He does render one speechless," Eliza agreed. "Sir Richard Tolliver felt the need to warn me that a man as comely as Mr. Bond would set his cap for me only because of my purse."

"Good heavens." Regina's ramrod-straight spine stiffened further. "Tolliver is blind and desperate. I paid a great deal of attention to Mr. Bond over the course of the day. He most definitely has tender feelings for you. Enough so he fears being unable to make you happy."

"How did you reach that conclusion?"

"Mr. Bond said as much to me."

Eliza's brows rose. "Did he?"

"He did indeed. Are you considering his suit?"

"To answer that conclusively, I would need to know him better."

Lady Collingsworth linked her hands together in her lap. "The responsibility I was given for you is a deep honor. As you know, your mother meant a great deal to me. I loved Georgina as I would a sibling. I wish most sincerely to do well by you."

"You have been wonderful." She wanted to say that Regina had done far better than her own mother would have, but she bit her tongue. She would never understand what the sweet, generous Lady Collingsworth had seen in the self-centered, mercurial Georgina. Whatever it was, it had inspired an abiding loyalty that persisted beyond the grave. Eliza learned long ago to voice no disparagement of her mother to Regina. To do so was to invite extensive reprimand and extolments of her mother's worth.

"You are kind to say so." Her ladyship smiled. "You look so like Georgina in that gown. I was taken aback upon first sight of you. For a moment, it felt almost as if time had moved backward."

Eliza didn't see the resemblance beyond the hue of her hair and eyes, but again, she said nothing. Then, she realized she should offer thanks for the voiced observation. Her ladyship would perceive it to be a compliment. "Thank you."

"You are a remarkably sensible young woman," Regina continued. "You are cautious and prefer not to leave anything to chance. But matrimony is all about taking chances. Do you know how much time Collingsworth and I spent together before he paid his addresses? If you consider only the moments we actually spoke to one another, it was no more than a handful of hours. There were parties and dinners and picnics and such, but always with others nearby impeding any chance for quiet, meaningful discourse. You speak of knowing someone well, but in truth there is very little you need to know. Does an attraction exist between you? Do you both wish to see the other happy or, at the very least, reasonably content? If you have those things, you have all you need to enjoy a comfortable marriage."

"And what if there are things he refuses to share with me? How can there be trust, if there are aspects of one another we don't know?"

"Are there not parts of yourself that you would rather keep private?" Regina challenged. "Things you would choose not to discuss? Of course there are. Women are entitled to their mysteries, and men are entitled to their secrets. Frankly, some secrets are painful and best left alone."

Eliza considered this information carefully. There were indeed things she would prefer never to discuss again. It stood to reason that Jasper, too, would have memories he would like to forget. The person he was today might have been shaped by past events, but they didn't rule him now. Why should they rule her?

"You can manage a man," her ladyship coached, "if you pander to his pride and innate sense of self-importance. Convince him that your idea is his and he'll follow it through. When handled correctly, marriage can be a useful enterprise."

"The effort you describe is altogether too much work, in my opinion." But perhaps worth the effort for a man such as Jasper Bond. Shockingly, Eliza was contemplating all the things she might have to concede if she wanted to have Jasper in her life for longer than the length of the Season.

"My dear child. You extract from life what you put into it." Regina leaned forward. "Your coin will be of little comfort to you during chilly nights and solitary meals. I want a happier future for you. Someone to look after you. Children to love. This is a man's world, Eliza. Whether we like it or not, there is no help for it. You think you have freedom and independence now, but marriage would grant you even greater license. And Mr. Bond appears to have means of his own, so you might have everything to gain and nothing to lose."

The carriage rolled to a halt outside the Melville town house.

Eliza caught her ladyship's hand and gave it an affectionate squeeze. "Thank you, Regina. You've given me a great deal to think about."

"I'm available to you, if you need me."

As Eliza climbed the steps to the front door, she recognized that a decisive shift had taken place in her world. It was as if she'd been sleeping in a moving carriage, content to move in any general direction. Now she was awakened and feeling the need to change course. Unfortunately, she had no notion of where she wanted to go. She was, however, beginning to think that wherever the destination, having Jasper with her would make the journey far more interesting.

Chapter 7

"This is the last one." Mr. Terrance Reynolds consulted the sheaf of notes in his lap. "As I mentioned during our last meeting, Miss Martin, your newest tenant creates perfumed soaps, bath oils, and candles to order. Business is slow at present, but having purchased some of Mrs. Pennington's products for my wife, I think that will soon change."

Jasper kept his gaze on Eliza, who sat on the opposite squab. It was nearing two o'clock in the afternoon. They'd been visiting her various properties for nearly three hours now, solidifying in his mind just how wealthy Eliza was. He could easily see how someone would find the lure of her fortune overwhelming, but a suitor would have to be capable of looking beneath the surface to discover it. In her business dealings, Eliza went to great efforts to hide her gender and, therefore, her identity.

"I'll pay a visit to this store," she said, looking out

the window of Jasper's unmarked, enclosed town carriage. "It will be interesting to see the scent the proprietress chooses to create for me."

Jasper wanted to tell Eliza that he liked the way she smelled already, but could not with Mr. Reynolds present. In addition to the safety considerations that prompted today's excursion, the exercise also brought to light how much he enjoyed talking with Eliza and listening to her view of situations. He missed being able to speak with her freely, but felt it best to keep the arrangement between himself and Eliza private. To Mr. Reynolds' knowledge, Jasper was a friend of Melville's and a possible investor in Eliza's proposed plan to modernize the amenities in a few of her older properties.

"How close are we to the store?" Jasper asked.

"A few blocks," Reynolds replied. "We're almost there."

Rapping on the roof, Jasper signaled for his driver to stop. "I'll walk from here. That will give us a sufficient length of time between Miss Martin's arrival and mine so it doesn't appear as if we came together."

An odd look crossed Eliza's features before she nodded. He made a note to ask her later what prompted it. Alighting from the carriage, he accepted the cane she passed to him through the open door.

"Pink and white striped awning," Reynolds advised.

"Thank you." Jasper saluted Eliza with a quick touch to the brim of his hat, then he set off.

Today, he'd learned more than just how wealthy

she was. Though neither Eliza nor Mr. Reynolds said so outright, Jasper noted that she leased her properties predominantly to women. He expected his investigation would prove her tenants to be mostly spinsters and widows. It was an honorable endeavor, and he admired her for undertaking it. However, the practice made it less likely that one of her tenants was to blame for her recent troubles. She would engender gratitude before malice. He would need to cast his net wider to include those whose rental applications had been denied. Meanwhile, every day that passed without a stronger lead aggravated him more. The work itself was not an issue. It was the threat to Eliza's safety that made Jasper dread every moment she was out of his sight.

In short order, he spotted the cheery awning and his waiting carriage nearby. This time, it was Reynolds who remained out of view while Eliza entered the store. One of the most important lessons Lynd had taught Jasper was to surround himself with trustworthy staff and to pay them well enough to keep them happy. *Better to have two people you trust with your life, than a dozen you can't vouch for.* Eliza appeared to have the same sensibility. Terrance Reynolds was paid handsomely. That fact was made obvious by the quality of his attire and his accessories, from his gold pocket watch to his leather satchel. In return, the man seemed genuinely fond of Eliza and intent on serving her interests well.

As Jasper entered the store, the bell above the door jingled to herald his arrival. The interior of the shop was perfectly sized for an establishment catering to the sense of smell. The air was fragrant without being overpowering. A variety of cloth-covered round tables were placed at set intervals around the room, displaying wares in colorful groupings.

He removed his hat.

"Good afternoon, sir."

Jasper found the speaker to his left, arranging items on a tabletop in front of Eliza. The shopkeeper was young and beautiful, blond and blue-eyed. As shapely as a prized courtesan, but with the face of an angel. He bowed in greeting, then shifted his attention to Eliza. The hue of her hair made her initially more arresting to the eye than the paler tresses of the proprietress, but she lacked the fullness of curves and classic beauty of the other. That didn't alter the fact that he found Eliza to be far more pleasing to look upon. From the first, she'd called to him on a physical level. There was raw magnetism between them, unique in its form. Bedding her would not be about the appeasement of his hunger, but a celebration of it. He'd never felt that for anyone else. With her it was the journey to be savored, not the destination.

"Miss Martin," he drawled. "Fancy meeting you here. It's a lovely day, wouldn't you agree?"

"I would indeed, Mr. Bond." Her eyes sparkled with genuine pleasure. The manner in which she looked at him always stirred him. She lacked the artifice to hide how much she enjoyed his appearance.

Jasper couldn't look away.

Eliza blushed when he continued to stare. She

caught her lower lip between her teeth and a wash of heat swept over him.

He could arouse her with a glance. Did she know what that did to him?

"Is there something in particular I can help you find?" the blonde asked, excusing herself from Eliza. She wiped her hands on the apron tied around her waist, then gestured at the goods around them. "Floral or fruity? Musky or spicy? If you tell me the age and gender of the person you're shopping for, I can help you find just the thing. Or I can create something unique."

"What would you suggest for a young woman of discriminating taste, high intelligence, and deep passions? Nothing ordinary or expected, please. She is neither."

"Is she a wife or a lover?"

He considered the inquiry a moment, both the boldness of the question and his possible answer.

"It's best if I ask," she explained, glancing back at Eliza. "Providing you with the best possible product will ensure both your future business and your referral, and I need one as much as the other."

"How can I argue with that, Miss . . . ?"

"*Mrs.* Pennington." In close proximity, she appeared to be no older than Eliza.

"Why don't I look around," he suggested, "while you assist Miss Martin?"

Once again, Mrs. Pennington looked over her shoulder. "She's selecting a half dozen of her favorite scented oils, which is what I would like you to do."

"I will start with the same offerings, then."

Mrs. Pennington gestured toward the back of the store. Jasper followed her prompting. As she opened up free space on a table, she continued to cast furtive glances at Eliza. Perhaps she feared thievery?

He held back and remained silent, not wanting to distract her from finishing her task as soon as possible. When she straightened, he listened to her instructions and assured her that he could whittle down the choices without further help.

When she left him, he watched her return to the front of the store and waited to see if she would eye him as often as she had Eliza. She did not. But Eliza did.

He'd never known it could be so arousing to be ogled. He supposed it was because he had never been ogled by the right person.

Once Eliza was home again, she stripped off her gloves in the foyer, then looked at the post lying on a silver salver atop the console table. She set aside the few letters for Melville that appeared to be of a personal nature and collected the rest, intent on taking them up to her room. She wanted nothing so much as something to eat and a cup of tea.

She was halfway up the stairs when Melville called her name from below. Turning on the step, she smiled at him. "Yes, my lord?"

"Could I have a moment of your time?" he queried, frowning while trying to straighten his crooked waistcoat.

"Of course." As she descended, her gaze met

the butler's. "Could you ask Mrs. Potts to bring tea to his lordship's laboratory?"

The servant's tall and lean frame moved quickly out of range of her sight.

Eliza followed Melville around the base of the staircase and collected his mail at the console. They passed her study door, then turned to the right at the end of the parquet-lined hallway. The room where his lordship spent much of his time was there. She made a chastising clicking noise with her tongue when she found the drapes drawn tight. A copious number of candles were scattered around the room, offering plenty of light . . . and smoke.

"It's a glorious day outside," she chastised, dropping the day's post onto one of the long, slender laboratory tables before moving briskly over to the windows. She drew the drapes aside, then systematically unlocked each of the windows lining the length of the wall and pushed up the sashes.

"Too bright," his lordship groused, blinking like an owl.

"You need sunlight. We humans don't thrive in dark places as mushrooms are wont to do."

"Mushrooms!" He snapped his fingers. "Brilliant, Eliza."

Melville quickly rounded his desk and began writing.

She pulled out one of the wooden stools that butted against a table bearing various-sized glass tubes and bottles. Waiting patiently, she blew out nearby candles that were unnecessary now that sunlight illuminated the large, disorganized space.

The multitude of colorful liquids in jars cast jeweled beams of light onto the floor. In that moment, it was possible to see how Melville could become entranced by the mysteries he researched.

When Mrs. Potts bustled in with tea service on a tray, the intrusion seemed to snap his lordship into a renewed awareness of his location and his visitor.

"Oh, Eliza!" his lordship cried, scratching his head. "I apologize."

Eliza laughed softly. "It's quite all right."

She enjoyed these quiet moments with her uncle. In addition to being the only family she had remaining, he did not seek to fill perfectly good moments of silence with inane chatter. She did not have to consider—and reconsider—everything she said, or phrase her words in ways that made them more understandable while also diluting their meaning.

Sliding off the stool, she stood in front of the tea service and began to prepare the tea.

"Montague paid a call on me today," Melville said.

"Oh?" Her brows went up. "Why does that make me apprehensive?"

"Because you know why he came. He asked for permission to pay his addresses."

Eliza's breath left her in a rush. "Did he give you cause to believe I would welcome his offer?"

"On the contrary, he made it quite clear that while you find him to be one of the more agreeable of your suitors, you are not inclined to wed him."

That made her smile. "Yet he made his request, regardless."

"He was concerned by speculation regarding events at Somerset House yesterday. Some talk of your accident not truly being an accident at all." His lordship accepted the cup and saucer she passed to him. "Why didn't you tell me about what happened?"

"There was no need to bother you with the tale," she protested. "It was unfortunate, but no harm was done."

Melville gave her a calculated look. "You hired a thief-taker to protect you because of threats to your person, yet you dismiss this egregious event out of hand?"

"Because the flagrant nature of the event makes it unlikely to be unrelated to the rest," she argued. "I could have been killed. What purpose would that serve anyone? And the location was so prominent, increasing the possibility of exposure. It doesn't align with the other attacks at all."

"Regardless, I granted Montague's request."

Eliza knew that tone; Melville's mind was set. "I suspected you had."

"My years are advancing. I would like you to have someone in your life to look after your well-being, someone whose loyalty is not bought with coin."

"I can look after myself." Wielding a pair of silver tongs, she prepared a plate for him, artfully arranging a freshly baked scone alongside slices of shaved ham.

"By hiring someone."

"Marrying Montague would be nigh on the same thing," she pointed out.

"With the addition of children and a permanent companion. Not to mention a title and the many responsibilities you would gain with it. You would be busy, fulfilled, and rarely alone."

"I enjoy being alone."

"I cannot bear the thought of it." Melville set his cup down. "I haven't forgotten our agreement. I know this is your sixth and final Season. You think you'll be happier rusticating in the country, but I disagree."

"Rusticating is not quite what I had in mind."

"I told Montague he had my permission to make the attempt to change your mind, and I wished him well. No harm in that, is there?"

"Would you be happy if I married anyone at all?" she queried, adding milk to her tea. "Or only Montague? You seem to like him quite well."

"I met his father once or twice." Melville shrugged. "He seemed to be a pleasant enough fellow. And Montague is determined to have you. There is something to be said for that. But if there's someone else you prefer, I would champion him over Montague."

"Thank you, my lord. I will keep that in mind."

"You're humoring me," he said dryly.

Eliza's lips curved against the rim of her cup. "I am not. In fact, this discussion has me seeing Lord Montague in an entirely new light. You are correct: there's something to be said for his determination. And yours. Which I think was his point. He wanted me to know he's serious, and he wanted to ascertain whether or not he would have your support. He said he understands me better now, and perhaps that's true. Flowers will not win me, but cunning and unorthodox methods . . . At the very least, I admire his approach."

Not enough to wed him, but she didn't see any benefit to reiterating that point. She was enjoying tea with her uncle far too much to ruin it by being unnecessarily contrary. She gestured at his plate in a silent urging to eat.

"Good girl," he praised. "How is Mr. Bond's investigation progressing? Is he equally unconcerned by large statues nearly crushing you?"

Just the sound of Jasper's name caused the tempo of her heartbeat to alter. "No. He was upset enough for both of us. If there's anything nefarious to be uncovered, he will find it. He would also like to meet with you."

"Yes, yes. Tell him to come by whenever is convenient for him. If he waits for me to remember to make an appointment, we shall never meet. I doubt I'll be of much help, however. I have never been with you when you've been accosted."

"He is investigating beyond the present," she explained. "He wishes to exclude anyone who might hold resentment toward you, Mother, or Mr. Chilcott."

"Ah, so . . . well, that's a reasonable avenue of inquiry."

They ate in companionable silence for a time, during which Eliza considered his comment about having a permanent companion. Up until now, she thought repasts such as she shared with

Melville were all she needed. They rarely spoke while eating, and she enjoyed that. She hadn't considered how the silence might be deafening if she was the only one to fill it. There was a large difference between sitting quietly with someone else and sitting alone. She realized there was a certain comfort in knowing one could speak if one wanted to and chose not to, rather than being unable to speak because no one was there to listen.

"What troubles you, my dear?"

"Nothing, my lord."

"I am aware denial is a common female response. But you are too direct for such evasions."

Eliza shook her head. "I've found it best to hold my tongue, if choosing to do otherwise is guaranteed to lead to fruitless argument."

"Ah . . . Your mother. You will have to speak of her sometime."

"I don't see why."

"Perhaps then," he mumbled around a bite, "you will stop thinking of her before making decisions."

"I do not—" she started to protest, then fell silent when he shot her a look. He was right, as always.

Eventually, Melville drifted back to his notes and Eliza slipped off the stool with the intent of moving upstairs. The day's post caught her eye and she scooped it up, carrying it over to the small, shallow basket where Melville kept his mail. It was nearly overflowing. She shook her head. She'd long ago learned to separate Melville's personal correspondence from the rest—so that out-

standing accounts were paid in a timely manner—
but clearly he was also neglecting to keep in touch
with those who reached out to him.

"What will it take," she asked, as she added to
the pile, "to motivate you to whittle this down?"

"What?" He looked up at her, then down at the
basket. "Good God."

"My thoughts exactly." She pulled five off the
top and brought them to him. "Can we start with
these?"

He sighed. "If you insist."

Eliza kissed his cheek. "Thank you."

"Ha." He snorted. "You are exacting your pound
of flesh for Montague."

She was laughing as she left the room.

Jasper leaned back in his chair and drummed his
fingertips on the desktop. "How long was he there?"

"About an hour," Aaron said, holding his hat to
his chest with both hands. He stood just inside the
doorway of Jasper's study, rocking back on the
heels of his boots. "Perhaps a little longer."

"You know why Montague paid that call," Westfield prompted from his usual spot on the settee.

"No, I do not. She refused him," Jasper bit out.

"All the more reason to gain Melville's support.
Don't be obtuse, Bond. Women bow to familial
pressure to marry men they don't want. It happens
all the time."

Jasper's fingers curled into his palm.

"Do you believe Montague is responsible for
Miss Martin's troubles?" the earl asked.

"I cannot be certain one way or the other."

"What will you do now?"

"Speak to her." How had she taken the news? How far would she go to make Melville happy?

The thought of Eliza with Montague did horrible things to him.

It was a new sort of torment to be unable to see her now, to be barred from her company by rules and dictates he'd ignored for years.

Straightening, he uncovered his inkwell and stabbed a quill into it. He dashed off a quick note, powdering the ink with fine-grained sand before folding. Then he sealed the whole and waved it at Aaron. "Take this to the Melville residence."

Aaron approached and collected the missive.

"Miss Martin may need you after she reads it. Linger to be sure and if so, assist her. When you've finished with that," Jasper went on, "I want you to look into a Mrs. Pennington, who runs a newly opened shop on Peony Way. Pink-striped awning out front, lovely blonde inside. There is something not right with her. Find out what it is."

"Will do, Bond."

After the young man left, Westfield stood and walked to the console to avail himself of Jasper's brandy. "It's unfortunate Montague made so bold a move. Had it been anyone else paying addresses, you could have killed two birds with one stone by encouraging her to marry the gentleman—Montague would be barred from Miss Martin's fortune, and you could wipe your hands clean of the business by entrusting her safety to her future husband. Assuming you would be able to ascertain that her betrothed was not our culprit, of course."

"Of course." The thought didn't improve Jasper's mood at all. In fact, it worsened with the understanding that foiling Montague and successfully completing his assignment had fallen behind his desire to possess Eliza.

"It might also explain why he sent along the missive today," Westfield continued. "The assurance that he would be buying back the marker to his mother's property was prompted by something."

"Like his father, he is arrogant to the point of idiocy." Unless Montague had something else shoring up his confidence . . . Jasper would research the possibility posthaste.

"What do you expect you can accomplish by talking to Miss Martin?" Westfield asked, turning to face him. "Does she trust you to play matchmaker as well as suitor?"

Jasper snorted.

"You are so touchy lately, Bond," the earl complained. "Perhaps you should take the evening off and indulge yourself at Remington's for a few hours."

"Montague can have any heiress he wants. Why is he so determined to have this one? Someone clearly on the shelf and possessed of a rare temperament? Someone who's told him she does not want him?"

"Perhaps that's the lure." Westfield sank into a chair in front of Jasper's desk. The earl looked both comfortable and bored, two states of being that were unknown to Jasper. "A woman can be a bloody nuisance when she is overly fond of a man. If Miss Martin is inclined to spend much of her time in the country, Montague could have all of the benefits of marrying an attractive yet mature heiress, with none of the detriments. I know you find it hard to believe, Bond, but sometimes there are sound reasons for doing something. Not everything in this world is motivated by some evil plan."

"It is with Montague."

"Are you quite certain the son is so like the father? Or does that matter to you?"

Jasper stood. "Quite certain."

"Look on the bright side. Perhaps Montague's move will speed things up a bit with your investigation. Now there's a more immediate timeline for the culprit to work against."

"It's a sorry thing indeed when the reason for celebrating is that a madman could now be feeling desperate enough to act rashly."

Westfield sipped his libation and watched Jasper carefully. "You are like a caged beast. There is such an air of disquiet about you. I have never seen you this way before. Is ruining Montague so important to you?"

It took Jasper a long moment to answer. He didn't want to share his state of mind; it was too personal and intemperate. "Have you ever wanted something so badly you couldn't imagine not having it?"

"Like what?"

"Anything at all."

"There was a gelding once." Westfield held his glass between both palms, warming the liquor with his body heat. "At Tattersall's. I underbid. I stewed for weeks afterward. If I had the chance again, I would not be so cautious."

"Had you ridden it?"

"No. But I watched him be put through his paces. I examined him myself. Beautiful animal. I knew the moment I saw him that we would suit beautifully together."

"Do you still regret the loss?"

The earl shrugged. "On occasion. Not often. It was some time ago. I tell myself surely there was something wrong with the beast and I'm fortunate to have avoided being saddled with it. Otherwise, fate would have seen fit to give him to me."

"I don't believe in fate. I believe we make our own destiny." Jasper rubbed his jaw, absently noting that he should shave again. It was early evening and his skin was no longer smooth. It might burn Eliza when he kissed her.

If she came . . .

"Certainly my situation is nothing like yours," Westfield said. "Your need is rather like a thirst, is it not?"

"Thirst . . . yes." It was clear the earl was mistaking Jasper's lust for Eliza for a lust for vengeance. Jasper chose not to correct the assumption. "That's apt."

Unfolding from the chair, the earl polished off the last of his brandy. "I will continue to assist you in your quest for revenge, Bond. You are not alone in this endeavor, whether you appreciate that or not."

How well the earl knew him to comprehend that he disliked being dependent upon anyone.

"You've done more than enough. The marker for Montague's property is my greatest wish realized."

"I'm merely your mask." Westfield's smile was grim. "You are the one who has interceded in every investment that might have saved him. You are the one who funded the seasoned gamblers capable of winning against him. You are the one who has worked tirelessly for years to earn enough to squander a fortune to ruin him. Remind me never to anger you, Bond. You aren't a very nice fellow to those you dislike."

"You are too honorable a man to do anything that would completely alienate me." With a smile, Jasper tossed the earl's words back at him. "Whether you appreciate hearing that or not."

"Good God, don't make that statement within earshot of others, please." The earl looked at the clock. "Should I return at ten o'clock to begin our shadowing of Miss Martin?"

Jasper considered the time. It was shortly after five. "Let's make it eleven, shall we?"

"You will hear no complaints from me," Westfield said as he made his egress. "I've spent more time with you over the last few days than I have with a woman. No offense, but you aren't nearly as charming."

"I should hope not," Jasper muttered, following the earl out to the hall en route to his rooms upstairs.

"I beg you to follow my lead and consider indulging in some female companionship yourself. It would be a relief to find you less surly this evening."

Jasper paused with his foot on the bottom step,

absorbing the now familiar thrum of anticipation he felt whenever time with Eliza approached. "Don't feel the need to be excessively timely," he said over his shoulder, before ascending the staircase two steps at a time.

"This coming from a man who is a stickler for punctuality?" Westfield called after him. "I believe you have caught the Melville madness."

Jasper thought that was apt, too.

Eliza wondered what the house looked like from the front. Alighting from the carriage in the mews afforded her only a backside glimpse of Jasper's home.

The young man who couriered Jasper's note to her urged her expeditiously through an iron gate and along a cobblestone pathway bisecting a garden that was immaculate, if uninspired. She was still absorbing the severity of the rear lawn when Jasper appeared. A shiver of delight moved through her.

He filled the doorway leading into the house, his broad shoulders and tall frame backlit by the interior candlelight. His stance was wide, allowing light to shine between his legs, detailing the length and power of his thighs. He was fully dressed, but the expert fit of his breeches left nothing to the imagination. For the first time, she found the sight of a man's body inflaming. From the moment she first laid eyes on him, she'd felt a disturbing and significant physical response to his proximity. It intensified daily, encouraged by every heated look and every casual touch.

"Eliza." There was something intimate about the way he said her name.

She gained the first stair leading up from the garden and he held his hand out to her. It was gloveless and looked so strong and capable. She decided she loved his hands.

She tugged off her glove before she accepted his assistance, wanting to feel the warmth of his skin. A frisson of heated awareness moved up her arm. His grip tightened for a moment, as if he felt it, too. Looking up at him from beneath the hood of her cloak, she noted the stark austerity of his handsome features. He seemed so somber. So grave.

"Is something wrong?" she asked, having been concerned from the moment his summons arrived.

"Come inside."

Glancing behind her, she saw that the young man who'd accompanied her had departed. There had been others with him, but they hadn't entered the gardens with her. Jasper's note advised her to ask his man to accompany her back, *if* she chose to visit him as he requested. Once she relayed her acquiescence, everything was arranged with amazing swiftness. She'd been squired from Melville's house through the delivery alley and seen into a hired hackney. The winding and repetitive route they'd taken ensured she wasn't followed.

Jasper led her inside and took her to a study. Her senses were engaged by the feel of the room the moment she entered it. The mixture of blue hues and mahogany wood was surprising; although

she couldn't say what else she might have chosen
for him. Large wingback chairs and overly stuffed
settees spoke of comfort as well as functionality.
She knew instantly that he spent a great deal of
time in this room, which made her want to explore
every corner of it.

He came up behind her and set his hands on
her shoulders. She stiffened, not with fear or apprehension, but expectantly. She heard him inhale slowly and deeply, as if savoring her scent.
The action suited him. He was a man firmly attuned to his baser nature, reliant on his senses and
instincts as all predatory and dominant creatures
were. She was attracted to that side of him, deriv-
ing a potent thrill from being capable of stirring it.

"May I?" he asked, referring to her cloak.

Eliza nodded.

Her hood was lifted and pulled back, exposing
her face to light from all around. He paused, his
frame emanating an unmistakable tension. The act
of removing her cloak suddenly became far more
revealing. She understood then that he hadn't sum-
moned her to discuss urgent business or anything
else. The divestment of her exterior garments was
the first step in the removal of all her clothing.

Her breath caught audibly and a fine tremor
rippled through her.

Jasper's chin came to rest atop the crown of her
head. His hands gripped her upper arms in a gentle yet unshakeable hold. "Will you stay?" he asked
gruffly.

She hesitated only a moment. "Yes."

Chapter 8

Eliza felt Jasper relax. She did not. How could she, having just agreed to give herself to a man she barely knew? For the first time in her life, she had ignored all reason and acted purely on feeling.

Just like her mother would have done . . .

She pushed the thought aside. She'd made her decision and she would not regret it. "What would you have done if I said no?"

"Changed your mind." His fingers deftly released the frog at her throat. Her cloak began to slip and he caught it with a flourish.

Turning to face him, she watched as he draped the black velvet garment over the back of one of the pale blue settees. "I'm agreeing to something I have no knowledge of," she pointed out. "Perhaps I will change my own mind."

Jasper stepped closer and cupped her face in his

hands. "If so, I will desist. But I fully intend for you to beg me not to stop."

The physical response she had to his words was so violent it took her by surprise. He took advantage, his mouth sealing over hers and taking it, his tongue thrusting fast and deep. Eliza caught his wrists to keep her balance, her body otherwise frozen by the onslaught. A whimper escaped her and was swallowed by his answering groan.

He released her as quickly as he'd caught her, stepping back and leaving her to stumble from the loss of his support. His chest lifted and fell rapidly. His gaze was heavy-lidded and hot.

"This is my study," he said in a hoarse voice. "When I'm home, this is the most likely place to find me."

Stunned by the sudden change in conversation and the distance between them, Eliza took a moment to register what he'd said. "It suits you," she managed.

"Come along." Jasper held his hand out to her.

He pulled her gently from the room and back out to the visitor's foyer. There was a longcase clock against the wall, a large console with a lone silver salver atop it, and a rack for Jasper's cane. It was a purely functional space, lacking any adornments.

"The parlor is here," he said, steering her across a round Aubusson rug covering the marble floor.

From the threshold, she saw a fire in the grate and playing cards scattered across two separate tables. It looked as if a gathering had recently been there and would be returning shortly. The room was decorated in shades of yellow and cream. There was a large quantity of furniture, all of which was oversized and sturdily built. Still, the space felt sterile and uncluttered.

"At any given hour," he said, "many of my employees can be found in here. The downstairs is often noisy, filled with bawdy conversations and raucous laughter. This is the first time this room has been empty in many years."

"Oh . . ." Eliza understood that he'd sent the men away because of her. "When will they be back?"

"Not for many hours."

Her palms grew damp, a reaction he couldn't fail to note with her hand in his. "Were you so certain of my capitulation?"

"Far from it, but I couldn't proceed as if failure was inevitable." He tugged her from the room. "There is also a dining room and ballroom on this floor, but I use neither, so they're unfurnished."

They moved toward the staircase and started to climb. With every step they took, her excitement mounted. Her breathing quickened and her face felt hot. There was an unmistakable finality to their upward progression, as if her fate had been set and she couldn't turn back now. Far from feeling trapped, she felt liberated. All afternoon, she'd thought of Melville and Regina and Montague. She had weighed their admonishments and advice. And she'd felt the mounting pressure to conform, to cede to the expected behavior and cast aside any lingering hope for independence.

"The third floor," he said, "has three bedrooms

and a nursery, which has been converted into a room for guests. Sometimes my men stay here, for various reasons. No one is here now. If you would like to see the rooms, I'll show them to you."

If he was trying to give her time to change her mind, it wasn't working. She was growing more agitated by the moment. Impatient. Restless. "Why?"

Jasper glanced at her. "Does anything about my home strike you in an unusual way?"

"It's lovely," she said. "Beautifully furnished. However, it is also oddly barren. Nothing adorns the walls or table surfaces. You've hung no portraits of loved ones or pleasing landscapes. I had hoped to learn more about you by visiting, but I've seen very little that tells a story."

"One has to *want* things in order to purchase them. There's nothing I want. There has been nothing I've seen in a shop window or in someone else's home that I have coveted." He paused with one foot on the next step. "I think you might understand that lack of wanting. You attire yourself for purpose, not for vanity. You did not refurnish Melville's study when you commandeered it. You replaced what needed to be replaced and made do with the rest."

"Many people find that art and sentimental objects provide comfort and enjoyment. I, too, own a few items that are impractical but give me pleasure."

"Am I such to you?" he asked, his dark eyes shadowed with some emotion she couldn't name. "An impractical pleasure?"

"Yes."

He started forward again. They reached the second floor landing and Eliza looked down the lone hallway, searching for and finding a lack of wall adornment. Aside from sconces to light the way, there was nothing to relieve the long expanse of soft green damask covering the walls.

His pace slowed from brisk to a near stroll. "I have only ever wanted intangible things—health and happiness for my mother, justice for wrongdoings, satisfaction in a job well done—things of that nature. I have never understood why others become focused on particular objects. I've never comprehended obsession or overwhelming need."

He spoke without inflection. There was nothing in what he said that betrayed any emotion, yet she felt a deeper undercurrent to his words.

"Why are you telling me this?" she asked softly, clutching his hand with both of her own.

"I'm the only one who uses this floor." He started forward. "Aside from my own rooms, the rest are vacant."

His repeated evasion of her questions was growing tiresome. She could not understand his mood. With her own emotions a confusing jumble, she didn't have the wherewithal to translate his feelings, too.

They reached a set of open double doors. Jasper gestured her in ahead of him.

Taking a deep breath, Eliza crossed the threshold. Like her room in Melville's house, Jasper's sitting room was predominantly burgundy in tone with occasional splashes of cream to alleviate the dark hue. But unlike her space, his was thoroughly masculine. There were no tassels or patterns to any of the materials, and no carvings in the wooden arms and legs of the chairs and tables.

The air smelled of him. She breathed the scent into her nostrils, finding it calming to her jangled nerves. Then, she looked at the open doorway to her left, the portal to Jasper's bedchamber, and her stomach knotted all over again.

"There are games women play," he murmured, his gaze hot enough to heat her skin. "Tests they devise to gauge a man's interest."

"What sorts of tests?"

"They make certain a man learns of their favorite flower or color or important dates, then wait to see if he will remember and gift them accordingly."

Her hands linked together nervously. Should she sit? Or remain standing as he did? She escaped into the conversation, not knowing what else to do. "The objects of feminine and masculine sentimentality are often widely different. To expect a man to assume what might be an unnatural form of sentiment to prove devotion is an unreasonable experiment with a high probability of failure. Why not accept his instinctual gestures of affection in whatever manner they are manifested? They likely mean more to him and reveal more about his character."

Jasper's smile curled her toes. "Do you have any notion of how sexually arousing I find your intellect? One day I should like you to expound upon this topic while I'm inside you. I suspect I would find it highly erotic."

A flush swept over her face.

He shut the door to the hallway and locked it. The soft click of the latch rippled through her.

"I tested you today," he said, with his back to her. "Considering how irritating I find such ploys, it astonishes me that I did so."

"Did I pass?"

Facing her, he shrugged out of his coat. "You are in my home, so I would say so."

He swiftly unfastened the buttons of his waistcoat. Eliza found she could not look away, despite the voice in her head that lectured about privacy and proper maidenly modesty.

She cleared her throat so she could speak. "You sent for me without telling me why."

"If Montague had sent for you, would you have gone?"

"Of course not. He does not work for me."

Jasper stiffened. When he returned to the act of shaking off his waistcoat, it was with notable impatience. "If Reynolds had sent for you, would you have gone?"

"No."

"But he works for you."

Clearly the expected responses were not the ones he wanted to hear. He wanted the truth.

"I would not have expended the effort for anyone else," she admitted, her mouth drying as he untied and unwound his cravat, baring his throat. The sight was intensely provocative to her. His skin was darker than her own, firmer. She wanted desperately to touch it, to feel him swallow beneath her fingertips.

He toed off his buckled shoes. "That was the test. I needed to know if you would place me in a different category from other men you know. I was also curious to see how deep your adventuresome proclivities were buried."

"I am far from adventuresome," she protested.

"You would like to believe that." Jasper tossed his cravat on the floor, then yanked his shirtsleeves over his head.

Eliza's knees weakened and she staggered over to the nearest chair, half-sinking and half-falling into it.

Dear God, he was beautiful. Astonishingly, breath-takingly so. She remembered how he'd urged her to touch him the first time he kissed her. He had been so hard beneath her questing fingers, like stone. She could see why. Her hand lifted to her throat. As dry as her mouth had been, it was now flooded with moisture.

She had never seen a rendering of a male body that could compare. The washboard-like cording of muscles across his abdomen and the light dusting of dark hair that thinned into a fine line were new to her. And delightful. Her gaze followed the trail to where it disappeared beneath the placket of his breeches.

Then lower . . .

He was hard there, too. Cupped by the expertly tailored doeskin, the outline of his erection was thick and prominent. The knot in her stomach tightened. He was such a blatantly masculine creature. Primitive in the most vital of ways. A male whose appetites were undoubtedly fierce and expansive. How could she, a woman who knew nothing about exploiting her own femininity, sate such a man?

When he didn't move, she jerked her gaze upward to find him staring back at her. A tight smile preceded him taking a seat on the opposite settee. He had allowed her to look her fill, she realized. Unashamed of the visible proof of his lust. Unabashed.

Jasper rolled down his hose, one leg at a time. "I *need* you to be adventuresome, Eliza. You wouldn't tolerate me and my profession for long if you were not."

"I do more than tolerate you," she rejoined softly, having lost the strength to speak louder.

He stood, and her eyes stung. She was enamored with the sight of him. Smitten as she'd thought she could never be. There was nothing she would alter about him, nothing she found fault with. In that moment, she was certain she would pay any price for the pleasure of looking upon him indefinitely. The sensations moving through her were drugging and addictive. She wondered helplessly if there was any way she could feel like this every day.

Approaching her with hand outstretched, he said, "From the moment I first saw you, I desired you and knew I had to have you. Since then, I have come to realize it isn't mere craving that drives me. It is wanting, Eliza. I *want* you. I've never wanted anything in my life, until you. Nothing. Do you understand what I'm saying? Gaining and losing a possession means nothing to me. There is always a replacement."

"I understand." She allowed him to pull her to her feet. "But I don't know what conclusion to draw from that understanding."

He gestured for her to face away from him. "I ceased trying to find reason in it. I cannot waste any more time trying to puzzle out what I don't know. I must act on what I do know—you are the one thing in the world I want, and I can have you. I'm also lacking the scruples that would prevent me from doing whatever is necessary to keep you. The details can be dealt with later, when I can once again think about something other than bedding you."

His fingers went to the buttons that secured the back of her gown and released them with laudable dexterity.

"Have I no say in the matter?" she asked.

He pressed his lips to the top of her bared shoulder. "If you intend to say you have no objections, speak away. Otherwise, I ask that you give me the next few hours before voicing anything that might make my task more difficult for me."

Eliza looked straight ahead, which was a straight-line view into Jasper's bedroom. The bed was directly in front of her, custom-made from the size of it. The back of her gown gaped open and he pushed it free of her shoulders, then down to the floor. "Step out," he ordered.

She obeyed, too overwhelmed to do otherwise. "You are giving me too much time to think," she groused, averting her gaze from the bed.

Jasper laughed softly, the moment of levity sufficient to lighten some of the incertitude preying on her. "Would you prefer to be ravished?"

"I would prefer not to have these fits of nerves."

"I should like to ravish you." He loosened her stays. "Not tonight, when I need both of us to have no doubt that you came to my bed willingly, but soon."

Crossing her arms over her chest, she held her loosened corset to her breasts. Jasper rounded her and backed up, putting distance between them.

"I'm almost naked," she bit out, wanting him to do *something*. Why was he standing so far away? Even if he extended his arms their full length, he wouldn't be able to reach her.

"I am highly aware of that fact." Reaching down, he stroked himself through his breeches, his long fingers rubbing along the length of the pronounced bulge.

"Have you no shame?" Her tone was curt, her emotions high. She was a virgin, for God's sake, and he was giving her too much breathing room. She was achingly aware of everything around her, when what she wanted was to be lost to the barrage of sensations he could so easily overwhelm her with.

"None at all. And I would like for you to have none either. Eliza . . ." His tone softened. "Did I not explain myself clearly? Don't you understand that you are uniquely appealing to me? You worry that exposing your body will make you vulnerable, but I'm the one who will be left raw by the experience."

She stood there for a long moment, lip quivering. He was forcing her to reason everything out during the one occasion when she didn't want to think at all.

Jasper watched her with those intense dark eyes, his body made golden by the flickering candlelight. How many times had he experienced this sequence of events to be so nonchalant? Dozens? More . . . ?

She would not be surprised. What woman could resist him?

She was resisting him. . . .

Her jaw clenched. He was right to avoid responsibility for her choice to be here. It was her decision, and she needed to claim it. Why should she tell herself that she was acting on instinct when that was a lie?

She was not like her mother. She was not driven to rashness by passion. She knew damn well what she was doing.

Eliza launched herself at him. Two running steps and a wild leap, and she was upon him. He caught her, laughing. Lifting her feet from the floor, he spun and strode into the bedroom.

"Not adventuresome?" he teased, setting her down at the foot of the bed. He looked at her with such an expression of proprietary pride that her throat tightened.

Pivoting on his bare feet, Jasper locked the bedroom door.

"I thought we were the only ones here?" she queried, her heart still racing from her leap off the proverbial cliff.

"You are assuming I'm locking others out, instead of locking you in . . ."

The thought of capture excited her. She had run willingly into the lion's den, and now there was no turning back.

He leaned back against the door, his palms pressed flat to the panels and one ankle crossed over the other. The perfect appearance of insouciant leisure. But he'd never been able to hide his predaceous nature from her. She had seen it from the first and she saw it now: the high color on his throat and cheekbones, the fine sheen of sweat on his chest, the flaring of his nostrils, and the narrowed, concentrated gaze.

One wrong move and he would pounce . . .

Reaching up, she began to pull the pins from her hair. She dropped them on the floor, one by one, as he'd done with his cravat. There was something oddly freeing in that carelessness. The act of tossing aside the trappings that restrained. Here in this room with Jasper, she could finally cast off the confusing strictures of society and be what she had always wanted to be—liberated and independent.

After the last pin dropped, she shook out her hair, relishing the tingling of her scalp. She was clad in only her loosened stays and pantalettes, but she was not embarrassed or cold. There was no way she could be, when warmed by a stare as heated as Jasper's.

He didn't move, barely blinked. As the silence lengthened, she lost courage and clasped her hands in front of her.

"You are so beautiful, Eliza." His hand lifted to his chest and rubbed, as if to soothe a pain there. "I adore your freckles. Do you have them everywhere?"

She bit her lower lip and nodded. "It is the bane of red hair, I'm afraid."

"I will kiss every one of them," he vowed. "They are delightful."

"Fustian," she scoffed. "No one likes freckles."

Jasper's eyes twinkled in the light of the bedside tapers. "Isn't there anything about me you adore? Any part of me you want to kiss?"

"I am mad for every inch of you," she pronounced with heartfelt fervency. "The way you smell. The cut of your hair. The line of your jaw. I'm especially taken with your hands. I can feel the strength in them when you touch me. You could crush my bones in your grip, but instead you are so gentle."

He held both hands out, offering them to her. She rushed forward, knowing his touch would calm and distract her. "Sometimes I fear crushing you," he confessed with a hitch in his voice.

Catching his hands with hers, Eliza pressed a kiss into each palm. "Is that why you stand so still?"

"Yes."

"What would you do, if you had no need for restraint?"

As before, he brought her hand to rest over his heart, allowing her to feel its racing. "I would pin you to this door behind me and take you, swift and hard. Then I would lay you on the floor, spread you wide, and have you again. Slowly. Deeply. Eventually, we might make it to the bed, but I couldn't guarantee it."

"It sounds . . . savage."

"You make me feel that way. If I could curb the need I have for you, I would. Perhaps, after tonight, it will be more manageable. I pray that's the case."

The roughness in his voice was a caress of its own. Freed from the pressure of her stays, the tips of her breasts throbbed and puckered tight. She was eye level with his chest, which made her wonder if his nipples were as sensitive as hers. The flat disks were surrounded by gooseflesh. Giving in to the urge, Eliza leaned forward and warmed one with a lick of her tongue.

"Bloody hell," he bit out, jerking violently.

Jasper spun her away from him in a dizzying pivot. The ripping of her stays was like a crack of thunder in the room, followed by the rush of cool air across her back and the soft tickle of her hair beneath her shoulder blades. Her pantalettes were next, the tie at her waist digging briefly into her flesh before breaking in half. The flesh-colored stockinette was rent into two halves that clung to her ankles by the fastenings there.

She'd barely registered that she was excited by his loss of control when a hand at her lower back steered her forward, straight up the short steps at the foot of the bed and onto the mattress.

On her hands and knees, she crawled across the burgundy counterpane, highly conscious of everything she was exposing to him in the process. His hand caught her ankle when she reached the middle of the massive bed, halting her. She dropped to her stomach in a bid for modesty. The remnants of her pantaloons were stripped from her legs and discarded.

Eliza didn't move, barely breathed.

"Are you frightened?" he asked gruffly.

She had to force herself to think about her feelings. "I d-don't know."

Jasper stretched out beside her, his arm extended above their heads. With his other hand, he urged her to roll to her side, so that her back was against his sweat-dampened chest. He leaned forward and rested his cheek against her shoulder, his silky hair brushing softly against her skin. His arm came around her waist and held her tightly to him. He didn't move. Eventually, she relaxed into his warmth, inhaling the scent of him, which was made stronger by the tremendous heat of his body. He felt fevered against her flesh.

It took long moments, but over time his temperature cooled and his breathing slowed.

"Jasper . . . ?"

His hand at her waist moved higher, cupping a breast. She tensed again at the unfamiliar touch.

"Shh," he murmured, gentling her.

The feel of his breath gusting across her ear made her nipple harden into his palm. A rough sound escaped him and his hand flexed convulsively around her.

"Let me show you what you did to me," he whispered, withdrawing enough to coax her onto her back.

Eliza stared up at him, awed anew by how handsome he was. How was it possible that such a man would find her so desirable?

She didn't care. She was just grateful for her good fortune.

With no further warning, he lowered his head and surrounded her nipple with the humid heat of his mouth. She arched upward with a gasp, startled by the violence of her response. His tongue curled around the aching tip, and his cheeks hollowed on a deep suckle. She cried out, her nails scratching into the velvet coverlet. His callused fingertips rolled her other nipple, then tugged. She began to pant.

"Jasper."

He growled and sucked harder, his tongue stroking the underside of the straining point with wicked skill. The flesh between her thighs pulsed in time to the rhythm of his mouth, clenching deep and feeling empty. Her hips lifted, seeking. The hand at her breast slid lower, across the flat of her belly and into the dark red curls at the apex of her thighs.

The shock of the caress froze her. She was too sensitive there, too wet and swollen.

"Touch me." His voice was so gruff, she barely recognized it.

He withdrew and caught her wrist, urging her hand to mold around the outline of his erection. He showed her how to move, rubbing her palm up and down his thick length. Heat rushed up her arm and spread throughout her body, easing her stiffened muscles. Exploiting her distraction, he resumed his quest, his fingers slipping through the lax barrier of her thighs. His palm cupped her, the breadth of his hand easily laying claim to the part of her that had always been intensely private.

His dark head lifted. He watched her reaction as his fingers moved, gliding through the slickness clinging to the entrance of her body.

"Open," he breathed. "Let me feel how wet you are."

When she hesitated, he took her mouth, his lips slanting across hers in a brazen seduction. His tongue followed the outer curve of her lower lip, tracing the shape before teasing the seam with flirtatious licks. She opened with rapacious hunger, her head lifting in an attempt to deepen the kiss. He pulled back, maintaining the provocative distance between them, denying her the full possession she sought.

Eliza made a frustrated sound and his fingers tapped lightly against her sex.

Challenged by his silent bargain, she spread her legs, draping one thigh over his so nothing was barred from him.

"Yes." His lips lowered to hers. "Be wanton . . ."

His tongue and fingertip breached her simultaneously, above and below. She writhed into the unexpected intrusion, moaning as sweat misted her skin. She gripped his erection with desperately clenching fingers. Bolder than she'd ever imagined she could be.

"So snug." His finger pushed inexorably deeper, then pulled back. When he stroked back into her,

her legs fell open, and her hips arched. "Snug and very hot."

Her fingertips found the plush head of his penis straining above the waistband of his breeches. She hungrily explored the satiny curve, fascinated with the heat and silky smooth texture. Moisture beaded on the crown. She wished she could clench the length of him, caress him fervently from root to tip.

"No more," he said harshly, pulling back from her.

She grasped for him to no avail. He slipped further down the bed, away from her greedy lips and tormented breasts.

"Jasper!" she protested, trying to sit up but losing the leverage to do so when he pushed his shoulders under her legs.

There was a blazing moment when she realized what he wanted, then her thoughts scattered beneath the lash of his tongue. An unvoiced protest died on her lips. She couldn't muster the will to stop him, even to appease her scandalized sense of modesty. Instead she moaned and rocked into his mouth, trying to find his rhythm so she could ease the terrible yearning within her.

"That's the way," he coaxed darkly, lifting her hips.

His tongue lapped through the tender folds of her sex, parting her, licking her with velvet roughness. He toyed with her, flickering over the knot of nerves with the pointed tip of his tongue. She bucked upward, knowing there had to be more. Wanting more. Needing it. She mewled in torment.

His finger returned, sliding easily through greedily clenching tissues.

"Oh . . ." she moaned, her eyes squeezing shut against the unbearable intimacy. "Oh, God!"

In and out. Pushing and withdrawing. Pumping. She writhed, and he pinned her hips with a heavy arm.

Two fingers. Her body shuddered violently at the unfamiliar stretching. His mouth surrounded her, tongued her, sucked her . . .

Eliza climaxed with a serrated cry, her fingers digging into the counterpane, her thighs quivering.

At the height of her pleasure, Jasper thrust his fingers deep and scissored them, rending the barrier of her virginity. She scarcely felt the pain, so lost was she to the wonder of his talented tongue.

He didn't stop, groaning as if he felt the same surfeit of feeling, prolonging the waves of sensation until she pushed his head away, unable to bear any more.

Chapter 9

Jasper pressed a kiss to a freckle on Eliza's thigh before sliding off the end of the bed. She curled onto her side, flushed and trembling, her slim, pale limbs drawn tight to her body. Her blue eyes followed his movements, looking dazed and sated at once.

His blood was raging, his cock throbbing. He yanked open the placket of his breeches and pushed them down. Kicking them aside, he took his penis in his hand and stroked the pulsing length. Crimson skeins of moisture—her virginal blood—clung to his fingers. The sight aroused him, luring his seed to leak from the tip of his cock.

He'd pushed her far and fast, needing to take her past the twin hurdles of inexperience and virginity so he could have her as he needed to. He had tried to warn her, attempted to explain, forced himself to give voice to a craving he didn't understand. Small comfort to a woman overwhelmed by her first physical attraction.

Jasper had taken advantage of that fact, remembering how riotous the flush of first lust was, how ill-considered and desperate it felt. He remembered it well, because Eliza made him feel that way again. Hot-blooded. Randy. Impatient.

With harsh strides, he went to the washstand and grabbed a handful of freshly laundered towels. On the way back to the bed, he caught up the bottle of oil he'd purchased at Mrs. Pennington's shop. He tossed the towels on the counterpane, then poured a small pool of the fragrant golden liquid into his palm. The bottle was set aside on the nightstand by Eliza's head.

Deliberately, he rubbed his hands together, releasing the scent of bergamot and spice into the air. He'd chosen a masculine scent on purpose, wanting it to linger in her mind after the night was over, goading her to remember the things he had done to her body. Thus far she hadn't been subject to the sorts of lewd imaginings he suffered through, but he intended that to change. Whether she was balancing her ledgers or dancing with blasted suitors, Jasper wanted her to be thinking of sex with him.

Eliza watched, riveted, as he gripped his cock at the root and stroked upward, pulling and stretching, swelling further until he was certain he'd never been this hard and thick. Ropey veins coursed the length of him, making him look as brutal as he felt. His bollocks were drawn up tight and hard, his seed churning with the need for release.

She made a soft, anxious noise.

"Are you frightened?" he asked for the second time that evening. Knowing she had to be. Aware that he would have been kinder to shield her from his size until she knew enough to appreciate it. But he was willing to cast aside what little gentlemanly considerations he had to gain what he wanted from her, using every advantage he possessed to distinguish himself from the others who hoped to win her and take her from him. She liked to look at him. And she was attuned to him on the most basic level. Her mind might shy away from his primitive display, but her body understood . . . and would react accordingly.

"Yes," she answered softly, her knees drawing closer to her abdomen. "I have always known you were too much for me."

"But you want me regardless. Face the other way."

Rolling, she gave him her back. She curled in a manner that drew her feet up to the lush curve of her buttocks. The discovery of her voluptuous derriere had been a delightful surprise when she'd crawled across his bed earlier. On the surface, Eliza appeared as moderate in form as she was in temperament, but even in this, her private landscape was the most picturesque. He was certain her backside was the most perfect he'd ever seen.

"Who knew you hid such a curvaceous bottom beneath your clothes?" he murmured, joining her and pressing a kiss to a cluster of freckles on her shoulder.

"You tease me," she accused without heat.

"You spoke of men who appreciate certain hues of hair." Jasper wrapped his body around her, pulling her against his chest with an arm around her slender waist. "Is it so hard to believe I might have my own preferences?"

"For freckles and buttocks?"

"You, Eliza. All of you." He inhaled sharply when she leaned into him, and he became further inflamed by the smell of her. "My patience is thinner than I would wish," he confessed hoarsely. "I must beg you in advance for greater license. You trust me with your life; will you trust me in this? Trust me to give you pleasure, even if I am rough or hurried?"

She looked at him over her shoulder. Her lower lip was caught between her teeth and her eyes were shadowed, but she nodded.

With no further preliminaries, he took his cock in his hand and arched his hips forward. Her breath hissed out when he tucked the thick head against her and slid upward, parting the slick folds of her sex and gliding across her clitoris. Up, then down. On the downstroke, the furled underside of his cockhead caught the swollen knot of nerves. On the upstroke, the swollen crest rubbed over it. He notched the tiny protrusion into the weeping hole at the tip of his cock and stroked himself from root to crown with his fist. A hot pulse of pre-ejaculate flowed over her sensitive flesh. She moaned, arching backward.

Jasper restrained her with a hand at her breast, fighting his turbulent need to pound into her and spew violently, expending his lust in a violent taking that would slake his craving. The sense of desperation was nigh intolerable. He couldn't shake the apprehension that she might be removed from his grasp before he was ready. It was too soon. His need for her too sharp . . .

Eliza's hand covered his.

Her nipple pebbled into his palm, tightening deliciously. He felt its sensitivity when he kneaded the whole of her breast. Her entire body trembled, and her hips pushed back. Her legs parted, one foot hooking behind his calf, giving her leverage to undulate against him.

She was finally unrestrained, and it was better than he'd imagined. She whispered his name. He pulled back, finding the clutching entrance to her body. There was a moment of hesitation; a brief second when reason reminded him that she was above him in station. Too good for him.

His jaw clenched. He pushed his cockhead deliberately into her tight, resisting flesh. She was scorching hot and drenched.

"Christ," he hissed, seared by the silken heat of her. The delicate muscles inside her bore down on the exquisitely sensitive head of his cock. A violent shudder wracked his frame.

Eliza's head thrashed against his chest. Her nails dug into the forearm he pinned her with. Her movements altered, writhing away instead of into him. She tried to close her legs, but he blocked her, moving his hand from her breast to her cunt in a lightning-quick lunge.

"Trust me," he said gruffly, pushing deeper. "Breathe."

Registering the tremendous strain in Jasper's voice, Eliza tried to obey, gasping air into seized lungs. He slid deeper, despite the panicked clench of untried tissues. She understood the use of the oil now. It gave her body no traction to deny him, no means of resistance.

Her eyes closed on a shuddering exhale. Her mind filled with the vision of Jasper standing beside the bed fully naked, skin gleaming, abdominal and chest muscles rippling from the rough movement of his hands on his magnificent erection. She knew how to judge proportions. She'd known she could never accommodate him, but she wanted to. Needed to.

He withdrew a scant inch. She sucked air into her burning lungs, and his hips lunged forward, tunneling his rigid penis into her. She made a broken sound, unprepared for the feeling of being so utterly possessed.

"God." He stilled, panting, his chest working like a great bellows against her back. His cheek nuzzled against her temple. "Am I hurting you?"

"No . . . Too full." Stretched to the point of aching, but she was not pained.

"You can take me." His fingers rubbed between her legs, starting a hot, sweet trickle of sensation in her core. "Let me in, Eliza. Don't fight it."

Eyes stinging, she gave a tentative, tiny swivel of her hips. He slid a fraction deeper.

"Yes," he purred, nudging forward then withdrawing. "Like that."

She forced her taut frame to relax, sagging back against his supportive chest and deliberately modifying her breathing. Slow deep breath in. Steady breath out. She concentrated on his touch, the way he expertly circled her clitoris with callused fingertips, urging pleasure outward across devastated nerve endings.

On her next inhale, he thrust, sinking into her until his thighs were pressed tight to hers. Her held fell forward on a low moan.

"*Eliza.*"

Dear God, he was so deep in her . . .

He pulled out with painstaking slowness, then filled her again. With every withdrawal and return, his movements became more fluid. Practiced. His expertise became apparent. He knew just how far to pull out, how leisurely to push in, how deep to penetrate to drive her mad for the feel of him inside her. Her enjoyment grew, until she sought the pleasure purposefully, writhing into his thrusts to feel the sweet fullness she craved.

A low rumble of approval vibrated against her back. "You like this."

She gasped at a particularly masterful stroke. The intimidating size of his erection was now something she relished. He was so long and thick. The largeness of him ensured that he rubbed and stretched every sensitive spot, awakening a voracious hunger. She struggled against him, resisting the position he kept her in that prevented her from increasing his depth and pace.

"Tell me you like this," he coaxed darkly, rolling his hips and fingers simultaneously, arousing her with consummate skill so she clenched greedily around him. "Say it."

"Yes." She whimpered in torment, aching every time he pulled out and left her empty. "But . . ."

"I can give it to you." His tone was rough and deeply sexual. "Tell me what you want, Eliza, and you can have it."

"More," she begged, shameless in her yearning. "Give me more . . ."

Jasper's hand cupped her swollen sex and pulled her back into a powerful lunge of his hips. Heat washed over her. His pace increased, the flat of his palm applying just enough pressure to stimulate her on the outside as well as within. Sweat coated her skin and his, making them slide along each other, releasing the fragrance of the oil and Jasper's scent into the air. The room became hot and the counterpane damp, creating a lush humidity that intensified the experience. He whispered lewd praise, his words slurring with pleasure, his abdomen and thighs flexing powerfully as he drove into her. Tears filled her eyes, the tension so fine she felt as if she might break at any moment.

"Please," she sobbed. *"Please!"*

"Right there," he groaned, holding still at the deepest point and grinding against her, screwing into her another fractional bit. "Right there."

She arched violently. The climax hit, her vision narrowing until it blackened completely. Her mouth opened in a silent cry of pleasure. Inside, she convulsed, tightening on him in the most intimate of embraces. Blood roared in her ears, drowning out all sound.

A thick wash of heat flooded the depths of her.

Jasper cursed and jerked against her, shuddering in unison with every wrenching spurt.

Eliza felt her name on his lips as he emptied himself inside her, his mouth moving against her shoulder in a sweetly broken litany.

There was no place in Jasper's life for Eliza Martin.

He lay on his side with his head propped in his hand, watching her as she napped. Strands of her beautiful hair clung to her damp forehead and cheeks. Her lips were parted, her chest lifting and falling in the measured tempo of slumber. She lay on her stomach, baring twin dimples in each curve of her extremely enticing buttocks.

Spread out as she was, naked and rosy-skinned and debauched, it was easy to imagine keeping her there in his bed. But it was only an illusion. His gaze lifted and swept around the nearly empty room. Aside from the bed and washstand, there was only a wardrobe and chair for furnishings. This evening with Eliza was the longest stretch of time he'd spent awake in his bedchamber since he took up residence in the house. In the normal course of his life, there would be laughter and loud voices filtering up from the lower floor. He would be adhering to a tight schedule, working as many hours as possible to keep income flowing. After all, there was nothing he wanted done that didn't require coin to see to it.

Try as he might, Jasper couldn't picture Eliza in any part of his home beyond this private space. The men who worked for him were coarse and sometimes ill-mannered. They would have no notion of what to do with a lady like Eliza. He had no dining table at which to feed her, no formal parlor in which she could entertain what few guests would deign to call on her here. His home was less than half the size of Melville's and located in a part of town that, while acceptable, had never been fashionable.

Things would have to change drastically . . .

Eliza made a soft noise. He looked at her and found her rousing. She blinked, then rubbed at her eyes. He watched her vision focus on him. Awareness swept over her face along with a heated blush. She grew unnaturally still.

"Ah," he murmured, smiling. "You look scandalized."

"You look smug," she accused, but with warmth in her eyes.

"Do I?" He stroked his hand down the curve of her back. How could he resist, when she looked at him as she was doing now? "If I do, so should you."

He knew some of her feelings were inspired by the aftermath of orgasmic bliss and gratitude for it, but some of them were more deeply rooted. God knew he had never expected nor wanted anyone to love him, but he'd have a better chance of keeping Eliza if her attachment deepened.

She looked at her fingers, which toyed with a wrinkle in the counterpane. "I did nothing."

Jasper tapped the end of her nose with his finger. "You'll have to take my word for it. There are many ways to have sex, ranging from horribly disappointing to quite nicely done. What you and I just experienced is another sort of matter altogether. It takes two people with singular chemistry to achieve such a delectable end."

Eliza remained strangely quiet.

"Sixpence for your thoughts," he said, aware of tension eating into his contentment. "Is regret setting in?"

"No. No regrets," she replied carefully, glancing at him. "The first day we met, you spoke of rare skills in sexual congress, and clearly you have them. What woman could regret ending up in your bed?"

"Your thoughts on the matter are the only ones that concern me."

"I fail to see how that can be true. I didn't even touch you. You were required to do all of the work—"

Laughing, he leaned over and pressed a kiss to her shoulder. "Sweetheart, that was far from 'work.'"

"I should have done something!" she protested, looking less shy and more animated. She set her chin in her hand, which elevated her torso just enough to bare the upper curve of her breasts. "I feel sorely inadequate."

Jasper was somewhat startled by the ferocity with which he was stirring again, simply from the sight of her and the thought of her deliberately arousing him. "Rubbish. If you had been any more adequate, the business would have been done before I was inside you. That's why I made a point of facing you away from me."

"You made certain I could not participate?" Eliza frowned. "I find that very unsporting."

"Unsporting?" He grinned, enjoying her immensely as always. In all of his days, he'd yet to bed a woman who wanted to put more effort into pleasing him. Leastwise, not any he hadn't paid for their services.

He gestured at his cock, which was half-hard. The semi-erection should not have been possible, not after the galvanic orgasm he'd been devastated by only a short time ago. "Men are easily enticed into the necessary physical state for sexual congress. It takes considerably more effort to arouse a woman. That's why so many are left disappointed—in the race to climax, men always run the distance faster."

"Disappointed? How can—"

"You asked me for more," he reminded. "Imagine if I had given you less, or worse, said I was finished and it was a shame you couldn't keep pace."

"Oh . . . But you would never do that."

"I would never do that," he agreed. Even if it meant nearly killing himself every time he had her.

She pushed up, stealing his wits with the unexpected view of her perfect breasts. They were neither large—as he'd erroneously thought he preferred—nor small. When she sat back on her heels with her hands on her knees, he found himself speechless.

Then, her eyes widened and she bit her lower lip. Red-faced, she made a move as if to leave the bed.

He caught her wrist. "What is it?"

"I need a towel," she whispered.

Sitting up, he grabbed one he'd thrown on the bed earlier. With his other hand, he gestured for her to widen her kneeling stance.

"Jasper . . ." Eliza was clearly mortified.

"It's mine," he said, tapping his shoulder in a silent order for her to put her hand there for balance. "Let me."

His cock hardened at the visible evidence of how explosively he'd climaxed. She was soaked with his semen. Thick trickles of it coursed down either thigh. He could hardly believe he was ready for her again. By all rights, he should be drained dry.

He cleaned her as gently as possible.

"You knew to have towels ready," she noted breathlessly, as he parted her delicately and dried the dark red curls between her legs. "I should have suggested sheep-gut condoms. I . . . I wasn't thinking clearly."

"It was my responsibility to do that."

"It's *my* body."

"Only in public and when you are dressed. When you're naked, your body belongs to me."

Her chin lifted. "Does your body belong to me when it's bared?"

"Clothed and unclothed, for as long as you'll have me." If he had his way, even longer than that . . .

Jasper looked her in the eye. "I always use French letters, Eliza. I haven't gone without one since I was young and too ignorant to know better. I assure you, that was many years ago."

"Did you forget tonight? Or find you lacked—"

"I never forget." He paused in his ministrations. "Tomorrow, when you're repaired and rested and feeling entirely in control of your mental faculties, we'll discuss everything that transpired tonight."

Her fingertips dug into his shoulder. "You deliberately spilled your seed inside me? Did you not think of the consequences I might face? Have you no care for me?"

Dropping the towel, Jasper caught her around the waist and tugged her against him. "I would do anything for you. Break any law, violate every rule, circumvent any competition—"

"Montague," she interjected, comprehension leaving her jaw slack. "You know he visited with Melville, and why."

"To hell with Montague," he said fiercely. "I want you. That's all there is to it."

"I gave myself to you freely." Eliza tried to wriggle away. "You didn't have to . . . *mark* me, as if you were marking your territory."

"I did." He gripped her with as much tenderness as her resistance allowed. "The moment you saw me, you knew what I was. My nature is no surprise to you."

"I hired you to protect me!"

Jasper inhaled sharply, cut to the quick by the truth of what she said. "Christ, Eliza."

He released her, but she didn't pull away. Instead she stared at him, breathing roughly. With her face and pale shoulders framed by gloriously hued tousled locks, she was the loveliest creature he'd ever seen.

"I'm sorry," he muttered, running a hand through his hair.

"Not for what you did," she surmised. "But because I'm unhappy about it."

There was nothing he could say to that. Lying to her was not an option.

The silence stretched out. They were only inches apart, both kneeling. He sat on his heels; she was upright, bringing them nearly eye to eye. He waited on tenterhooks, wondering if she would want to leave and what he could do to convince her to stay. Seducing a woman in a temper often led to hot sex, but the fury afterward was hotter still. He couldn't risk pushing her any further away.

Damnation, he would give anything to know what she was thinking . . .

"I can almost hear your brain working," Eliza said, studying him. "Care to tell me what thoughts occupy you so completely?"

"My brain isn't as refined as yours, so I am at a loss for what to do. Tell me how to sweeten you toward me again."

"I'm mystified by the ferocity of your possessiveness. You could have anyone." She swallowed hard. "The only thing distinguishing me is my fortune. Is that what you covet so strongly?"

"You don't believe that," he scoffed. "And I will point out that you, too, could have anyone."

She gave his shoulder a little push. "Lie down."

Jasper fell to his back without reservation, willing to do whatever she required to redeem himself. However, there was nothing repentant about his cockstand, which eagerly extended almost to his navel. He'd progressed from nearly erect to flagrantly so the moment she became aggressive.

"Since your body is now mine, by your own admission," she murmured, "I should like to examine it."

He lay unmoving, submitting . . . for now.

Eliza gestured at his penis. "I should like to see it at rest sometime."

"Little chance of that happening. Merely thinking of you makes me hard." He should, perhaps, couch his sentiments more delicately, but since his lust for Eliza was raw, it was more honest to word it thusly.

She reached out and caressed his biceps. When the muscle twitched beneath her touch, she pulled back with a squeak.

Jasper caught her hand and put it back. "Don't be frightened or shy. Whatever you do, I promise to enjoy it."

"I do not want you to simply *enjoy* it," she argued, meeting his gaze. "I want to be exceptionally good at pleasing you. I want to be memorable."

Jasper exhaled in a rush, the allusion to temporariness goading every proprietary instinct he possessed.

Eliza's fingers moved featherlight over the flesh of his upper arm. Then, she grew bolder and squeezed.

"You are so hard," she whispered. Her gaze moved over his chest and abdomen, followed by her hands. She lingered over his stomach, tracing every ridge of muscle. "And large. You are like a great, sleek beast. A virile animal."

A visible shiver moved through her, which set off an answering response in him. "You like that about me."

"I shouldn't. You are too wild and undisciplined. I'm not woman enough to tame you."

"You wouldn't want me tamed." He caught her hand again and urged it to his cock, prodding her fingers to wrap around him. Her tentative touch was like lightning, causing the hair on his legs to prickle. "Part of you may be appalled at my primitive approach to certain matters, but part of you wouldn't have me any other way."

"You are very arrogant."

"I take no credit for your attraction. My parents are responsible for my appearance, and my ruthlessness is equally inherent. I am, however, grateful they win your regard. Contrary to your opinion, you are the perfect female for me."

Her other hand joined the first, cupping him. Her hands were so slender; she could not circle him in her grip.

"What wins your regard?" she asked, tracing a thick vein with her fingertip.

"Your honesty and good s-sense," he hissed, shuddering as she clasped the head of his cock in her palm. "Your agile mind and independent thought. And the way you respond to me physically. By God, I cannot get enough of that. You melt for me, softening all those hard edges you use to keep others at bay."

Eliza's tongue followed the curve of her lower lip. Her eyes had grown heavy-lidded, betraying how well she enjoyed touching him so intimately. Or perhaps it was what he'd said. Jasper reached up and cupped her breast, his thumb and forefinger surrounding the delicate peak and tugging. She made a soft noise of pleasure.

"Lie atop me," he said hoarsely.

She hesitated, looking unsure. He showed her the way, steadying her with his hands on her waist as she draped her slim body over him. Cupping her nape, he pulled her lips down to his. He kissed her with open-mouthed hunger, drinking her in with deep draws on her tongue. She kissed him back with equal fervency, her lips slanting across his, her hands clutching the counterpane on either side of him.

He groaned, feeling ravenous but wanting no more than this for now. It wasn't enough and yet it was too much, the act of kissing both erotic and sweet. The feel of her slight weight stretched across him was one he adored, and the sudden smattering of tiny kisses she pressed all over his lips made him laugh with delight.

"I'm sorry," he said again, knowing he could never give up this intimacy. He was willing to grovel to keep it. "I will make mistakes. I don't know how to do this, how to be what you deserve."

Eliza kissed him quiet. "We'll show one another how to be what the other needs," she breathed. "I want to be the one who gets inside you. The one you cannot forget . . ."

Jasper thrust his fingers into her hair and took her mouth in a long, deep kiss. He had no notion of what time it was, and he didn't care. He just knew he didn't want it to end.

Chapter 10

Eliza had never fully appreciated the restorative properties of salt baths. However, Jasper insisted she take one before leaving his home the evening before and suggested she might avail herself of one in the morning as well. Having taken his advice, she felt much better, although there was still lingering soreness in unmentionable places.

She was also starving, as she often was after strenuous activity. She ate far more at breakfast than was usual and remained at the table for some time after Melville excused himself. With the late morning sunshine slanting through the window at her back, Eliza read the paper and chose not to think about all the many things she should be thinking about. Instead she chose to dissect the waltz in her mind, remembering the way it was taught to her and improving upon that teaching method.

Jasper would be calling later for his first dance

lesson. She was eager for him to become proficient so she could share a dance with him in public. A thrill moved through her at the thought of being in his arms in full view of everyone. It would be a delicious challenge to be decorous at a time when she would be so physically stimulated.

Eliza turned the page and tapped her foot to a tune playing in her head. After returning home at ten o'clock the night before, she'd stayed in. She was perfectly content to read the various renditions of last night's events in the gazettes, having previously come to the conclusion that the printed tales were often more entertaining than the reality.

"Eliza."

Glancing up, she smiled as her uncle reentered the room. "Yes, my lord?"

He rounded the long wooden table with a frown. Today was one of the few days when every piece of his attire was the way it should be, signaling a hard-won victory for his lordship's valet.

"The Earl of Westfield is here," he said, pausing beside her.

"Oh?"

"He has expressed an interest in paying his addresses to you."

Eliza blinked up at him. "Beg your pardon?"

"He wants to wed you. And speak with you. He awaits you in the parlor."

She folded the paper carefully, her thoughts rushing forward and stumbling all over themselves. With her brain arrested by confusion, her attention moved to the delicate lace runner that bisected the table. Her gaze slowly shifted to the brass candelabra that stood in the center. The antique piece was surrounded by a ring of pink roses, just as she was surrounded by sudden marriage proposals.

Melville cleared his throat and pulled her chair back from the table. "I was not aware you and Westfield were well acquainted."

Eliza stood. "I hardly know him."

"It would be an excellent match, much more advantageous than marrying Montague."

"Absolutely," she agreed, linking her arm with his and following his lead toward the door. Westfield was handsome, wealthy, and widely respected. He was also a friend of Jasper's, which made his offer decidedly more curious.

"How do you feel about this?" his lordship asked as they left the room.

"I wish I knew. Perhaps I'll have a better idea after I speak with him. How did you respond?"

"I wished him luck."

"What about me? Do you wish me luck, too?"

"I wish you happy, dear. In whatever form suits you best." He kissed her cheek. "Now, go on. Don't keep Westfield waiting."

Eliza set off on her own toward the front of the house. It was late enough in the day that the sun no longer shined directly through the glass around the front door. The familiar stillness of her home was usually comforting, but today it emphasized the disturbance created by the earl's visit. A second offer of marriage in as many days. She could hardly credit it.

As she entered the formal parlor, Eliza collected that Westfield's reason for visiting wasn't the sole cause of her unease. His physical presence was palpable. His person fairly crackled with a vibrant energy very much at odds with Jasper's quiet, intensely watchful air.

"Good morning, my lord," she said.

"Miss Martin." Westfield stood. He was as tall as Jasper, though not as broad or muscular. If pressed for a description, she would call him "elegant" and very dashing. "You look radiant."

"Thank you. I should return the compliment and say you look quite nice."

He grinned. "How are you faring this fine day? I hope you're well. You were missed about town last night."

Eliza chose to sit in the pale yellow velvet wingback facing the doorway. She lowered herself into the seat and smoothed her floral-patterned muslin skirts. The earl settled opposite her with practiced grace, a man of understated power and privilege. She decided that "polished" was a more apt descriptor than "elegant." Jasper had a sharper edge to him.

"I'm well," she answered. "I stayed in by choice, not due to any malaise. I don't enjoy the events of the Season as much as others do, I suspect."

She mentioned her sentiments deliberately, knowing Westfield would need an accomplished hostess for a wife if he hoped to achieve his political and social aims.

"Not surprising," he said, "considering what a danger they have become to you."

"Beg your pardon?"

"I'm aware of the nature of your association with Mr. Bond."

Eliza was too startled to blink. "Oh."

"Please don't hold his disclosures against him. He confided in me because he knows I am trustworthy."

"He may trust you with his own personal matters, but trusting you with mine is an avenue I wish he'd discussed with me." She wondered how much information the earl was privy to. Considering he was offering marriage, she expected he was aware of more than she was comfortable with.

"I appreciate your concern, I assure you." He paused as the tea service was brought in and placed before Eliza on the low table between them. He eyed Mrs. Potts with what appeared to be astonishment, a reaction Eliza was quite used to. The housekeeper was tall and slender as a reed, her arms seemingly too frail to support the weight of the heavy service. But she was far stronger than she looked, capable of lifting items even Melville struggled with.

After Mrs. Potts left, Westfield continued. "My intention is to help you and Bond. And myself, of course."

"By offering to resolve a temporary problem by binding me to a permanent one?" Eliza turned her attention to the preparation of tea.

"You just called me a permanent problem," he pointed out dryly.

"Not *you*," she corrected, measuring the tea leaves. "Marriage to you. We know very little about each other, and if we were to consider what we do know, I doubt we'd find ourselves to be aligned."

"I know I'm appreciative of the way you responded to a statue nearly braining you," he argued, leaning forward. "I thought you displayed considerable fortitude and courage. You proved yourself capable of addressing any situation presented to you, Miss Martin, and that is a trait I've not previously been wise enough to consider."

Taking more time and care than necessary, Eliza balanced a strainer atop the lip of a cup. Her mind was focused on identifying how she felt about Jasper's betrayal of her confidence. She knew she shouldn't take the matter lightly—not after the examples of foolish choices her mother had made in the throes of an infatuation—but she found herself making excuses for Jasper. Attempting to find a mitigating circumstance she could accept. Surely he had good reason for sharing what happened between them the night before, if only she could think of it. It was difficult for her to decide whether she was showing good faith or poor judgment.

"I understand my desire to remain unencumbered by marriage is incomprehensible to most," she said finally. "All young women are expected to select a husband as they would a new bonnet or pelisse, because a spouse is as necessary a female accessory as outerwear. But I need no support, financial or otherwise. I have most of what I need, and I can afford to buy the rest. Frankly, my lord, while your solvency is most refreshing, I don't see what use I would have for you personally."

"No?" His mouth lifted on one side in a manner

she knew many women would find appealing. "You would be free of the suitors plaguing you, including Montague, who is becoming impatient. Bond has only your best interests at heart, but he's blinded by his own personal motivations, and now they are contributing to your dilemma. Seeing you safely wed to someone he can trust is the most responsible way to address your situation."

"I dislike talking in half-measure, my lord. I lack the talent required to translate and decipher. Since I don't believe you would offer marriage in the name of friendship, regardless of the circumstances, I should like for you to speak bluntly and honestly."

Eliza chose not to elaborate on what those circumstances might be, because she still wasn't certain how much the earl knew. If he was aware of her indiscretion and the possible ramifications, it would explain his address. But what would motivate a man in his position to step into such a situation?

Westfield waved off her offer of sugar. "I'm not being completely altruistic. You are sensible, attractive, and willing to take extraordinary measures to accomplish necessary tasks."

"I'm certainly not the only female to meet those qualifications."

"You are wealthy, intelligent, and determined," he enumerated. "You have sufficient breeding, but come unencumbered by tiresome, troublesome, or expensive siblings. You speak your mind and force me to speak mine. What more could I ask for?"

"Desire? Elevated feelings? Youth?" She could tell by the momentarily blank expression on his face that her first suggestion took him aback. However, she felt the question was warranted by his offer.

"Four and twenty is a perfectly acceptable age. As to the rest, a lifetime is a long time to commit to another individual. I'd rather not enter into such an extended association based on higher sentiments."

"That isn't why you make this offer. You see an opportunity in me, yes. But finding a suitable wife is not all you want."

Westfield straightened. Although his gaze didn't narrow, his focus did. "What else would it be?" he drawled.

It was the drawl that proved her point. "Perhaps you seek a shield or a barrier. Someone to deflect attention from you. Or an innocuous person to fill a hole you find painful."

"Can I add 'imaginative' to the list of your attributes?"

The sound of masculine voices in the foyer drew Eliza's attention to the open parlor door. A moment later, the butler appeared with a calling card borne atop a salver. A quick glance at the clock on the mantel told her it was Jasper. He was timely as usual, arriving just a few minutes early.

She nodded at the butler in a silent acknowledgment that he should show Jasper in. "Mr. Bond is here, my lord."

When Jasper appeared in the doorway, her fingers linked tightly within her lap. For such a large man, he moved with an effortless silence. His attire was notably understated, comprised of shades of gray. His Hessians were polished to a shine rivaling the luster of his gleaming hair, and he stood with a widened stance, a position that emphasized how solid he was. How well-anchored and stable.

Jasper drew to a halt just inside the threshold, looking at Westfield in a way that said he wasn't surprised to see the earl visiting. Either his men watching the house had informed him, or he'd known from Westfield. Eliza didn't know how she felt about the latter possibility.

What she did know was that their relationship was irrevocably changed. Although he was dressed from his neck to his toes, in her mind's eye she saw him as he'd been last night—flushed and disheveled, naked and vulnerable. He had been so open then, so willing to bare his thoughts and feelings, even when he didn't understand them. The knowledge of that hidden side to him created a nearly unbearable yearning. A part of her believed she "knew" him. It was not reasonable for her to feel thusly, considering how little about his life and past was known to her, but it wasn't her mind making the determination.

From the way he was looking at her, he was remembering the night before, too. But if he felt the same deep connection, why had Westfield come to call on her?

"Miss Martin." Jasper bowed, his voice lingering in the air for a delicious moment. He straightened and pivoted to face the earl. "My lord."

Westfield stood. "Bond. How fortuitous your arrival is."

"Is that so?" Jasper looked at her. "Why?"

Eliza understood from Jasper's low tone that he was in a volatile mood. She hesitated a moment before answering, unsure how to relay the events of her morning. "Lord Westfield has come to offer his assistance."

Visually, there was no change in Jasper's countenance, but his clipped response spoke volumes. "With what?"

She looked at Westfield, turning the conversation over to him.

Jasper's arms crossed.

The earl smiled. "I'm simply following through with what we discussed last night. Seeing Miss Martin wed might resolve the problems of everyone involved."

"Wed to whom?"

"To me, of course."

"Of course." Jasper shifted slightly, in the manner of a stirring beast.

Eliza, who was uncertain of what was transpiring, thought it best to keep her own counsel.

Westfield's smile began to fade as the silence stretched out.

Jasper glanced at Eliza. "Have you answered him?"

"Not yet, sir."

"Why the delay? Westfield is suitable in every way."

Stiffening against a sharp pain in her chest,

Eliza lifted her chin and replied, "Perhaps I was waiting for your endorsement, Mr. Bond."

"Damned if I'll give it to you," he snapped.

She blinked.

The earl looked equally stunned. "Now, see here, Bond—"

"What is your answer, Eliza?" Jasper stared hard at her.

She looked at his hands, noting the whiteness of his knuckles as he gripped his biceps. She forced herself to look away and give Lord Westfield her full attention. Her fingers were linked so tightly, they hurt. Even lacking refinement in social graces, she knew what she was about to do was wrong in many ways, but she also knew Jasper needed to hear she wanted him as well. He required it said aloud, with a witness. As confident and aggressive as he could be when in his element, he was as lost as she was when it came to intimacy.

After a deep inhalation, she said, "As honored as I am by your address, my lord, I must decline. My feelings are engaged elsewhere."

Westfield's brows rose.

"Right, then," Jasper said, breaking his stillness. "Out you go, Westfield. I'll see you this evening. Come early. You and I have matters to discuss."

Frowning, the earl stood. "My offer will stand through the end of the Season, Miss Martin. As for you, Bond"—Westfield's face took on a hardened cast—"we do, indeed, have matters to discuss."

Eliza was vaguely aware of holding out her hand to Westfield, who lifted it to firm lips and kissed the back. She might have said something inane, he might have as well, but she was so taken aback by the intensity with which he stared at her that she missed the rest. It was a searching look, one she couldn't answer.

He left shortly after, with Jasper following him to the front door. Eliza took the brief moment of solitude to take a fortifying drink of her now tepid cup of tea.

Equanimity. She missed it. Feeling so unsettled and confused was anathema to her. This was exactly the sort of situation her mother had so often wallowed in, the sort of situation Eliza long promised herself to avoid.

"Eliza."

"What did you tell him?" Her head lifted so she could see Jasper's face, then lowered again as he sank to one knee in front of her. Her heart thudded violently. Her free hand fisted in her lap.

He urged her grip to relax by gently prying open her fingers. "The only thing Westfield knows is the reason why you hired me. I needed someone who had invitations to the events you attend, so I could gain entry."

"Of course." As he massaged her palm, the tingles that coursed up her arm weren't entirely due to a returning flow of blood. "You didn't know he intended to—"

"No."

"I thought, perhaps, it was your way of protecting me from the consequences of last night."

He took the cup from her other hand. "I'm not

that selfless. Regardless, the memory belongs only to us, and I would never share it."

She swallowed hard. "Why are you kneeling in that way?"

A slow, self-deprecating smile curved his mouth. "If I'm able to secure Melville's blessing, would you have me?"

"*Jasper.*"

"Westfield is correct. It would solve many problems. I would have greater access to you, the person who wishes to harm you would have less access, we would have more time to—"

"We hardly know one another!" she protested, while a rush of warm and sweet feelings tightened her chest.

"We have honesty and desire." He brought her hands to his lips and kissed the knuckles. His eyes were dark, his words delivered with heartrending earnestness. "You have money and breeding; I work in trade, and my blood is worthless. But I would spill it for you."

Eliza sucked in a shaky breath. "What are you saying?"

"Marry me."

"I don't want to marry."

"But you want me." Jasper reached up and cupped her nape, his thumb stroking across her throbbing pulse.

"Why can't I have you without a ring?"

He snorted. "Only you would prefer to be a man's mistress instead of his wife."

"You should prefer me that way, too!"

"While other men line up to ask for your hand and claim rights to you that are mine? I think not."

"In a month, the Season will be over—"

"But our relationship will not be. You don't yet see it, but you are visibly changed by what transpired between us last night. The more I have you, the more obvious it will become, and other men will be drawn to that new awareness in you."

She absorbed his words, startled to think that the lush languidness she felt might be obvious to others. Studying Jasper, she searched for signs of change in *his* appearance.

His mouth curved. "I am down on one knee, Eliza. If that isn't a reflection of change, I have no notion what would be."

"Please do not make light of this. You don't want to marry either. You said you have no place in your life for a wife."

"I can make a place for *you*. We've both thought of matrimony in terms of how it would limit our lives, but marriage can be useful in some regards. A married woman has far more freedom than a spinster."

"How would it be useful to you?"

"It would settle me." His touch moved downward to cup her cheek. "In the last few days, I've been pulled in two directions—between work that must be done and thoughts of you. If you were mine, you would be close and protected. I could focus on the tasks at hand in the thorough manner I'm accustomed to."

She gripped his other hand tightly in her lap.

"Perhaps it would be best for both of us if we went our separate ways and resumed our lives as we knew them."

"Eliza." He made a frustrated noise. "Don't ask me to come to you as Montague and Westfield did, with practical reasons and sound arguments. If pressed, I would have to say we have no business in one another's lives and we would be mad to marry."

"I know."

"But I can make you happy. We are alike in many ways, yet different enough to complement one another. You can show me how to be more circumspect; I can afford you the opportunity to be as adventuresome as you like."

An odd sort of delight bubbled within her. Like champagne, it made her slightly giddy. "I'm not nearly as confident in my ability to make you happy. Most people find me to be aloof and too quiet. I am proficient with the piano-forte, but I'm a terrible singer. I—"

He laughed and leaned forward to kiss the end of her nose. "I don't want to be entertained. I want you. Just the way you are."

"You worry about the possibility I might be with child," she argued.

"I take that very seriously, yes. But why ask for marriage now, instead of waiting to be certain?" Jasper leaned back. "Tell me truthfully, Eliza. Is your fortune an obstacle between us? Do you think it matters to me?"

She shook her head without hesitation. When he continued to seem expectant, she spoke the negation aloud, "No."

"Good." He released her, and set both his hands on his upraised knee. "Let us make a bargain, shall we? I will secure Lord Melville's blessing, and you'll say 'yes' to me—"

"Jasper, I would swiftly bore you."

"Then," he pressed on, "the banns will be read. That will give us the time we need to find the source of your trouble, discern whether or not you are increasing, and spend some time together. If, after all of that, you still believe we don't suit and cannot be happy together, we'll break the engagement at the end of the Season. Is that reasonable enough for you?"

"It isn't easy to break an engagement."

"But it can be done."

"You claim not to be reasoned about this, yet you present me with a practical plan that affords me the opportunity to reach solid conclusions." She sighed. "I'm faced with two difficult choices: Make a decision now with too little information, or progress further than I ever intended in order to gather the information I believe we both need."

"If only you were impulsive," he teased. "I might have been able to convince you to elope with me and spare you all the rumination."

"How can you be so confident about this?" she complained. "Why can I not have some of that surety?"

"I make my decisions here"—he tapped his abdomen—"and they are usually instantaneous. You make your decisions here"—he tapped her temple with his index finger—"and that takes more time. I'm trying to give you that time, Eliza, while staving off my own impatience. An engagement is the compromise we reach."

Worrying her lower lip, Eliza struggled to find the courage to say what she shouldn't.

"Talk to me," he urged.

"I cannot decide if it's desire goading me to agree against my better sense, and I'm also concerned that as the novelty of bedding me becomes less engaging you will want me less and less, until eventually you no longer want me at all. After we are bound to one another, it will be too late to realize we had only lust, which was quickly sated."

His nostrils flared. "If the possibility of waning interest concerns you, I can prove I desire you for more than sex. I won't ask you to give yourself to me again until we are wed, but I'm available to you whenever and wherever you want me. Chivalry and mores are no restraints to me. I learned long ago never to spite myself; the only person who loses is me. You should know of that aspect of my character, I suppose, before you wed me."

To be wanted so keenly . . . Eliza finally understood why her mother had been addicted to the feeling. It was so very tempting. And Jasper was irresistible.

To have him whenever she wanted. The thought of commanding sex from him, at any time and in any place, was impossibly arousing.

"Eliza," he murmured, drawing her focus back to him. "Give yourself permission to take what you want, for once. You might enjoy it more than you think."

That was partially what she was afraid of. But her fear wasn't a strong enough deterrent to mitigate her memories of the night before and the lingering happiness she'd felt upon waking.

"Speak to Melville," she said. "Then, ask me again."

Chapter 11

"I would never have expected this of you," Westfield said, rocking back on his heels.

"That makes two of us," Jasper said dryly.

The Valmont ballroom was larger than many,
but the broad expanse and thirty-foot ceilings did
little to ease the crush of guests. Worse than the
crowd was Jasper's realization that he was an object
of curiosity. Having spent the entirety of his life
avoiding notice whenever possible, he found it decidedly uncomfortable to be the center of attention. But the news of the notoriously reticent Miss
Eliza Martin's betrothal to a man few people had
ever heard of was apparently the most interesting
item of discussion. His appearance was being examined by nearly everyone, as if the reason he'd
won her could be determined visually.

Mindful of Eliza's pride, he had dressed with
care. While he'd elected to wear black to minimize his size, his coat and breeches were flawlessly

tailored. The materials used were exceptional, as were the diamond in his cravat pin and the sapphire in the ring on his right hand. The result was understated yet expensive elegance, which he hoped mitigated any speculation that he wanted Eliza for her fortune.

"You are completely inappropriate for her," the earl went on.

"Agreed."

Jasper looked for Eliza and found her. She appeared composed, if slightly irritated. The frown marring her brow betrayed both her peevishness and bemusement. He smiled, appreciating her artless honesty.

"She would be better served with me," Westfield said. "How can any woman live the life you do, Bond?"

"I expect Miss Martin and I will discover the answer as time progresses."

Westfield stepped forward, then turned to face him, effectively taking up the entirety of his view. "Is there anything you will *not* do in your quest to ruin Montague?"

"This has nothing to do with Montague."

"Of course it does."

"On the periphery," Jasper conceded, sidestepping to resume his viewing of Eliza.

"Wait." The earl moved in front of him again. "Were you talking about her last night? That nonsense about wanting something badly?"

"Yes." He wanted her now. Eliza had worn another of her mother's gowns, this one in a lovely rose hue. It was as simple in cut as the sapphire gown she'd worn days ago, but the bodice was provocatively low and the waist perfectly snug. The slender beauty of her figure was a joy to behold.

"Bloody hell." Westfield looked over his shoulder at Eliza. "Do you love her?"

"I enjoy her, and I can make her happy."

"I doubt you can. Not for the long term. And how does enjoyment signify? I enjoy half a dozen women any given fortnight, yet you don't see me proposing to any of them."

"Therein lies the difference between us," Jasper drawled. "There are very few things I've enjoyed in my life, and none to the degree with which I enjoy Miss Martin's company."

"Now, you have me intrigued," Westfield complained. "I'll forever be wondering what I missed about Miss Martin."

"No, you will not. You'll forget about her in any other capacity than as my wife, and that will be the end of it."

"Hmm . . ." Westfield turned around, searching. "I have yet to see Montague. I should like to know how he's taking the news of your engagement."

Jasper didn't care what Montague thought.

The moment the realization hit, his spine straightened and his breath hissed out between his teeth. Shifting his position, he canted his body away from Eliza, his hands flexing at his sides. Soon, he would be able to put Montague behind him, but not now. Not yet. The earl had still to pay for his sins and the sins of his father.

Eliza. She made him forget himself, which was one of the reasons why he needed her. But she couldn't serve that purpose now. Not yet. His plan was in the final stages after years of frustrated waiting and endless hours of work.

"*Mr. Bond.*"

Turning his head, Jasper watched as Sir Richard Tolliver approached. Although Jasper had believed Tolliver couldn't be any thinner, it appeared he was tonight. His dark coat hung loosely on his shoulders and his modestly embroidered waistcoat gaped a little just above the top button. "Good evening, Sir Richard."

"I hear congratulations are in order," Tolliver said, looking far from congratulatory.

"They are. Thank you."

"How fortuitous that Miss Martin should decide to marry so soon after you returned to her life. Almost as if she were waiting for you these last few years."

"Poetic," Westfield drawled. "Perhaps if you'd shared your talent for romantic thought and turns of phrase with Miss Martin, you might have had more luck with her."

"What talent did *you* share?" Tolliver shot back, glaring at Jasper.

"Be very careful when maligning me," Jasper warned softly. "Should you inadvertently cast aspersions on Miss Martin's character, I assure you, I won't take it well."

Tolliver's foot tapped against the floor. "Your long familial friendship with the Tremaines makes it decidedly odd that Miss Martin can share little about you."

"Cannot? Or will not?" Jasper challenged. "She understands the value of privacy. It's one of the many qualities she and I have in common. Now, cease being a nuisance. Go find a new heiress to woo."

Tolliver remained in place for a long moment. Finally, he spoke between clenched teeth, "Good evening, Mr. Bond. And to you as well, my lord." He turned about and stalked away.

"You're making friends already," Westfield said, staring after Tolliver. "I have to say, I never guessed he had such forcefulness in him. Perhaps his feelings for Miss Martin were true after all."

"Nothing so sublime." Jasper rolled his shoulders back. This was what he'd wanted—to attract the attention of whoever was endangering Eliza. But he hadn't anticipated the feeling of jealousy. Tolliver had roused his proprietary instincts and his discomfort was certain to worsen as time progressed.

The sound of Montague's name being bandied around them drew Jasper's attention toward the farthest entrance. "He came," he murmured. "I'd begun to doubt he would."

"Look at this place." Westfield gestured with a jerk of his chin. "Lady Valmont hasn't enjoyed a gathering of this size in many years. The curious come en masse to see Miss Martin's transformation and the man responsible for it. She changed her appearance for you, did she not?"

"She did it for the investigation. At first." Jasper gave himself permission to look at her again. He was torn between his two goals—winning Eliza's hand

and staying focused on his vengeance. "Tonight, I think she did it for me."

"So she was being truthful when she said she had feelings for you?" Westfield snorted. "What in God's name does she see in you?"

"I wish I knew. I would show her more of it."

Montague's progress through the room was marked by a noticeable ripple in the throng. He was heading toward Eliza, who stood on the opposite side of the room.

Jasper started in that direction. Westfield fell in line. They worked their way through the crowd, their path repeatedly blocked by one inquisitive well-wisher after another.

"Is your marriage a sign that Montague's destruction is now assured?" the earl asked.

"Not yet. I have learned he's forming a pool of investors for a coal mine speculation." Jasper grabbed a glass of lemonade from the tray of a passing footman.

"Is that what shored up his confidence about his finances and prompted him to contact me about retrieving his marker?"

"I hope to know the answer tomorrow. Either he's falling deeper into ruin or digging himself out of it."

Westfield grabbed his elbow and pulled him to a halt. "Bond."

Jasper's brows rose in silent inquiry.

"Have you considered embracing your new life with Miss Martin and leaving Montague's future to fate? In my experience, deserving fellows have a way of finding their own sorry end."

"*I* am Montague's end," Jasper said, before tossing back the contents of his glass. He started forward again, lamenting the beverage's inability to make the scrutiny directed his way more tolerable.

"I am so happy for you." Lady Collingsworth beamed like a proud parent. Dripping in sapphires and adorned with white plumes in her hair, she carried herself with the sort of regal confidence that supported such accessories instead of depended upon them.

"Thank you." Eliza ran a hand over her unsettled stomach.

"I admire you for following your heart," Regina went on. "I know how difficult the decision to marry was for you."

"I've tried to understand why it is so hard for me and not for so many others. Certainly I am not privy to information other women do not have."

"Of course you are. Only you lived with your mother."

Eliza's eyes widened. It was the closest the countess had ever come to speaking harshly about Georgina.

"Why do you look so surprised, dear? I'm aware of how you feel about your mother and her choices. She wed two different men because she cared for them, and neither marriage ended well. The fact that her second husband was a fortune hunter sealed your opinion of matrimony. I understand the preconceptions you had to overcome before accepting Mr. Bond's proposal." Regina looked past Eliza, focusing on something or someone behind her. "I can only hope that the indecent way he looks at you had a hand in your capitulation. I do believe his regard elevates the temperature in the room."

"Regina!" Eliza resisted the urge to glance at Jasper, knowing if she did, she would become flushed and distracted. All evening long, he'd been staring at her as if she was naked.

"Stuff," the countess retorted. "What happens in the privacy of the marital bed is of equal importance to what happens outside of it. A marriage cannot thrive if there is disharmony in the bedroom."

"Can it survive if pleasure is all there is?"

"My dear girl, pleasure is what is lacking in most marriages. Don't take it for granted."

"It seems so frivolous a reason," Eliza muttered.

"You are too smart to make frivolous decisions. I'm certain if you made a list of Mr. Bond's good and bad points, you would find the good far outweighs the bad."

No longer able to resist looking at Jasper, Eliza turned her head to find him. En route, her attention was caught by a familiar tall figure. The Earl of Montague was cutting through the crowd, his handsome face lit with a charming grin. Although he was frequently held back by those who wished to greet him, it was obvious he was on a direct path to her.

"Montague seems to be in good spirits," Regina noted. "It was good of you to tell him directly about your engagement to Mr. Bond."

"Leaving the matter to Melville would have been too distant and insincere." Eliza offered a smile to Regina that was filled with heartfelt gratitude. "I wouldn't have had the courage to meet with him without you. Thank you for accompanying me."

"Accompanying you where?"

Eliza was warmed by the sound of Jasper's voice behind her. The occupants of the room receded, her awareness of the noise fading into insignificance. She faced him. "To the park this afternoon."

"For a meeting with Montague?"

"Yes. To tell him about our engagement."

A shadow passed over Jasper's features. "You should not have done that."

She stiffened at his tone, unaccustomed to being gainsaid. "It was the least he deserved."

"You have no notion of what he deserves."

"Bond." Westfield's low, warning tone stole Eliza's attention. She looked at the earl, who stood just beyond Jasper's left shoulder. Like Montague, Westfield cut a dashing figure, and when he looked at her, his eyes were kind.

Two peers. Both were attractive, solicitous, and willing to marry her. Yet she had chosen the wild commoner of indeterminate origins. A man she could never hope to tame. She felt a frisson of disquiet over her decision.

Jasper's jaw tensed, as if he sensed her sudden confusion. The affection that had been in his eyes when they'd first reunited this evening was far less evident now. To her, the distance between them seemed almost tangible.

Regina cleared her throat. "Perhaps you might accompany me to the drinks table, Lord Westfield. My throat is dry."

"Of course." The earl shot a meaningful glance at Jasper, before leading Lady Collingsworth away.

Jasper stepped closer to Eliza. "How can I protect you when you deliberately put yourself in danger?"

"What danger? I met with Lord Montague in public, with Lady Collingsworth in attendance. Your men were certainly somewhere nearby. Or were they not? Is that why your mood is so foul?"

"You hired me to investigate your suitors. Then you meet with one privately to tell him he's losing any chance of laying claim to your money, putting him in a desperate position!"

"What could he have done?"

"Abscond with you. Hold you for ransom. Anything."

"Montague?" she scoffed. "A man of his station would not—"

"You don't know him, Eliza, or what he is capable of."

"And you do?"

"Stay away from him."

Her brow rose. "Is that an order?"

Jasper's jaw clenched. "Don't turn this into a battle of wills."

"You are attempting to limit my freedom. It's unreasonable to expect me not to fight for it."

He caught her by the elbows and tugged her scandalously close, as if they were alone and not surrounded on all sides by prying eyes. "I am attempting to keep you safe."

"Your advice is duly noted." Eliza knew she was goading his temper, but his clipped responses made her wonder if she wasn't giving him precisely what he wanted. He seemed to be spoiling for a fight.

"You must heed me." His eyes were so dark, they were nearly black.

"Your concern is unfounded. I foresee no occasion where Lord Montague and I would have cause to meet again outside of social settings."

"Cause or not, I want you to keep your distance." He released her. "From Tolliver, as well."

Irritation swelled within her. "Tell me why."

"Tolliver is not taking the news of our engagement well."

"And Montague? He smiled when I told him and wished me happy."

"He cares for no one's happiness but his own."

"And I'm just to take your word for this, with no explanation provided?"

"Yes."

"Already exerting your husbandly right to control me in whatever manner you see fit?" Her grip on her fan tightened to the point that the wood creaked in protest.

"I will not allow you to turn a discussion about your safety into an argument about independence and the drawbacks of matrimony."

"Won't allow. I see. Is this acceptance and rejection of acquaintances reciprocal? Can I forbid you to meet with Lord Westfield?"

"You are deliberately baiting me."

"I am simply attempting to discern where the boundaries are, and if they apply equally to both of us."

"Westfield is no danger to anyone."

"Maybe I know something you do not," she challenged. "Of course, if I follow your example, I don't have to share what I know with you."

She looked away to hide the prickling of tears and saw Lord Montague approaching. Her shoulders went back.

"Miss Martin." Montague kissed the back of the hand she extended to him, then released her with a stately dip of his head. He looked at Jasper. "Mr. Bond. May I extend felicitations to you?"

Jasper's lips curved in a teeth-baring smile. "You may, my lord. I accept them with pleasure."

Eliza knew the rigidness of her posture betrayed the oppositional nature of her conversation with Jasper, but she was too frustrated to care overmuch.

"Is it too much to hope, Miss Martin," the earl said, "that you might still have room on your dance card for me?"

"The next waltz is yours."

A tic in Jasper's jaw filled her with acrimonious satisfaction.

She'd deliberately withheld the evening's two waltzes. Not for Montague, but as a token gesture for Jasper. She had intended for her next waltz to be with him, even though it would take weeks for him to learn the steps and absorb them into memory.

"It appears I, too, am fortunate," Montague said. "Although not to the same degree as you, Mr. Bond."

"So it seems." Jasper's features were set in hard lines.

The orchestra played a few brief notes to alert the guests that the next dance would soon begin. Eliza gratefully excused herself and searched for her partner, Baron Brimley. As she moved away from the terrible tension emanating from Jasper, her breathing became easier. Reason returned to her, swiftly followed by regret. She disliked that they'd quarreled. Worse, she disliked herself.

Jasper watched Eliza walk away with undue haste and berated himself for sparking their first argument. He *knew* he had to tread lightly with her or risk her thrusting issues of money and independence between them, but he'd been discomfited into acting rashly. The surprise of learning that she'd met with Montague drove him to be harsh and unyielding, yet his ignorance was his own fault. Lynd had called upon him unexpectedly, and Jasper made the mistake of delaying the daily reports in order to accommodate his old mentor.

How could he have been so careless? He lived by rigid schedules and timetables for a reason—they kept things running smoothly and without startling incidents. Compounding his error by expelling the anger that should rightly have been self-directed only made the situation worse. He'd now caused a rift between him and Eliza that he could ill-afford.

"You have Byron's brooding countenance mimicked to perfection," Montague said. "I didn't try that tactic when attempting to woo Miss Martin."

Jasper's head turned slowly, his expression altering to reveal no emotion whatsoever. He and his half-brother were nearly of a height. The similarities between them were numerous enough that Jasper shifted slightly to put more distance between them. "I cannot say I'm sorry you lost her to me."

Montague smiled and rocked back on his heels, blissfully oblivious to the resemblance between them and the reason for it. "You are somewhat of a mystery, Mr. Bond."

"Ask me what you want to know. Perhaps I'll answer you."

"How do you feel about coal?"

A ripple of satisfaction moved through Jasper. Could acquiring the information he needed be so easy? "It's a necessity. Life would be miserable without it."

"My thoughts exactly." The earl's smile turned into a grin. "I have a speculation you might find interesting."

Jasper pushed Eliza from his mind and managed a smile. "You have the entirety of my attention, my lord."

By the time the Earl of Montague collected Eliza for their waltz, her ire had vanished. Still, she was completely out of sorts. For the first time, she understood that she'd lived her life without conflict after her mother passed on. No one disagreed with her because there were no points of contention; she was not obliged to explain herself nor meld her viewpoint with anyone else's. The result of her unchallenged independence was that she was sorely unprepared for arguments. Her entire body responded negatively to discord. She had a headache, and her stomach was upset, even though she was no longer angry.

"I've never seen you look lovelier, Miss Martin," Montague murmured, as he set his hand at her waist.

"Thank you." She stared at his cravat, noting its elaborate style and thick starching.

Montague had dressed flamboyantly in peacock blue velvet and a multi-colored waistcoat. His attire was far removed from Jasper's more somber style, and yet the earl's height and physical coloring were uncannily accurate substitutes for Jasper. The similarity caused Eliza to focus on how the earl made allowances for her shorter stature when an upraised arm position dictated it. He was a highly accomplished dancer, leading her expertly through the steps. She took mental notes for use in Jasper's dancing lessons, grateful the preoccupation afforded her some respite from her emotional turmoil.

"You have aroused my curiosity," he said.

"In what regard?"

"Your matchmaking skills."

Eliza frowned. "I didn't say I possessed any. Only that I could find someone more suitable for you than I."

"Suggestions?" His dark eyes were laughing.

"I believe any unmarried woman in attendance tonight would fit that criterion."

"For shame," he cried, laughing, and thereby turning heads toward them. "To foster hope, only to dash it with a cruel jest."

"Fustian. You could have anyone."

"Except for you."

It took her a moment to realize he was teasing her. "How about Audora Winfield?" she offered.

"Her laugh drives me to madness."

"Jane Rothschild?"

"I frighten her. She stammers and turns red. The best we've managed were short stretches of time at a house party where I spoke incessantly to fill the void and she nodded vigorously to everything I said."

"Poor thing. Perhaps more time spent with her will alleviate her nervousness?"

"Too torturous for both of us, I think. Certainly too much work."

"Lady Sarah Tanner?"

He shook his head.

"What fault does she have?" Eliza asked.

Montague hesitated a moment, then said, "She is . . . overbold."

"Oh. I see." She found herself at a loss. There were others, she was sure, but she couldn't name them offhand. "Perhaps you would be best served by waiting for a new Season and new debutantes?"

"As recently as yesterday, I would have said I could not afford to wait that long."

"And today?"

"Today, I have renewed hope that I can buy the time necessary to find a suitable replacement for you. I believe I have found a solid investment with a high probability of return. Mr. Bond might join me in the pool. We have plans to discuss it further tomorrow."

"Do you?"

Why would Jasper consider investing with Montague when he claimed not to trust the earl and knew him to be insolvent? It was unreasonable. And that wasn't her only concern. What was Jasper's experience with investments? Did he know what he was involving himself in?

In the morning, she would ask Reynolds to look into Montague's speculation and assess its potential. Then, she'd approach Jasper directly and ask him to explain. If he refused to answer, she would give him an ultimatum—share with her or lose her.

They could progress no further as a couple with so much unsaid between them.

Chapter 12

"I'm sorry."

Eliza turned away from the French doors leading to the rear garden and faced Jasper. He entered the Melville ballroom with a determined, forceful stride. There were over one hundred feet of marble floor between them, but she felt his presence keenly.

"Close the door," she said.

He drew to a halt. The massive room was dimly lit, with only the indirect morning sunlight at her back offering any illumination. She heard him take a deep breath before turning around and returning to the door.

As the click of the latch echoed through the room, she asked, "Did you sleep well?"

"No." Jasper resumed the long walk to where she stood, passing the many mural vignettes without looking. "But then, I've never slept well. There is too much to be done and not enough time in the day."

"I didn't sleep well either." She absorbed the rush of sensation she always felt upon first sight of him. Interspersed between the Georgian-era vignettes of a picnic party were long, slender mirrors framed by cream-colored molding. The result was many Jaspers filling the room. Her reaction was equally magnified.

"I apologize for last night," he said again, reaching for her and pulling her into his arms. Lowering his head, he sealed his mouth over hers.

There was nothing remorseful about his kiss. It was hot, fierce, and lustful. Jasper's tongue teased her lips open, then licked inside. The taste of him exploded across her senses, awakening a powerful need to possess him.

Eliza caught him to her with fevered desperation. Her arms encircled his shoulders, her fingers pushed into his silky hair and cupped his nape. Her breasts swelled against his chest, the lingering soreness between her legs forgotten in a rush of slick moisture. She wanted to bare his skin, rub her open mouth across it, caress him with her hands and uninhibited undulations of her body.

He groaned and twisted his mouth away.

"Jasper . . . ?"

"I handled myself poorly." He rested his temple against hers. "I know you won't tolerate being dictated to."

She no longer wanted to talk, but knew they must. Sexual passion could not be all they had. "H-how do you know that?"

"Because I pay attention to you." He set her away from him. "And I'm a good judge of character."

"You have me at a disadvantage. I know nothing about you beyond your livelihood and your wish to marry me."

"You know how I look without my clothes on. And how I feel inside you."

She wanted him inside her now. Ached for the feeling of fullness and delicious friction. The incendiary rush of climax and the repletion that followed.

Eliza linked her hands behind her back and circled him, her green skirts swaying around her legs. "That isn't enough for me in quiet, contemplative moments. I think of you and how I act when I'm around you, and I do not recognize myself. You are the catalyst for the changes in me, yet you're an enigma. Can you understand how difficult it is for me to experience such upheaval with no foundation upon which to lay it?"

He turned his head to keep their gazes connected. "I know it appears as if I haven't altered as much or sacrificed as much as you have."

"You aren't the only one sorry about their behavior last night. I said and did things I regretted almost the moment they happened. I was irritated with you and reacted unthinkingly."

"Relationships are fraught with such behavior. It's perfectly normal."

"It will not be normal for us, or I want nothing to do with it."

His stance widened. "What are you saying?"

Slowing in front of him, she eyed him from head to toe. He was dressed for riding in snug doeskin breeches and polished Hessians. The powerful muscles of his thighs and calves were clearly delineated. He crossed his arms, as if in preparation for a confrontation, and his flexing biceps strained the seams of his dark gray coat.

He was the most attractive, sexually alluring man she'd ever crossed paths with.

"I cannot hide how I want you," she said huskily. "I want to be in your bed even now, despite the fact that it's the middle of the morning. I want you so badly I burn with it."

"Eliza."

"See how you've changed me, that I can say such things aloud? But desire alone won't be enough impetus to wed you. I could insist on an affair instead." She rounded him again. "I agreed to your proposal because you've been honest with me. Although you haven't revealed much of yourself, what you have shared up to this point has been truthful."

Jasper caught her arm as she came around. "I'm different with you, as well. I am learning to adjust. You will, too."

"Not unless you become more than a stranger to me. You once said your past and future are irrelevant. But since then, you've asked me to blend your future with mine. To create a joint future. *Our* future. In order for that to happen, you have to show me the road upon which you travel. I cannot be led along blindly. If you won't commit to sharing, then we are finished before we begin."

"The future is shaped by the past." His throat worked on a hard swallow. "My past will alter your view of me. The risk of you turning away from what I am is too great."

Eliza cupped his cheek. With every inhale, she smelled the beloved scent of his skin. "What kind of life would we have together, if we continue to do and say things to each other we lament? It's the worst sort of dishonesty. I've seen it before, and I know it ends in sorrow and misery. I don't want that for you, or for me. I do not want that for *us*."

He caught her hand and kissed her palm. "You speak of your parents."

"There was so much left unsaid between them. Their infatuation brought them together, but it wasn't strong enough to bear the weight of their façades. They quarreled often and said unkind things. Eventually, apologies were no longer enough to mend the rift between them. How could they be, when they continued to repeat the mistakes they apologized for?" Her fingertips drifted across his firm lips. "If only they'd been honest about themselves and what they needed. Perhaps they could have made each other happy."

"The moment you walked away from me last night, I regretted my brusqueness. I considered climbing through your bedroom window just to reassure myself that you would still receive me."

"Would you have revealed the truth to me then?"

Jasper offered a rueful smile. "I doubt it. Surely, the convenience of finding you in bed would have distracted me."

"How swiftly you tell the truth when it's not tied to your past."

He urged her closer and pressed a kiss to her forehead. Then, he walked away and spoke over his shoulder. "Pull the pins from your hair. I'll speak for as long as it takes you to let it down completely."

"What game is this?"

"I intend to learn how to dance with you. We cannot have every lesson delayed by interruptions, despite how pressing they might be. We need a way to measure the time spent."

"Your pocket watch will not suffice?"

"That isn't nearly as fun."

Reaching up with both hands, she obliged. Slowly. Pulling out one pin and carefully lowering her arm to drop it on the floor.

He gave an approving nod, then began to follow the length of the wall. "There are some individuals who lack empathy for others. They are unable to create or sustain emotional connections, and their vision of the world is limited to their own viewpoints."

"My stepfather was such a person. Chilcott was entirely self-absorbed."

Jasper's voice rose to compensate for the growing distance between them. "In addition to that defect of character, Montague is also cursed with aberrant sexual appetites."

Eliza paused in the act of withdrawing another pin. "How do you know this?"

"I have crossed paths with women who've had the misfortune of catching his eye. He prefers un-

willing partners and the infliction of pain. My
understanding is he cannot perform otherwise."

"Unwilling . . ." Her stomach turned at the
thought of being forced to share the intimacies of
sexual congress with someone who was cruel and
malicious. "How does one acquire such deviant
tastes?"

"Through the blood, perhaps? Or a defect of
the soul." He shrugged. "Who knows?"

Her hands fell to her sides. She walked toward
him with her hair loosened and threatening to fall
around her shoulders. "Why didn't you tell me this
earlier? How could you keep such things from me?"

"When could I have told you?"

"Don't be coy!"

He altered direction to meet her halfway, his
booted steps more silent than her slippered ones.
"I would give up a great many things to spare you
such sordidness. I knew you were decided against
marriage, which made the possibility of your ever
learning of Lord Montague's activities very slim indeed."

"I would not have met with him yesterday if I'd
known!" As she reached him, her hands went to
her hips. "And you and I would not have quarreled."

"I also feared what would happen if he discovered you knew of his darker nature. Your face is so
expressive. You will not be able to hide your con-
demnation, and he's a desperate man. His good
name is all he has left. He cannot afford to have it
sullied by gossip."

Although she didn't approve of his methods, she

hadn't the heart to argue about his reasoning. He wanted to protect her in every respect. "Do you think he's the one who has been plaguing me?"

"I wouldn't put it past him." Jasper beckoned her closer with a crook of his finger. "He is teetering on the verge of utter ruination. He's gambled away or sold every non-entailed property, and he does not have the means to support the holdings he has left. His debts are such that he's being denied credit. Soon, he will have nowhere to turn."

"And yet you're considering investing with him?" Eliza stepped into his open arms. "What are you thinking?"

He set his chin atop her head. "I want him ruined. I cannot allow him to find a means of salvation. If feigning interest is required to glean the information I need to thwart him, it's a small price to pay."

His tone was so vitriolic, it didn't sound like Jasper at all. Eliza leaned back to study his features. "Why?"

"Retribution for a . . . friend."

Jealousy stung her. "A lover?"

"No." His hands stroked the length of her spine. "Before you there was sex. You have been my only lover."

Her fingers straightened his already immaculate cravat. "Will I always be?"

"Are you asking if I'll be steadfast? Of course."

"You answer so easily."

His beautiful mouth curved with amusement. "As if I practiced my response for just such a question? And here I thought we'd established I have yet to tell you a falsehood."

Eliza looked up at him from beneath her lashes. "I find the thought of another woman enjoying you as I have to be extremely vexing."

"Vexing," he repeated, grinning.

"Intolerable," she amended.

"We certainly cannot have you vexed. Therefore, I must be faithful."

Unsatisfied by his response, she goaded him. "I shall follow your lead in this aspect of our association, as I have in everything else."

"Why, Miss Martin," he drawled. "I do believe that was a threat."

Her gaze dropped to where her fingers lay against white linen. "Only if you stray."

He laughed. Picking her up, he spun her around.

"Jasper!" Wide-eyed, she looked into his face. Something in his expression flushed her skin.

"You delight me." His voice was slightly husky.

"You confound me. And charm me."

"And arouse you."

"Too easily." She ran her hands through his hair, unable to resist its thick silky texture.

"I want you even when we're not together. Can you say the same?"

"Yes, in the moments when I'm not questioning myself for jumping into a situation with my eyes closed."

Jasper set her down and touched her falling hair with reverent fingers. "Your mind wants to make sense of what you feel. I've forsaken any effort to understand it, but you will not. It's one of the many things I admire about you. Just promise me that when you have doubts or concerns, you'll come to me as you did today. Tell me what you need, and I will find a way to give it to you."

Eliza believed him. He made her feel as if she was important to him. Necessary. She'd never been necessary to anyone before. It was a novel feeling, one she was still attempting to assimilate.

"What I need," she began, catching his hand in hers and setting her left hand on his shoulder, "is for you to learn how to waltz. I want to dance with you."

He positioned his hand at her waist. "From the very first, you listed dancing as a requirement in your suitors."

"I'll enjoy dancing with you best of all." Eliza smiled. "You have that air of danger about you, and a very seductive way of moving. The inherent sensuality of the waltz was made for a man such as you."

His smile made her pulse race. "I want to commission a new gown for you to wear during our first public waltz. Will you wear it?"

Pleased by the thought of a gift, she nodded. It had been a long time since someone who cared for her bought her a present. Melville rarely knew what day of the week it was; special occasions were beyond him.

"I cannot wait," he purred, his spine straightening beautifully. "Teach me quickly."

"It will be my pleasure." Her tone changed, became more clipped and direct. "There are nine positions in the German waltz. However, we must start with a rule: this precise distance between us should always be maintained."

"You're too far away," he complained, shooting a pointed glance down at the floor between them.

"Stuff. The waltz is the only dance in which pairs are set apart from the assemblage and focused on each other. There is no way to be more intimate."

"Without a bed."

Eliza bit back an indulgent smile. Certainly she shouldn't encourage his roguish tendencies, but she adored them. He was unlike any man she knew— wicked in all the best ways.

"Pay attention," she said sternly. "Your feet should be turned outward when stepping"—she demonstrated—"and the lift of your leg should be pronounced."

Although he continued to make provocative statements, Eliza remained focused. She walked him carefully through the steps. At first, he seemed almost afraid to move. When she pointed it out, he groused, "Damned if I'll trample you."

But he soon learned to appreciate her responsiveness. He became more confident and sure-footed. The steps became more natural, his arm movements accomplished with more flourish. She praised him when his form was perfect, and teased him when it wasn't.

As time passed and they continued their exertions, his scent of spice and bergamot filled the air between them. The advance and retreat of the steps became foreplay to her. The twisting movements limbered her, while the too-brief moments of proximity began to titillate her senses. His powerful shoulder flexed beneath her hand, reminding her of how delicious he was when naked and passionate and aroused. Her breathing quickened.

Jasper watched her with an enigmatic smile. "I like this."

"The dance?"

"The way you follow my lead. The feel of your body moving in just the way I want, with only the slightest urging."

"You like being in control."

Jasper paused mid cross step. Their faces were turned toward one another, their lips only inches apart. "And you like me in control."

"Perhaps"—she lowered her gaze to his lips—"being out of control is my aim."

His hand tightened on her waist. "Are you propositioning me, Miss Martin?"

"What would you do if I did?"

"Anything you want."

He sidestepped, so that their bodies were aligned. Face-to-face. Jasper was such a large, strong man. She felt so delicate when she was with him, yet never overpowered.

"You know what I want," she whispered, blushing.

"A kiss?" He gently pulled another pin from her hair. "An embrace?"

"More."

"How much more?"

She bit her lower lip.

Jasper caught her chin. "Shyness has no place between us."

"I don't want to be . . . overbold."

"Sweetheart." His tone was soft and warm. "Can you still be unaware of how I relish your esteem and desire? Haven't I told you how deeply they please me and how much satisfaction I derive from them?"

"As if I'm the only woman to admire you," Eliza said wryly.

"You're the only woman whose admiration has value to me."

"Why? There's nothing special about me. Whatever pleasing traits I possess are better represented in other females."

"Not in the combination with which you are blessed." His hand drifted from her jawline and closed around her breast. He studied her reaction as his thumb circled a highly sensitive nipple. "I love that you are beautiful and clever and carry a constant desire for me. You could not be more perfect."

Her body responded instantly to his expert touch—her nipples tightened into aching points and the flesh between her legs throbbed with need.

"Tell me what you want," he coaxed, anchoring her with a hand at her hip. With two fingers, he rolled and tugged the erect point of her breast, the pressure too light to offer any relief.

She felt pliable and wanton. Intoxicated. They'd been alone for an hour, only inches apart; his body had been in motion the entire time. Watching him move was a seduction in and of itself. She couldn't keep herself from wanting him. Her infatuation was far too great to be moderated.

"I want you naked," she breathed.

A soft rumbling came from his chest, sounding suspiciously like a purr. "Why?"

Her hands moved of their own volition, catching the lapels of his coat. "Take this off."

His wicked smile made her toes curl. He shrugged out of the expensive garment and let it fall to the floor. "Better?"

"Not nearly." She caressed his arms through his shirtsleeves. Looking behind him at the mirror on the opposite wall, she drank in the view of his buttocks and thighs. The sight, smell, and feel of him were all aphrodisiacs to her.

He glanced over his shoulder. "You surprise me in all the best ways. Should I hang a mirror above our bed?"

"Jasper . . ." A shiver of mortified delight moved through her. "I would never be able to look."

"I think you won't be able to look away. Shall we prove it?"

Eliza stilled. "Here?"

"Would Melville disturb us?"

She shook her head. "How . . . ?"

Her mind rushed forward, planning how they could manage a coupling without a bed.

"Your nipples are so pretty," he murmured, drawing her attention to her bodice. She was shamelessly, visibly aroused. "So tiny and petite."

He stayed her when she moved to cover herself. "Unfair for you to hide when I cannot."

She followed the gesturing sweep of his hand

and found the bold outline of his erection straining the placket of his breeches. A soft sound of yearning escaped her. She wished for nothing more than to be naked with him, his powerful body flexing and working atop hers, his long thick penis pushing deep into her. Despite her lingering soreness, the lure of orgasm was too potent to be denied.

He stroked himself brazenly through the doeskin. "You cannot have this again so soon."

"Why not?" she demanded, her gnawing desire making her audacious.

"You're sore, and I'm not in possession of a condom."

Knowing he was vulnerable to her, she closed the distance between them. With one hand at his nape and the other gripping his buttock possessively, she rubbed against him like a cat.

Jasper's chest vibrated with a chuckle, stimulating her already tender nipples. "Vixen," he murmured, bending his knees and notching his erection against her swollen sex. He worked her against him, stroking where she ached with the stone-hard length of him.

"Yes," she panted, her nails digging into his skin. "I want this."

His lips moved against the shell of her ear. "You can't have it, I told you. But I can make you come. Would you like that, Eliza?"

"Please." She felt feverish.

"Are you wet for me?"

"Jasper!"

"Show me." He backed away. "Lift your skirts and bare yourself."

Despite the extremity of her desire, Eliza was still mortified by the request. It was one thing to be in his arms and lost to his skill. It was quite another to stand alone and lewdly display herself. "I cannot."

His eyes were so very dark. "I promise to reward your courage."

She fought against years of training and memories of her mother's promiscuity to blossom as he wished her to do. She'd always believed intimacy was built through time and familiarity. Now she knew it could also be based simply on trust.

She clutched her skirts in her hands. "I suppose you've seen countless pantalettes before."

The corner of Jasper's mouth twitched. "Countless? How debauched do you think I am?"

"Enough to ask me to do this."

"True enough," he conceded with a regal bow of his dark head. "But I did not *ask*."

She might have taken him to task for his arrogance, if her brain hadn't leaped in another direction. *So rare is this particular skill that many a woman will disregard other considerations in favor of it,* he'd said the day they had first met. And she'd laid claim to a man who possessed such expertise and wanted to practice it on her. How foolish was she to deny herself?

Before she altered her mind, Eliza yanked up her narrow skirts.

The way he looked at her caused the hairs on her nape to stand on end. "How brave you are," he praised.

Emboldened by his admiration, she untied the

ribbon that secured her pantalettes around her waist. The lace-hemmed linen fell to the floor and pooled around her ankles.

"Sweet Eliza," he murmured, his foot deliberately catching on his discarded coat and sliding it across the floor to a spot directly in front of her. "You are more generous than I deserve."

He sank to his knees.

As he stared at the dark red curls between her legs, Eliza became so aroused she could no longer stand still. She swayed slightly, and he caught her hip with one hand. With the other, he caught the waistband of her pantalettes and silently urged her to step out of them.

He kept her legs wide by gripping her ankle and keeping it in place. The hand at her hip moved between her legs, parting her and stroking gently through the slickness of her desire.

"I believe you were made for me," he said huskily, rubbing her flesh with a callused finger. "Look how wet you are."

Her hips rolled into his teasing caresses. "Jasper . . ."

Leaning forward, his breath ruffled her damp curls. She tensed in anticipation.

He licked his lips and purred, "Let's see how wet you can get."

Chapter 13

Eliza watched as Jasper leaned forward and licked lightly across the quivering flesh exposed by the spread of his fingers. The sensation was exquisite torment. Her thighs shook with the strain of yearning for orgasm. The sight of him on his knees, servicing her with such tenderness, was too stimulating to bear. He was so beautiful. So big and strong. So confident and self-possessed. To see him subjugating himself to her desire filled her with a sense of feminine power she'd never known.

And Jasper had introduced her to that power. Shown her it existed. Reveled in her wielding of it. She cherished him for that gift and his confidence in giving it to her.

Cupping the back of his head, she held her breath in anticipation.

"Open to me," he said softly, tapping the top of his shoulder.

It took the space of a heartbeat to comprehend

what he wanted. He held out his hand to help her balance and she carefully, hesitantly lifted one leg. As the back of her knee settled over his shoulder, the thrill of dominance increased. Heat raced across her skin. The lush weight of her breasts strained her bodice. The illicitness of what they were doing only added to her excitement. Her entire body felt ripe with erotic promise, fluid and languid, restless and alluring.

Jasper tilted his head back to look up at her. His expression—lust laced with fondness and admiration—tightened her chest. "You've discovered your ability to enslave a man. And you like it."

She ran her fingers through his hair, grateful she had the right to do so. "With you, I seem to like everything."

He caressed her thigh with a firm, yet gentle grip. With a turn of his head, he pressed a kiss to the skin above the tie of her stocking. His tongue flickered, so swift and fleeting she wondered if she imagined it.

"Don't tease me," she pleaded. "I am already overwrought."

"Patience is a virtue."

"Do I look virtuous to you?" she cried, so frustrated by desire she had to look away.

It was then that the mirror behind him snared her attention. Her breath caught sharply at the reflected view—her leg slung dominantly over Jasper's broad shoulder, her toes pointed from the delicious expectation, her hands cupping his head and urging him toward the eager flesh between her thighs.

"Are you watching?" he asked with a dark note of devilish provocation.

"Yes . . ." Eliza stared, unblinking, as his head canted to the side and he leaned into her. A second later, his mouth was on her, his firm lips surrounding her clitoris in a heated embrace. The flat of his tongue rubbed across the distended knot of nerves, and she cried out as tiny spasms rippled through her.

Jasper pulled back, licking his lips. "One day soon, I will spread you across my bed and feast on you for hours, just to hear the sounds you make when I pleasure you."

His words created a vision in her mind that inspired a heated rush of moisture. He hummed with approval and leaned forward, his hands cupping her buttocks and holding her still. The restraint he'd shown so far disappeared in a voracious assault of lips and tongue that destroyed any remaining rational thought.

Driven to wildness by his ardor, Eliza held his head and rocked into his working mouth. In the mirror, her reflection was both aggressive and wanton, her calf flexing against his back, urging him on. She was red-faced and gasping, her eyes glassy and her hair in disarray. She looked ravished and debased and more sensual than she ever thought she could be.

She looked like a woman who might enslave a man like Jasper Bond.

He hefted her higher with effortless strength, forcing her to balance on the tips of her toes. His tongue pushed into her and she moaned, pleasure sizzling across oversensitive nerve endings. Stabbing fierce and fast, Jasper breached the clenching tissues and drank the flow of silky liquid that welcomed a deeper, thicker penetration.

All the while the mirror starkly displayed her frantic writhing. She ground her throbbing flesh against Jasper's mouth, riding his thrusts in a mindless quest for orgasm. His tongue withdrew, and he caught her clitoris in a hot, wet kiss. With suction and the pointed tip of his tongue, he set off a climax so intense her vision blackened. Sobbing in the grip of violent shudders, Eliza hunched over him, attempting to pull away from his fervent suckling but unable to escape him. As the gripping ecstasy eased, the circle of his lips tightened, hurtling her headlong into another furious release.

Her nails dug into his shoulders. Tears burned her eyes and sweat bloomed from her skin in a humid mist. As she listed and began to fall, Jasper shrugged out from under her leg and caught her to him, tumbling backward so she sprawled across him.

She clung to him weakly, breathing his name.

"Shh," he soothed, his hands stroking her trembling back. "I have you."

He did. Completely.

Jasper stared up at the murals of circling olive branches surrounding each of the three massive chandeliers in the Melville ballroom. He knew time was rushing by while he lay on hard marble with Eliza draped bonelessly atop him. However, he didn't care about the time or the discomfort of his position. There was nowhere else he would rather be. Aside from a bed, perhaps . . .

"Jasper?" Eliza's normally clipped voice was passion-hoarse. He enjoyed the sound so much, he was prompted to press a quick hard kiss to her forehead.

"Um?" His fingers played with the disheveled strands of her tumbling hair.

Her head lifted and she looked at him. "How can you imbue so much smugness into one little sound?"

"Should I not be smug? You just melted in my mouth."

Gaze narrowed, she rose to a kneeling position beside him and set her hands on her knees. Her expressive face took on a look of examination and calculation. When her focus settled on his groin, his subsiding cockstand swelled to renewed life. He almost held his breath, wondering how far she would go.

"I cannot allow you to leave with that," she pronounced.

He grinned, adoring her. "Oh? But it is attached, I'm afraid. Fortunately, we are to be married, and you'll soon have more frequent access to it."

She gave his shoulder a push. "Not the penis itself. The erection, you vexing man."

"Ah . . . I always have one when I part ways with you."

Her blue eyes widened. "You do not!"

"I do. Not to this extent, but to some degree."

Eliza appeared to consider this information carefully. "Have you always been so randy?"

"Not prior to meeting you. My natural appetite for sex was previously sated by twice-weekly visits to Remington's." He rubbed a strand of her hair between his thumb and forefinger, remembering the flaming tresses spilling across his pillows.

"Courtesans?" One of her hands lifted to rest on his abdomen. "Have you never had a woman who was special to you? One to whom you were attached enough to see more than once?"

"There are some who are . . . easier to pass the time with. They eschew conversation and work diligently. If they're available, I will choose one of them over the others. But attachment? No."

"Sex without affection? That sounds very lonely to me."

"I don't know what loneliness is." It was not in his nature to discuss feelings and such. Jasper shifted uncomfortably, but answered directly. The more he revealed, the less hesitant Eliza became. That result was worth any discomfort. "There are goals to be met and work to be done. There is no time in my day to wish for things I don't have. Except for you."

"I will never understand why you like me so well." The tiny dimple he'd first noted on the day they'd met winked at him. "But I won't complain about my good fortune."

Enamored with that dimple, he grabbed her hand and tugged her toward him. "Kiss me."

"You like kissing. Not that I'm complaining. You are very accomplished."

"I never liked the act prior to meeting you. Now, I cannot get enough. Sometimes the urge to kiss you is so fierce I have a damnable time resisting it."

Her eyes widened. "Truly? I cannot fathom your disregard. I love your lips. And your kisses."

"I never considered my mouth a particularly erotic part of my anatomy. There are other places on my body I preferred directing attention to."

"Can I kiss you somewhere else?" A blush swept upward, over her chest to her cheeks. "Here, perhaps."

Her hand moved lower and stroked him through his breeches.

"Bloody hell," he hissed, unprepared for his impossibly swift reaction to her boldness.

"Too much?" she whispered, withdrawing.

"No." He caught her retreating hand and put it back, mentally kicking himself for startling her away from an act he wanted as much as his next breath. The level of trust she was displaying—from speaking freely to indulging his lustful whims—humbled him. He'd done nothing in his life to deserve her.

"Have your wicked way with me," he urged. "I beg you."

Eliza raked him with a heated glance, from head to toe. He felt that gaze like a tangible caress. "Teach me how to please you. Show me the way to be the only woman you will ever need or want."

Jasper yanked the placket of his breeches open and pushed his smalls out of the way. His cock sprang free of its confinement, straining toward his navel in a display of brute male arrogance.

"My God," she breathed. "Every part of you is magnificent."

The awed note in her voice sent relief rushing through him, swiftly followed by rampant desire. He watched as she reached for him, her slim white hands enclosing his scorching length in cool satin skin. His neck arched, his teeth gritting together in a bid for control. A few pumps of his hand and he could finish this. He was primed to blow after Eliza's earlier display of total abandon. Her scent clung to his lips, filling his nostrils with every drawn breath, spurring his lust to previously unattained heights.

Her fingertips slid delicately up and down his cock, exploring. Jasper exhaled in a rush. His bollocks were drawn up tight, his seed churning and pushing its way up his shaft to leak out the tip.

Eliza touched the first drop, then lifted her finger toward her mouth.

"You might not like it," he warned. "Some women do not."

Her brow arched defiantly. Her mouth formed an O, and she pushed the glistening fingertip inside. She hummed softly, and that was his undoing.

"Put your mouth on me," he said gruffly. "Wrap your lips around the head."

She bent over him without hesitation. Her hair—still partially pinned—drifted over her shoulders, with some freed pieces falling to pool on his stomach. He reached up with one hand and pushed her hair out of the way of his view.

He watched her lips part, her head lower, his cock disappear inside her . . . Her mouth fastened on the plush head, and he groaned raggedly. The drenching heat and gentle suction were torturous.

"That's good," he gasped. "Take more."

Her lips slid farther down, pushing his cockhead deeper into the narrowing channel of her mouth.

"Suck. Ah . . . yes, like that." Sweat dotted his brow and upper lip. "God . . . your tongue . . ."

A moan vibrated along the length of his shaft.

Any worry he'd had that she would find the act distasteful vanished with that sound. Her hand pushed into his breeches and cupped his testicles. Her avid tongue rubbed the underside of his cock. Her head bobbed up and down his length, her mouth sucking so forcefully it was audible. The wet smacking echoed through the massive room, then rippled through him in a wracking shudder.

As frenzied as she'd been in her own extremis, she was similarly ravenous for his. Eliza worked his cock as if starved for the taste of him. The sight of her fervor, the feel of her hands and mouth, the sounds she made . . . it was all so erotic he lost himself to her.

"You make me so hard," he growled. "Desist. Let me finish this."

In response, she took him as deep as she could, her tongue pinning him to the curved roof of her mouth. She sucked him so vigorously his thighs shook with the pleasure.

"Christ." His hips lunged upward. The first furious spurt of semen felt as if it was wrenched from his spine.

Eliza swallowed deeply and worked her hand on him, pumping his seed up the length of his shaft and into her eager mouth. Groaning and sweating, Jasper clenched his jaw shut and fucked his cock through her swollen lips, spewing his lust in an orgasm so intense it was painful. The rush of climax was endless, his cum spilling over her stroking tongue in thick, creamy washes. She took every wrenching pulse with unmitigated greed, urging him on with muffled moans.

Jasper collapsed to the floor with arms outstretched, muscles twitching from his calves to his shoulders, his lungs fighting for every serrated breath. His cock began to soften, as exhausted as he was, but she didn't cease her ministrations. The tip of her tongue dipped into the tiny hole at the crown, drinking the last bit of semen he had left. He closed his eyes, drunk on the repletion sinking into the very marrow of his bones.

"Come here," he murmured, needing to hold her.

As she curled against his side on the marble and entwined her legs with his, Jasper didn't recognize the feeling gripping his chest in a vise.

It was hours later when he realized the sensation might have been joy.

"Good morning, Miss Martin."

Eliza welcomed the distraction provided by the

arrival of her man of affairs shortly after eleven o'clock two days later. Jasper had sent a note, excusing himself from their scheduled morning meeting, and while it expressed regret, the missive gave no explanation for why he'd canceled. The last time they spoke at length was during yesterday's dance lesson in the ballroom—a space she would never think of in the same way again.

"Good morning, Mr. Reynolds," she replied briskly, closing her ledger and smiling.

He stared at her, blinking, as if taken aback, which brought to her attention how readily she smiled of late.

Clearing his throat, he took a seat in front of her desk. She was pleased to see he'd procured a new satchel. Unlike his previous one, this one was made of butter-soft burgundy leather ornamented with gold hardware. He was a wonderful employee, one who worked hard and performed well, and she paid him accordingly. It was good to see him indulging himself.

"I understand congratulations are in order," he said.

"Yes. Thank you." Eliza linked her fingers on the desktop. "How is Mrs. Reynolds?"

"Very well."

He told a story about his wife's social pursuits that Eliza made every effort to appear interested in. She was grateful when he moved on and said, "I've also received word from my brother."

"Oh?" A quiver moved through her tummy. Jasper's agreement to be more forthcoming about his situation put her in an awkward position. She'd grown more and more apprehensive about sending Tobias Reynolds to Ireland. Although she had engaged Tobias before beginning an intimate relationship with Jasper, she was nevertheless circumventing the man she intended to marry by researching his past without his knowledge or consent.

Reynolds settled more comfortably into the chair. "He arrived safely and has begun the initial inquiries."

She reminded herself to trust her instincts. "I would like to recall him. I have the information I need."

"If you're certain . . ."

"I am. He'll still be paid the agreed-upon fee for his time, of course."

"I never doubted it." His fingers curled and uncurled around the wooden arms of his chair. "May I speak freely, Miss Martin?"

"Always," she assured. "I value honesty above all else. I'd expect you would know that by now."

"I do. However . . ." He inhaled deeply, then exhaled in a rush of words. "Have I been remiss in my duties or disappointing in some way? Have I given you cause to distrust me?"

"No." Her spine straightened with alarm. "Why would you have such concerns?"

"You've always asked me to investigate your suitors. Therefore, I was startled to learn of your engagement to a gentleman whose circumstances I was not asked to explore. I know he is a friend of Lord Melville, but he's also a possible investor and even in that capacity, you did not ask me to verify his solvency."

Eliza was impressed. "Your thoroughness is laudable, sir."

"I'm relieved to hear you say so." He leaned forward. "I had only yesterday and this morning to inquire, but I must confess, what little I've gleaned has made me uneasy."

"Uneasy?" Certainly Terrance Reynolds wasn't the only enterprising and curious individual in town. What could be learned about Jasper through cursory inquiry?

"His residence is in a less-than-fashionable area of town. He has all manner of disreputable-looking individuals coming and going as they please. I'm not yet certain, but I believe he engages in trade. I suspect he makes a comfortable living, but it's doubtful he has your means."

"Few do. Regardless, Mr. Bond counts the Earl of Westfield as a close acquaintance."

"There is that," Reynolds conceded. "Frankly, your betrothed is a bit of an enigma."

Much obliged by his loyalty, Eliza felt it best to offer a truthful explanation for Jasper, so Reynolds would no longer be troubled. "Mr. Bond is a thief-taker."

"A thief-taker!" There was a pause, during which he blinked rapidly. Finally, he said, "Not one of the better-known ones."

"No, of course not. It would have been impossible for Mr. Bond to assume the guise of a viable suitor if he was a familiar personage. I found him through a referral."

"Found . . . ? You *sought* a thief-taker? I don't understand."

"Do you recall when Mrs. Peachtree experienced monetary troubles earlier this year?" she asked, referring to a tenant who'd suspected one of her employees of pilfering from the till. "You reported that she hired a Runner. When my situation arose, I approached her for his name and engaged the same man. However, Mr. Bell was unable to assist me. He referred me to Thomas Lynd, who suggested Mr. Bond would be more suitable."

"Dear God." Reynolds flushed. "You've done so much without my assistance . . . I cannot help feeling superfluous."

"Quite the opposite. You're an excellent man of affairs, sir, and valuable to me. Therefore, I was unwilling to endanger you. You see, I have recently found myself to be prone to accidents of a disturbing and suspicious nature."

"Accidents!" He paled. "What . . . ? Why . . . ? Damnation! *Who* would have reason to harm you?"

"That's what I hired Mr. Bond to discover."

"I wish you'd seen fit to include me. Tobias and I could have overseen a thief-taker or Runner on your behalf. You could have avoided the ruse of an engagement to Mr. Bond."

"It isn't a ruse." She lamented the shadow of confusion that swept over his features. "My relationship with Mr. Bond is twofold."

Reynolds began to shift uncomfortably in his seat. He looked pained.

"If you have something to say, sir," she prompted. "Please feel free. I respect your opinions and viewpoints as they relate to my business matters."

He cleared his throat again. "I find the novelty

of the series of events leading to the hiring of Mr. Bond to be . . . dubious. The circle begins when you're subjected to incidences causing you to fear for your safety. Then, you hire a thief-taker. The result of which leads to the thief-taker successfully wooing you into accepting his proposal of marriage, despite his lack of suitability. I cannot help wondering if the end ties back to the beginning in a manner more closely related than surface appearances indicate."

"You're wondering whether it's possible Mr. Bond is the source of my problem, as well as the solution to it? No, do not look chagrined! It is a fascinating hypothesis. I'm embarrassed I didn't think of it myself." She leaned back in her chair and allowed her mind to toy with the idea. "Mr. Bond would indeed be quite clever if he arranged to create circumstances necessitating his hiring, then used his employment to gain access to wooing me. However, considering my former aversion to marriage, I cannot see how anyone would imagine such machinations would be successful."

"Your financial means and familial circumstances would certainly make the effort worthwhile. What would Mr. Bond have to lose? At the very least, he would be paid to solve a mystery of his own making, ensuring a satisfying conclusion for you and a financial reward for him."

Eliza smiled. "I'm congratulating myself for hiring such a creative thinker for my man of affairs."

Reynolds looked embarrassed. "You have always been so circumspect, especially about your suitors. Please allow me to continue investigating Mr. Bond.

I'll accept no fee for my services. Putting your mind at ease is the very least I can do."

"I am not uneasy, Mr. Reynolds. Trust is of equal value to me as honesty. I've extended mine to Mr. Bond without reservation, and I have no wish to erode that foundation with needless doubts."

He nodded. "As you wish."

"Thank you, Mr. Reynolds. However, I do have something for you to look into. The Earl of Montague is creating an investment pool. I should like to know what speculation has garnered his interest and how you assess its viability."

"Are you interested in joining the pool?"

"Not at this time. Lord Montague approached Mr. Bond about it, and I'm concerned as to whether or not the investment is sound."

Reynolds withdrew his weekly report from his satchel and stood. "I'll begin my inquiries straightaway."

Eliza accepted the papers with a brisk nod. "Godspeed, sir."

He gave a slight bow. "To you as well, Miss Martin."

For the hour following Terrance Reynolds's departure, Eliza worked diligently on a list of garments and items she would need for her trousseau. Her desire to replace her entire wardrobe with gowns of brighter hues and more provocative lines was just another sign of how much she'd changed since meeting Jasper. It was not an alteration of character she took lightly.

After contemplating the matter thoroughly, she understood that Jasper wasn't the entirety of the reason why she was able to abandon long-held attitudes and beliefs. Her own ability to trust him enabled her transformation. She'd watched her mother falter through one relationship after another, spiraling deeper into melancholia with every failed romance. Whatever it was Georgina had been seeking in a partner, she'd been unable to find it. Eliza now suspected a lack of trust and honesty was to blame. All this time, she'd thought avoidance of romantic entanglements was the solution. In truth, the answer was simply to find a partner whom she could trust. Now she had only to cultivate her bond with Jasper through transparency and forthrightness.

A soft rapping on her open study door drew Eliza's attention from the papers on her desk. Robbins stood on the threshold with the post in hand.

"Excuse me, miss."

The butler entered and set the salver on the edge of her desk. "Will you be taking tea here, or with his lordship?"

"With Melville, thank you."

Eliza stared at the unusually large pile of letters in front of her. She shifted through them, separating Melville's correspondence from her own. The majority of her post was invitations, far more than she was accustomed to receiving. Confused by the sudden influx, she collected Melville's missives and stood. She went to her uncle's study and discovered him absent, then moved on to the conservatory. There she found him watering the plants he experimented with. The afternoon sunlight poured in through the many windows, warming the enclosed space and creating a noticeable humidity.

"Good afternoon, my lord," she said upon entering.

Melville presented his cheek to her, and she pressed a kiss to it. "Eliza," he said breathlessly. "Remember the splicing I shared with you? Look how it's thriving!"

Eliza examined the two disparate plants, now connected at the stem. It made her think of her relationship with Jasper. "Beautiful. I can see why you're so pleased."

"Normally these plants grow best in a tropical climate, so I am doubly pleased by the success." He beamed with pride, then noted the letters she carried. His smile faded, and he held out his hand with a sigh.

She handed the post to him. "Are you making any progress with responding to those who write to you?"

His wince was answer enough.

She shook her head. "Do you never miss the company of others, my lord?"

"I have all I need right here." He set the mail atop potting soil scattered on the table.

"Perhaps others need *you*. Clearly they continue to extend their friendship to you, even though you don't reply."

Melville's well-being was a growing concern to her. What would happen to him when they no longer shared a roof? She was his sole human connection to the world at large. Would he soon become completely estranged from Society, reliant upon the gazettes for news? It broke her heart to think of it.

He returned his attention to watering his plants. "Were you not determined to live a solitary life until a short time ago? Content with quiet walks, good books, and uninterrupted time with your ledgers?"

"I have you."

"For how long? Eventually, I will move on to my reward."

Eliza drew swirls in the soil with her fingertip. "The time you speak of is still far away."

Melville glanced at her, but blessedly did not continue to speak of his demise. Instead he said, "Regardless, I am relieved to see you out of your mother's shadow. It does my old heart good to know you've found someone with whom to share your life."

"My mother's shadow," she repeated softly. "Have I moved out of it? I resemble her, and I've chosen a man similar to my father. Perhaps I have assumed her shadow and made it my own?"

"You have her beauty," Melville agreed. "But also a steadfastness she lacked. Your footing is solid. Georgina's was often unsteady."

"You mean to say she was irresponsible."

"I mean to say she was unstable. She could not maintain an even keel. She listed from one side to the other." He flicked a small bug off a plant leaf. "Georgina is the reason I acquired an interest in horticulture. My hope was to find some combination of herbal elements to tame the mercurial quality of her moods."

Eliza remembered those fluctuations all too well. Georgina would be giddy with happiness one week, then unable to rise from bed the next. "You think her ailment was physical? I have always believed she simply had poor judgment."

"I was willing to consider any possibility. I would've searched the world for the key to her happiness, just as I would do for you."

"Mr. Bond makes me happy. The only worry I have now is for you."

He reached over and patted the back of her hand. "I'll be well, so long as you are."

Turning her hand over, she squeezed his. "Shall we retire to your study for tea?"

"Is it time already?" As if cued, Melville's stomach grumbled with hunger. He set the watering pot down and dusted off his hands. Then, he proffered his forearm to her.

"Don't forget the mail I brought you."

He groaned, but gathered up the post. "You are certainly stubborn like your mother."

They exited the conservatory and strolled the distance to his study in companionable silence. When they stepped into his private domain, Eliza took in the space where her uncle spent the majority of his day and knew she would miss these moments with him. For all his idiosyncrasies and foibles, she loved him dearly. She wondered how much time she might have to visit with him once she lived with Jasper. When Melville retreated to the country, would he be alone for months at a time? Now that she thought of it, she suspected Jasper spent all of the year in London due to his trade.

Melville set the latest post atop the leaning pile of mail in the basket by the door. Unable to bear the additional weight, the mass shifted to the side and dozens of letters tumbled to the floor. "Bloody nuisance," he muttered, squatting to pick up the wayward missives.

Eliza joined him, raking letters toward her with widespread fingers.

"How odd," he said to himself.

"What's odd?" she queried.

"This seal."

She focused on the black wax seal gracing the letter he held out to her. "It looks to be a sword crossing over . . . something."

"An hourglass."

"Interesting. To whom does that seal belong?"

"I've no notion. But there is another one . . ." He dug into the pile at his feet and withdrew a second letter bearing the same image in black wax. "See here."

He opened the letter, dropping the others to the floor in the process. As he read, he frowned. Then, he grew very pale.

"What is it?" she asked, alarmed.

"It appears to be a threat of violence"—Melville held the letter out to her—"against you."

Chapter 14

Standing, Jasper set both palms flat on Eliza's desk and surveyed the five open letters spread out before him. They were obviously all penned by the same female hand. The delicate swirls and flowing script were clearly the handiwork of a woman.

He glanced up at Melville and Eliza, both of whom sat in chairs facing him. "Are there more?"

"Those were all we could find," Eliza said, looking remarkably composed.

"Do you have any notion of when the first of these arrived? Or the last?"

She shook her head.

Jasper's fingertips drummed on the desktop. "This changes everything."

"Yes," she murmured. "It certainly does."

Each missive warned Melville to retire with Eliza to the country or she would pay the consequences, completely contradicting Eliza's original assumption that she was being pushed toward matrimony.

He looked at the earl. "Would you, perchance, be able to assist with the procurement of a Special License?"

Eliza jolted visibly. "Beg your pardon?"

"Special License?" the earl asked, frowning and scratching his head. "Who's getting married?"

"I will take that as a 'no.'" Jasper was certain Melville's hair was even more of a fright today than it had been the previous times he'd seen it. "Perhaps Westfield can be useful in that regard."

"Jasper." Eliza no longer looked placid. "What are you about?"

Straightening, he set his hands on his hips. "It appears there's a woman out there who perceives you to be a threat. It's likely she has an interest in one of your suitors."

"An unhealthy interest."

"One can only hope that it's Montague who has enamored her to the point of violence."

She shot him an arch look.

His smile was unapologetic. "Regardless, taking you out of competition could likely remove you from danger straightaway."

"Perhaps the news of my engagement will suffice, if we give it a chance to spread?"

"I would rest easier if you and I resided under the same roof." In truth, he doubted he would rest at all if they shared a bed, but that was a topic for another discussion.

Melville nodded. "Quite right. I've proven to be unsuitable for the task of protecting you."

Eliza's gaze dropped to her lap.

"Eliza." Jasper made every effort to keep his voice

modulated. "I should like to hear your thoughts on the matter."

She took a deep breath. "I'm not prepared to leave Melville at this time."

"Is he your only concern?"

Her head lifted. "Am I overlooking something else?"

"No." He relaxed. "I could take up residence here with you until the end of the Season. As your husband."

The softness that stole into her eyes when she looked at him was worth far more than the concession deserved, but he wouldn't complain about that.

"Would you?"

"I will do whatever you need."

"Thank you." Her smile lit up the room.

A surge of adrenaline pushed through him. Eliza would be his within the week. "Make whatever arrangements you need, but please avoid leaving the house whenever possible."

She nodded.

"I will see to my end of things." He cast one last glance at the letters laid out before him. Fury resurfaced with biting swiftness. He would find the author of the threats and ensure that the culprit never posed a hazard to Eliza again.

Marriage would not be the end of his hunt.

Jasper urged his horse away from Lambeth Palace. He cast a final look at the brick gatehouse and Lollard's Tower, then set his hand lightly over the Special License tucked into his coat's inner pocket.

Drawing abreast of him, Westfield said, "You have yet to tell me precisely what the letters said. Since their contents incited our mad rush to the archbishop, you have to know I'm overset with curiosity."

"The missives were brief. A few lines each, almost in rhyme, with the same admonishment to retire from the city. Two made indirect references to sidesaddles and the Serpentine, both of which relate to accidents Miss Martin experienced."

"Nothing about the falling statue at the Royal Academy? Perhaps it *was* an accident."

"Perhaps. I'm at a disadvantage in many respects. I don't know if the letters arrived before the events, which might suggest violence was not the culprit's first choice. Or if the letters arrived after the fact and served as taunts."

"Written by a woman, you say?" Westfield whistled. "There is some sense in that. A man who wished to prevent her from marrying could simply compromise Miss Martin."

"I doubt she would have conceded, despite the damage to her reputation. She has an aversion to being managed and a limited appreciation for Society's mores."

"Truly?" The earl tugged the brim of his hat down as a shield against the late afternoon sun. "The more I learn of her, the more I like. Who would have thought a spinster's sixth Season would cultivate such drama and intrigue?"

"Which begs the question: why now? Melville's correspondence has been accumulating for years. His housekeeper was able to present a small trunk of past letters, and there were no threats prior to this Season."

"I assume you won't be abandoning your work in favor of a honeymoon?"

The mention of a honeymoon was all it took to fill Jasper's mind with lascivious thoughts. "If only I were so fortunate."

"You are extremely fortunate."

Jasper's brows rose. "Oh?"

"You knew precisely what you wanted, and made certain you attained it."

Directing his gaze forward, Jasper pondered the somber note in the earl's normally droll tone. "Is all well with you, my lord?"

"Of course. Nothing is ever wrong in my world, Bond. There are no surprises. No challenges. Equanimity rules the day."

"There is something to be said for that."

"Yes, it's boring."

Laughing, Jasper urged his mount into a canter, leaving the Thames behind. There was a great deal to be done before he could end the day. "You are welcome to stay in my world for a while longer, if you prefer. Never a dull moment."

"Wait until you're married," Westfield drawled.

Jasper entered his house to the sound of raucous laughter floating out of the downstairs parlor. Behind him, Westfield barely stepped onto the marble floor of the visitor's foyer when Herbert Crouch caught sight of them.

Herbert, who'd been leaning against the parlor doorjamb as if awaiting them, pulled his hands out of his pants' pockets and straightened. He was one of Jasper's most seasoned employees; old enough that his two grown sons also worked for Jasper. He lumbered over with a broad grin that peeked out from the frame of a bushy, unkempt beard.

The Crouches were an odd-looking lot as a whole. Herbert was of a height with Jasper, but considerably broader. Many of his progeny were near giants; the top of their sire's head barely reached their shoulders.

Herbert mussed his wheat-colored hair with a meaty hand, disrupting the perfectly molded shape of his hat's interior. "I 'ave news that might be interesting."

Gesturing toward his study, Jasper passed his hat and gloves to his butler, but kept his coat on. The Special License in his pocket wasn't something he was willing to allow out of his immediate reach.

He settled behind his desk. Westfield moved over to the console to help himself to the Armagnac. Herbert sank heavily onto one of the settees.

With libation in hand, Westfield faced the center of the room and leaned back against the console with his hip. He crossed his legs at the ankle and enjoyed a deep swallow of brandy. "How fare you, Crouch?"

Jasper studied him. The earl seemed to be imbibing more of late. If he continued along the same vein, Jasper intended to bring the matter up for discussion. It was not a subject he looked forward to broaching, but the health of his friend warranted his concern.

"As well as can be expected, mi'lord." Herbert didn't smile, which was unusual for him. Jasper knew the commoner was ill-at-ease conversing socially with an earl.

"How are Mrs. Crouch and your brood?"

"All are well. The missus is increasin' again."

"Again? Dear God." Westfield took another drink. "How many children do you have now?"

"Eighteen. Until the birthin'."

"You are a stronger man than I, Crouch."

Herbert gave an awkward pull on his beard and looked at Jasper almost pleadingly.

Jasper took pity on the man and said, "Before you begin, it is important to know we're now looking for a woman."

"I knew it!" Herbert slapped his knee.

"Of course you did." Jasper was more than satisfied with the strengths of his crew. Herbert in particular had an instinct for hunting, becoming quite dogged when he sensed something was amiss. "What did you uncover?"

"I still 'ave a few more questions of my own to answer 'bout some o' the renters, but there's one I'm fair certain isn't what she says she is."

"Who?"

"Vanessa Pennington. Aaron and I 'ave asked around, but we can't find any proof of a Mr. Pennington. No ring on 'er finger, no papers or letters, no portraits—"

"Perhaps she keeps such sentimental items in a private place," Westfield suggested.

"I checked," Herbert said.

"How—?" Westfield paused. "Forget I asked."

Jasper's mouth curved. "Her residence is above the store, yes?"

Herbert nodded. "Aside from the agreement to rent the space from Miss Martin, I couldn't find anything with the name 'Pennington' on it. But I did find several receipts and such addressed to 'Vanessa Chilcott.' "

"Chilcott." Jasper leaned back heavily into his chair. "Bloody hell."

"A ne'er-do-well clan of thieves and miscreants." Westfield straightened and took the seat opposite Herbert. "Perhaps their past success with Lady Georgina has made them bold in regards to the Tremaine family."

"How is Vanessa Chilcott related to Miss Martin's stepfather?" Jasper asked.

Herbert lifted one sturdy shoulder in a shrug. "Aside from praising her face and figure, the other shopkeepers in the area 'ad little to say 'bout her. She keeps to 'erself."

Westfield snorted. "I've been told the Chilcotts are all remarkably good looking. Which is not enough to make *me* foolish, but clearly the same cannot be said of everyone, or the family wouldn't be so successful in their subterfuges."

Jasper averted his gaze. Eliza was too intelligent to miss seeing the parallels between her relationship with him and her mother's with Chilcott. She had to overlook prejudicial experiences in order to extend her trust to him, which made her credence all the more valuable. He would have to tread carefully or risk losing something priceless.

"I want Miss Chilcott watched at all hours until further notice," he told Herbert. "I want to know whom she speaks to, where she goes, and what hours she keeps. And I need to know how she's related to Miss Martin."

"I'll see to it." Herbert pushed heavily to his feet.

Jasper watched the man depart, then looked at Westfield. "I visited the Pennington store with Miss Martin, and she had no notion the proprietress was anything more than a stranger. Miss Chilcott, however, appeared to be greatly interested in Miss Martin."

"That's to be expected." The earl made a careless gesture with his hand. "She is residing and conducting business in space owned by Miss Martin."

"Miss Chilcott should not be aware of that fact. Miss Martin takes great pains to remain anonymous, conducting most transactions through her man of affairs. She believes it eases the way for everyone involved if her gender remains unknown." Jasper rapped his knuckles against the desk in frustration. "Damnation. If I'd retained the sales receipt from my purchase, I could have compared Vanessa Chilcott's penmanship to that of the letters Melville received."

"I still don't understand why Miss Chilcott would want to prevent Miss Martin from marrying. Pettiness?"

"There is an obligation created with their business relationship that doesn't exist otherwise," Jasper reasoned, "a legal agreement between two parties with responsibilities and ramifications on both sides. As a former step-relation, whatever grievance Miss Chilcott may have against Miss Martin clearly has no weight or she would have pursued it legally. Without legal basis, there's no possibility of restitution. But as a tenant, if she was to create a circumstance in which Miss Martin was seen as liable for damages or loss of income, Miss Chilcott could possibly negotiate a financial settlement."

"I see. Miss Martin is accountable as a landlord in ways she isn't as a relation-by-marriage. Exploiting their business association for monetary gain wouldn't be too far outside the realm of possibility, considering the Chilcott family's larcenous reputation."

"My thoughts exactly. It would also explain why Miss Chilcott hid her true identity."

"But would an assumed guise withstand further scrutiny in a court of law?" Westfield queried.

"Assuming I'm correct, I doubt she intends her plan to go that far. If she was able to gain leverage of some sort against Miss Martin, I believe the result would be a quiet exchange of funds in order to maintain the business anonymity Miss Martin prizes. However, if Miss Martin had a spouse, *he* would have greater license to mount a public defense, because he would have no reason to hide."

"Extortion is a nasty business. Best not to have anything requiring concealment."

Jasper's foot tapped restlessly. "I'm due to retrieve the balance of my purchases from Miss Chilcott's store—customized items requiring preparation time."

Westfield set his glass on the low table with a dull thud and rose gracefully to his feet. "I'm coming with you, of course. I should like to see what happens next."

"Let us hope you see the end of Miss Martin's troubles." Jasper pulled out his pocket watch and checked the time. He cursed.

"Running behind again, are you?" There was laughter in the earl's voice. "Tardiness is becoming a habit with you. Here I thought you would corrupt Miss Martin's finer points, but perhaps the opposite is true."

Jasper might have been chagrined if not for the fact that the swifter time passed, the sooner Eliza would be his wife. "Step lively, Westfield."

But haste didn't help him achieve his aim. Although they arrived at Miss Chilcott's shop within posted business hours, the proprietress was not in evidence.

"Shoddy way to run a new business," Westfield muttered, tilting his head back to eye the pink-striped awning.

"Only if you mean to make a success of it. By your accounts, the Chilcotts aren't ones to work for their keep."

Jasper waited for Peter Crouch to return from checking the rear exterior staircase leading to the domicile on the second floor. When the young man appeared, he was shaking his head.

"Damn and blast," Jasper muttered. "I cannot wait for Miss Chilcott to return. I'm to meet Montague at Remington's in an hour to discuss his idiotic mining speculation."

Westfield looked at him. "Despite an imminent wedding and the nefarious Miss Chilcott, you still won't allow Montague to meet his own fate? You know as well as I he's destined to destroy himself."

"He and his family owe me far better than that. I want his destruction to come by *my* hand, and I will not rest until I've seen the deed through to the last."

The earl sighed and turned away from the building. "I'll accompany you to Remington's, then part ways with you for the evening. With the announcement of Miss Martin's engagement to you, you won't be needing me to gain entry to anyplace you choose to go. I, however, am in dire need of a strong drink and a soft woman. Or two."

"Easy on the drink," Jasper said, walking back to his horse.

"And ride hard on the woman? Excellent idea."

Neither man could see the eavesdropper in the room above them. She sat on the floor beneath the barely raised sash and listened to the masculine voices drifting up to her. A smile curved her lovely lips. With a rapacious gleam in her blue eyes, she began to plan . . .

It was difficult for Eliza to refrain from fidgeting when she knew she was to be married the next day. However, the Cranmores' ballroom was not the place to appear anxious.

A few years had passed since she'd last been invited to a Cranmore event. Lady Cranmore was a consummate hostess whose entertainment innovations were often copied, and her expertise was widely evident tonight. Tulle and ivy wrapped Ionic columns. Harp players filled every corner with music when the orchestra was quiet. Outside, the rear lawn was dotted with dramatically blazing torches. The result was one of Grecian decadence, and everyone in attendance appeared to be in high spirits.

Eliza, however, was feeling high-strung. She was filled with a mixture of exhilaration and apprehension such as she'd never known. Tomorrow, she would be wed. After so many years of making certain she did nothing as her mother would have, she was no longer allowing Georgina to rule her actions from the grave. Which made every aspect of the coming day momentous.

"I am so pleased," Lady Collingsworth said, looking at Eliza with bright eyes. "I must confess, when you told me you would be married tomorrow, I doubted I could do justice to the occasion with such short notice."

Personally, Eliza thought nothing more than family and close friends were necessary, but she guessed that saying so would only disappoint and hurt Regina. "Thank you," she said instead. "You're too kind to me."

"Stuff." Regina waved one gloved hand carelessly. "I had given up on your ever marrying. I'm so very happy you found someone precious to you after all."

"Precious," Eliza repeated, her head turning to find Jasper. He stood on the edge of the ballroom speaking with Montague. She'd previously taken note of Westfield's absence.

"You are full of surprises lately," Regina murmured. "To think . . . Secret proposals from *two* of the most eligible bachelors of the ton. Absolutely delicious. Does Mr. Bond know who his competition was?"

"Yes."

"Lord Montague is being laudably gracious. Look at him speaking so civilly with your betrothed. And what a pair they make. From this distance, one could almost imagine them as brothers."

"My understanding is that the similarities between the two exist only on the exterior."

Regina leaned closer. "Your tone is intriguing."

Eliza lowered her voice to a whisper. "Have you ever heard anything of a worrisome nature about Lord Montague?"

"Such as?"

"Never mind. There are some things it's best not to know."

"You cannot initiate such a topic, only to abandon it!"

When it became apparent Eliza would say no more, Regina snapped open her fan with a flourish. "Hmph . . . With your engagement, I'd hoped that poor Rothschild girl would finally capture Montague's attention, but you have me wondering if he's not such a prize after all."

"Jane Rothschild?" Eliza frowned.

"Over there." Regina gestured to where Miss Rothschild was hovering behind a column near Montague and Jasper. "See how she stares at him, looking so forlorn? I've noticed her lingering in his general vicinity, as if she hopes he'll notice her. Her behavior is sadly untoward, but exception must be made for her common origins."

Jane was a pretty girl with soft brown hair and eyes, and a rather curvaceous figure. An air of melancholy clung to her. Perhaps it was the way her mouth turned down at the corners, or how she shifted so restlessly, as if the disquiet inside her was so great it manifested itself physically.

"Montague told me he attempted to court Miss Rothschild," Eliza said, "but she was unreceptive."

"I cannot believe that," Regina scoffed. "Her parents would pay a fortune for an earldom, and her actions speak for her."

Eliza could argue with neither point. Curious, she excused herself and moved toward the other woman. Why would Montague say Miss Rothschild was averse to his suit, when it appeared she was in fact openly seeking his regard? It was a puzzle, especially considering how dire Montague's financial situation was reported to be and how wealthy the Rothschilds were.

As she drew closer, Montague parted from Jasper and moved toward the open doors leading to the moonlit garden. Jane prepared to follow the earl outside, but Eliza spoke out.

"Miss Rothschild. How are you this evening?"

Jane cast an almost frantic glance at Montague's back, then faced Eliza with a weak smile. "I'm well, Miss Martin. Thank you for inquiring. Congratulations on your betrothal."

With proximity, Eliza noted Jane's wan complexion and the dark circles under her eyes. "Thank you. Would you care for something to drink? A lemonade, perhaps?"

"No." Jane looked out the door again. "I'm not thirsty."

"Miss Martin."

Jasper's voice drew Eliza's attention. His gaze was blatantly inquisitive.

Jane bolted. "Excuse me, Miss Martin. I wish you a good evening."

Eliza gaped as the woman hurried out to the garden.

Drawing abreast of her, Jasper queried, "Is everything all right?"

"I doubt it."

He leaned over her, his proximity far too close to be seemly, but she couldn't complain. The thrill she felt at his nearness was worth any censure.

"What do you know of your stepfather's relations?" he asked.

"Extremely little. I avoided speaking with him whenever possible."

Jasper's gaze moved over her face, searching. "What was it about him you disliked so intensely?"

"You would have had to know my mother to understand. She was . . . erratic. Impulsive. What she needed was a firm hand, such as my father's, but Mr. Chilcott was overly indulgent. He encouraged her wild notions and sudden changes of agenda. His enabling of her behavior led to their deaths. She decided they absolutely had to travel north to celebrate the passing of six months of marriage. She ignored warnings of muddy roads due to torrential downpours, and he didn't have the sense or will to stay her."

"I see."

Eliza looked out to the rear lawn, but could no longer see Jane Rothschild or Lord Montague. The Cranmores had a heterogeneous garden featuring a hedgerow maze, a pagoda, various-sized obelisks, a re-creation of a Grecian temple ruin, and a gazebo covered in climbing roses. It was an expansive outdoor space that could not be seen fully while standing in the ballroom.

"What are you looking for?" Jasper asked.

"Escort me outside."

With one brow arched in a silent show of curiosity, he offered his arm and led her to the garden.

They reached the gravel-lined path beyond the terrace and began to stroll. There were several groups of guests enjoying the many sights, but the distance between parties was sufficient to keep the conversations private.

"What, precisely, are we doing?" he inquired.

Although she was focused on finding Jane Rothschild, Eliza was taken by Jasper's warm tone. She glanced at him. "We're searching for a quiet corner."

"Are you attempting to compromise me, Miss Martin?"

"I confess, the notion is tempting. If you were of a mind to steal a few moments of my time away from prying eyes and ears, where in this garden would you go?"

He raked their surroundings with a considering glance. "Not the maze. Nor the gazebo. The temple might have promise, if you could restrain those sweet whimpers of yours that drive me to distraction."

"You are not quiet in your pleasures either."

"Because of you, love. Only with you."

Her breath hitched at his endearment. Embarrassed by the depth of her reaction, she looked away . . . and noted footprints moving off the pathway onto the adjacent lawn. She tugged Jasper's arm to stay him, then pointed at the ground.

His lips pursed, contemplatively.

Only two prints were visible before the rest became hidden by low-lying ferns. A large Italian alder spread its branches above them, providing a slightly shadowy cover from the moonlight.

Releasing him, Eliza looked around to be sure no one was watching, then she followed the trail by stepping deliberately into the preceding footprints. She knew Jasper was with her even though she didn't hear him behind her. As she approached the tree, she picked out the sound of voices. One was feminine and pleading, the other masculine and biting.

Jasper caught her elbow and pulled her to the side, then urged her to crouch behind a boxwood shrub. Eliza bunched up her pale green skirts to keep the hem from becoming damp and dirty. They were on the far side of the tree from where they'd left the path. She couldn't see the other couple from their vantage, but the sound was much improved.

"You cannot leave me in this state!" Jane cried.

"I can do anything I desire. Haven't we already determined that?"

The identity of the speakers was clear to Eliza. When she looked at Jasper, she knew he recognized Montague's voice, if not Jane Rothschild's.

"You leave me no choice," Jane said, with steel in her tone. "I shall tell my parents what you did to me at the Hammonds' house party. They will know I carry your child."

"Is it mine?" Montague rejoined smoothly. "I think not. You are a promiscuous piece of baggage. I'm certain I can locate others who would attest to sampling your dubious charms."

Jasper jolted physically, eliciting Eliza's concern. Reaching out, she set her hand atop his forearm and found it to be hard as marble. He looked stone-faced and furious, his jaw clenched so tightly the tautness of the muscles was visible. He did not, however, look the least bit as surprised as she knew she did.

"I was untouched," Jane said with more dignity than Eliza thought she would manage under similar circumstances. "You forced this child on me. You must make this right. Your misdeed can no longer remain hidden."

"Rape is a serious allegation, Miss Rothschild. In fact, I find it so egregious I'm considering leveling an allegation against you in response: *scandalum magnatum.* While antiquated, it would still serve to protect my good name. You would go to prison, Jane, for libel against a peer of the realm. Not the most hospitable accommodations for a woman who is *enceinte.*"

"You're a monster. Vile and debased. Filled with the devil's own taste for depravity and lust."

"And you want to wed me." Montague laughed. "What does that make you?"

"Desperate," Jane hissed.

Eliza swayed with a rush of nausea. Jasper grabbed her elbow and stood, dragging her up with him. He propelled her away from their hiding spot and back out to the pathway, nearly running into Sir Richard Tolliver and his sister, who were strolling away from the manse.

"I say," Tolliver muttered. "What were you doing back there, Mr. Bond?"

Jasper moved to step around the siblings. "We were momentarily lost."

"Lost?" Tolliver snorted. "Ridiculous. Have you no care for Miss Martin's reputation? Certainly my sister and I will be discreet, but you should—"

"Your discretion is appreciated. Excuse us." Jasper gave a quick bow and set off toward the house, forcing Eliza into an indecorous pace to keep up.

As they fled, she glanced behind her. Tolliver was engaged in spirited debate with his sister. Chagrined to have been caught stumbling out of the bushes with Jasper, Eliza was turning her gaze forward again when a shifting shadow beneath the alder caught her eye. A chill moved through her.

Had Jane Rothschild noted their departure? Or worse, had Montague?

Chapter 15

"Forgive the delay, Mr. Reynolds." Eliza hurried into her study. "I wasn't expecting you this morning."

Reynolds rose swiftly to his feet. "My apologies, Miss Martin. I have some information I feel you must know, and I thought it best to bring it to you directly."

"Oh?" Rounding the desk, she sat for the first time since breakfast. She shot a quick look at the window, noting the persistence of the early morning drizzle. In her opinion, the gray and overcast sky was ill-fitting for her wedding day, but she thought it matched Jasper's mood of the evening before. He'd seen her safely back to Lady Collingsworth, admonished her to stay far away from Montague, and departed in a rush. She was anxious to see him again and ascertain how he was feeling on the day of their wedding. "My curiosity is duly aroused."

Her man of affairs remained standing for a few

moments longer; his attention caught by the parade of footmen and hired staff flowing past the open doorway. "I don't recall ever seeing such a flurry of activity on the premises."

"Mr. Bond and I are to be married late this afternoon," she explained, somewhat startled to realize she would rather return to the interrupted fitting for her wedding gown than participate in a discussion of business matters.

"Married?" Mr. Reynolds lowered himself into his chair. "So soon?"

"Why wait?"

"I wish you happy, Miss Martin. But I'm also exceedingly grateful I called on you this morning."

"Thank you, sir. I appreciate your sentiments."

He nodded. "As for why I'm here . . . By some stroke of good fortune, my father's employer, Lord Needham, recently learned of a business associate who was approached by Lord Montague to join the investment pool you asked me to look into. My father began an investigation into the viability of the speculation at that time, which was a few days ago. Sadly, it would appear it *isn't* sound, and we recommend against participation."

"I see." Eliza couldn't muster even a modicum of concern for Montague. She was still horrified to realize how consummate his façade was, how perfectly it shielded him, and how ugly he was behind it.

"Considering Lord Montague's financial state, I wondered why he would risk his few remaining funds on such a risky prospect. Once again, my father was of great assistance. It seems Lord Needham was a player in a card game that also boasted

Lord Westfield and Lord Montague as partici-
pants. Lord Westfield was the victor, and the winnings included the deed to a property in Essex
that has been in the late Lady Montague's family
for generations. Montague is said to have been
overwrought at the loss, which was instigated in
large part by Westfield. I assume the property has
sentimental value. It's Montague's last remaining
unentailed holding. He sold everything else long
ago."

"Instigated?" She frowned. "In what way?"

"Montague was prepared to withdraw from the
game when Westfield put a deed into the pot. He
then went to great lengths to goad Montague into
doing the same by making thinly veiled references
to Montague's poor financial situation. It esca-
lated to the point where Montague was faced with
the choice of folding under the cloud of insol-
vency or continuing in an effort to maintain the
guise of affluence."

"Dear God," she muttered, somewhat disgusted
by the carelessness inherent in gambling. She val-
ued her financial security too deeply to leave its
fate up to chance. "I still don't see how Westfield
can be held in any way responsible for Montague's
stupidity."

"The property Westfield wagered is actually
deeded to Mr. Bond."

Eliza went very still for a moment, then she exhaled in a rush. "Well . . . that alters the situation a
bit, does it not?"

The Earl of Westfield was an extremely wealthy
man who owned both entailed and unentailed

properties. If he wished to gamble with such high stakes, he didn't require Jasper's means to do it. Jasper, however, held a deep dislike for Montague, and he'd apparently been aware of the earl's dissolute and immoral private life. He would insist against Westfield risking anything in the process of providing assistance, and so would supply the property to be wagered to mitigate any possibility of loss.

What had Montague done to garner Jasper's wrath? And how far was Jasper willing to go to gain whatever recompense he sought?

Reynolds continued. "Westfield also ensured Montague's bet by offering unusual terms: if Montague lost, he would have until the end of the Season to buy the marker back. Albeit at considerable expense, far more than the property is worth."

"Montague thought he had little chance of losing the deed permanently." Her hand lifted to her knotting stomach. Would Jasper go so far as to marry her to prevent Montague from gaining access to her funds, which the earl could then use to recover his marker?

"I believe the investment pool Lord Montague is forming is actually a means to gather the funds necessary to regain his mother's property before time runs out. He can tell the investors later that the speculation was unsuccessful, resulting in a loss, or perhaps he intends to marry or gamble successfully to repay the investors without the pressure of an end-of-Season deadline."

"It is tremendously hazardous to play such games." In truth, she couldn't care less whether or not Montague was ostracized. It was the very least he deserved. She spoke only to fill the silence, absentmindedly attempting to hide how unsettled she felt.

"Montague seems to have little choice." Reynolds looked grim. "I cannot help wondering how involved Mr. Bond is in this affair. Is he assisting Lord Westfield? Or is Westfield assisting him? And why?"

She kept her face impassive. "The Rothschilds would gladly take Montague as a son-in-law, but he resists. If he was of a mind to recover his deed, he could do so through Jane Rothschild's dowry."

"Montague would never marry Miss Rothschild," he scoffed. "Both of her parents are of common stock. Montague has approached only tradesmen to invest in his pool, and he refuses to gamble at tables where commoners are seated."

"I am astonished at how little I knew about someone I saw with fair regularity."

"Is the same not true of the man you intend to marry today?"

"No." She said no more. There was no need to explain her or Jasper's personal affairs.

"With his participation in Westfield's wager, Bond, too, is playing a hazardous game against a peer of the realm. And his profession . . . will he continue it? If so, doesn't that present a separate set of challenges? The danger he faces daily will be brought home to you. Those he angers will seek you out—"

"Is that all, Mr. Reynolds?" she said sharply. She could hardly tolerate hearing him speak so reasonably about a matter she was too emotionally invested in to view impartially. Where was her good sense? Her reason? Her desire for self-preservation?

"I've angered you. That was not my intent." His stiff posture deflated. "Providing you information with which to make decisions has been my position for so long, it's now second nature to me. But I should know better than to step into your personal and private affairs."

Eliza immediately regretted her harsh tone. "This is as uncharted for me as it is for you. I will never hold your concern for me against you. Your loyalty is why I retain you, after all."

"I promise to speak no more on the matter. Not ever."

"Please, rest easy, Mr. Reynolds," she said softly, because her throat was too tight to allow for greater volume. "I didn't make my decision regarding Mr. Bond lightly."

"I understand. Your feelings are engaged. I should be celebrating your good fortune, not questioning it. Lord knows having my wife, Anne, in my life has made my world a richer place." He managed a smile. "There is risk in love, but it can be worth taking."

Eliza searched her own heart, something she was not accustomed to doing. She'd always questioned what purpose feelings served when the reasonable course of action was best decided with the mind. But it seemed her heart refused to be denied. Even now, it raced with something akin to panic at the thought of losing Jasper. Despite everything she'd learned from her mother, and everything she knew from observation, and everything years of dealing with her own business affairs had taught her, she couldn't imagine turning away from him now. Despite whatever his goals or motivations might be. Despite the heartache she invited by proceeding with marriage to a man who hid so many things from her.

She—a reasonable woman who prized her equanimity to the point of excessive caution—was faced with the realization that the only avenue she could bear taking was the most hazardous and unreasonable one.

She'd given Jasper her trust, and she would not take it back. She couldn't. She loved him too much.

"I brought this for you."

Jasper turned away from his bed, where several garments were laid out for his selection. He smiled at Lynd, who entered through the sitting room door. His mentor held a folded square of white cloth in his hand. When Jasper accepted it, he saw the letter *L* embroidered in the corner.

"It was my grandfather's," Lynd explained, shoving his hands into the pockets of his overly elaborate coat of fine wool. He rocked back on his heels in an uncustomary nervous gesture. "It was passed to my father, then to me. I want you to have it on your wedding day."

The monogram distorted as Jasper's eyes stung. Lynd was the closest thing to a father he'd ever had. It meant a great deal to him that Lynd regarded him as a son. "Thank you."

Lynd waved the gratitude away with a shaky hand.

That telltale sign of deep emotion goaded Jasper to step forward and embrace his old friend. There was a moment of crushing, then back slapping.

"Who would have thought you would marry an heiress?" Lynd said in a gruff voice. "And an earl's niece in the bargain!"

Jasper set the kerchief carefully on his bed. "I'm not certain *I* will believe it until the vows are said and the deed done."

"The chit is fortunate to have you. If she has a brain in her head, she knows it."

"She's the most intelligent person I know. Oddly humorous. Lacking all guile." Glancing around the room, Jasper remembered Eliza in the space. "And passionate in ways one would not expect."

"I certainly would not expect it," Lynd muttered. To which Jasper laughed.

Lynd studied him with an odd half-smile. "She has changed you. I didn't realize until this moment that this is a love match."

Jasper breathed deeply. He hadn't named his feelings for Eliza. Perhaps he'd been afraid to. He wanted and needed her, and he could have her. He'd been content with that.

Turning away, he gestured at an ensemble of light gray breeches, a silver-threaded waistcoat, and a charcoal gray coat. "What do you think of this?"

Lynd drew abreast of him and set his hands on his hips. "Have you nothing less plain?"

Remembering Eliza's commentary on Lynd's

need for a proper tailor, Jasper hid a smile and shook his head. "I'm afraid not. This is for you, you see. I cannot have you better dressed than me at my own wedding, can I?"

Wide-eyed, Lynd looked at him. "You would have me at your wedding?"

"I would not have the wedding without you. Who will stand beside me, if not for you, my old friend?"

Lynd's nose reddened, swiftly followed by his eyes.

A knock came from the open doorway. Jasper looked over his shoulder. Patrick Crouch stood on the threshold with the top of his head nearly touching the lintel. "There is a woman 'ere to see you. I told 'er you weren't seeing anyone today, but she mentioned Lord Montague and I thought I should tell you."

"Is she still here?"

"Aye."

Jasper moved to the chair by the door where he'd tossed his coat earlier.

Lynd cleared his throat. "I'll come down with you."

They descended to the ground floor and took up positions in Jasper's study—Jasper leaned into the front of his desk, while Lynd settled into a wingback with one ankle set atop the opposite knee. In short order, a petite brunette entered the room. She was lovely, with sable-dark hair and cornflower blue eyes. Her back was ramrod straight and her head held high. She declined to pass her fur-lined cape and muff to the butler, and spent a long moment sweeping the room from one end to the other with an examining glance.

Finally, she returned her attention to Jasper and said, "Mr. Bond, I presume."

"Yes."

"Mrs. Francesca Maybourne." She brushed off the immaculate damask of his settee with a gloved hand before perching delicately on the edge. She fluffed her rain-dampened skirts with little regard for Jasper's rug.

Lynd rolled his eyes.

Jasper crossed his arms. "This is my associate, Mr. Lynd. How can we help you, Mrs. Maybourne?"

"I trust I have your discretion," she said in a clipped tone.

"I would not be successful in my profession if I weren't discreet."

She weighed his assurance for a second, then nodded. "My sister is in trouble, Mr. Bond. I'm at my wits' end trying to help her."

"Can you elaborate?"

She met his gaze directly. "Eloisa is young and impetuous. She has yet to learn how to deny herself anything. Recently, she began a flirtation with the Earl of Montague. I thought it was ridiculous, but relatively harmless. After all, my sister is a married woman."

Jasper's brows rose.

"However, it has come to my attention that Lord Montague is a scoundrel of the worst sort." Mrs. Maybourne's nose wrinkled, which softened her sharpness somewhat. "My sister came to me this morning in tears. It seems Lord Montague asked her for a token of her affection. I was horrified when she told me this! To give irrefutable evidence of an indiscretion . . . I cannot imagine what she was thinking."

"What was this trinket?"

"A sapphire and diamond necklace, sir. One of great value. And if that were not bad enough, it's a family heirloom on her husband's side. There is no doubt he will notice its loss."

"Has she asked for the necklace back?"

"Many times. Prior to today, Lord Montague said he would return it. Then, this morning, he said he intended to sell it. He gave her the name of the jeweler and said she could contact the proprietor any time after three o'clock this afternoon to repurchase it." Mrs. Maybourne sighed and wrung her hands. "The necklace is worth a small fortune, sir. There is no way for her to obtain the funds necessary to reclaim it without her husband becoming aware."

Jasper's lips pursed. He glanced at Lynd. Montague had devised a way to obtain the funds needed to buy back his marker. Yet by some twist of fate, the knowledge had been brought to Jasper. It seemed he was destined to destroy Montague.

He looked back at Mrs. Maybourne. "You want me to retrieve the necklace before he pawns it."

"Yes."

"Perhaps he already has."

She shook her head, causing thick glossy curls to sway around her piquant face and long, slender neck. "I pray that's not the case. I approached a Runner, but because a peer is involved, he refused the commission. Mr. Bell recommended you, sir. In the interim, he ascertained that the necklace had not yet been brought into the store as of an hour ago. He agreed to watch the premises until you make an appearance. Perhaps you will arrive too late. I won't hold anyone but my sister responsible for such a lamentable end. But if God is kind, you will precede Montague and find a way to bring this debacle to a successful resolution."

"This is no easy task you set," Jasper warned.

"My sister cannot afford to buy the necklace, Mr. Bond. But she and I are capable of affording you."

"Bond." Lynd uncrossed his legs and leaned forward. "May I have a word with you?"

"Time is of the essence!" she cried.

Lynd managed a ghost of a smile. "It won't take but a moment."

Jasper followed Lynd out to the foyer. "What are the odds that this should fall in my lap?"

"Tony Bell is a good man. Certainly an excellent source of new business." Lynd stopped in the center of the circular rug and turned around. "Let me manage this task for you. You cannot take this on today, yet the opportunity isn't one you can allow to slip through your fingers."

Growling, Jasper ran a hand through his hair and damned the timing of this unexpected boon. "I cannot send you out to accost a peer. If things go awry, the penalty could be your life."

"That's what masks are for, my boy." Lynd grinned. "I'll put on that suit you have for me, and add a wig. If Montague attempts to identify me later, he'll describe a very different fellow. With any luck, I will even arrive at the wedding on time."

"Montague is my cross to bear."

"Bloody hell." Lynd shook his head. "You know how I feel about this vendetta you wage—it cannot help your mother now. That said, you are so close to achieving your final aim, and I would rest easier knowing you've put the past behind you. But I'm not certain you can do so until you see this matter of Montague's property through to the end."

Jasper's head fell forward. For all of his life, the one thing he'd needed was justice for his mother. And now, with the end in sight after years of planning, he could no longer deny he wanted Eliza more. He wanted her so badly that when faced with the choice of foiling Montague or getting married, the latter was the event he couldn't bear to miss. Even while the thought of Montague slipping through his fingers caused his gut to knot and sweat to mist his skin, the response was only a shadow of what he felt when contemplating the loss of Eliza.

Torn, he spoke gruffly. "I'm certain I will not rest easy until I've seen my plan through to the end. Montague's ruination is all I have lived for, for so long. How can I abandon the cause in the final hour? How could I face my reflection in the mirror every morning, knowing I deserted my life's goal only days before fruition?"

"By having something else in your life more fulfilling," Lynd posited. "You are young yet. There is a world out there to be explored. I know that's what your mother would have wished for you."

A thought that had eluded Jasper previously came to him in that moment. Was it possible that the tutoring she'd secured for him had not been for his father's benefit at all? Perhaps a secure and brighter future for her son had been the true aim.

Regardless, it wasn't his mother's wishes—whatever they may have been—that decided him. He made his choice based on the instincts that had saved his life so many times before.

"I cannot lose Eliza," Jasper said with total, unequivocal conviction. With her, he had no sordid past. There was only the future, one he looked forward to and . . . needed. "If you can see to Montague, I'd be eternally grateful. As for myself, I have a wedding to attend."

"Right, then." Gesturing toward the study, Lynd said, "You deal with the matter of the retainer and collect the necessary information. I'll change my garments."

"Thank you." Jasper clasped him on the shoulder.

Lynd flushed. "Consider it a wedding gift. Now off with you. There is work to be done and vows to be spoken."

Jasper arrived at the Melville house precisely at three o'clock. Eliza delayed the donning of her wedding gown for his arrival and rushed to the lower floor to meet him. She came to a halt partway down the last flight of stairs, arrested by the sight of him. He'd dressed in the same garments he wore on the day they'd met, and the sentimentality of the gesture touched her so deeply her chest ached with it. His dark hair was slightly windblown and his cheekbones burnished by the cold. He was beautiful in every way. Flawless to her eyes.

Smitten, she sighed. Jasper heard. His gaze lifted to find her, and she watched his expression change, becoming fiercely focused.

"Eliza."

She barely heard her name, but she felt it. She rushed down the remaining steps and stopped a few feet away from him. "How are you?"

"Better, now that I'm with you."

Eliza gestured toward the parlor, then led the way. As always, she knew he followed even though he moved silently. She sat, and he took a seat beside her on the settee.

They were to be married in an hour. She felt more joy than apprehension about that.

"I am so glad you came early." She fought the urge to reach for his hand. "I've been worried about you since we parted last night."

He nodded. "Montague is very much like his father. The manner in which he spoke was difficult to tolerate."

"His father . . . ?"

"I've come to you now because we have something to discuss before the wedding, something you must know before we say our vows to one another. I can only pray you'll still have me, once the truth is out."

Eliza was made wary by his tone and her own

lingering anxiety from Reynolds' visit. "You can tell me anything. I want to support you, Jasper. You no longer have to carry your burdens alone."

His dark eyes were contemplative and somber. "It's my goal to commit myself to you unencumbered. I am working diligently in that regard."

She was waiting patiently for him to continue when a violent pounding came to the front door. The sound echoed through the lower floor and brought them both to their feet.

Somehow, without appearing to run, Robbins reached the entrance before they did. The butler opened the door and revealed one of Jasper's crew, the handsome young man who'd escorted her to Jasper's home the night she shared his bed. Aaron yanked off his hat when he saw Eliza. His wild eyes caused her alarm.

Jasper quickly outdistanced her with his longer stride. "What is it?"

"The store. It's ablaze."

"Pennington's?"

Eliza's heart lodged in her throat. "What is ablaze? What's happening?"

"Stay with her," Jasper ordered, running down the front steps to where a footman held the reins to Aaron's mount. Catching the pommel with both hands, he vaulted into the saddle and galloped away.

As he disappeared from view, Eliza stared out the open doorway, confused and frightened. Aaron stepped into the house, panting. She caught him by a thick biceps before he moved past her. Their gazes met directly. "Where has he gone?"

"To your property on Peony Way."

One meaningful glance at Robbins was all it took to set things in motion. Within twenty minutes a carriage was hitched and brought around front. During that time, Eliza spoke with Regina and Melville, explaining the delay and assuring them all would be well. She ignored admonishments to await Jasper's return.

"We're to be married in half an hour," she argued. "Regardless of the circumstances or location, I intend to be with him at that time."

Aaron followed her down the front steps to the street. "He wouldn't want you there. For your own safety."

"While he risks his own for me?"

"Bond is not unprepared for this event. I'm certain the situation will be well in hand before we arrive."

"Then he should have no cause for objection." She pulled together the sides of her hastily donned pelisse and secured the buttons.

Eliza was tying the ribbon to her bonnet when a familiar figure rode up to the house and drew to a halt.

"Don't tell me I missed the nuptials," Westfield called out, pushing up the brim of his rakishly angled hat.

"Mr. Bond and I will return shortly, my lord." She accepted the footman's assistance up the carriage steps. "Please see yourself inside. Lady Collingsworth will receive you."

The earl dismounted and approached, catching either side of her carriage's doorframe with both hands and leaning in. All levity was gone from his features. "What has you so anxious?"

"One of my properties has caught fire. Mr. Bond has gone on ahead."

"To Peony Way," Westfield said.

Eliza blinked, understanding that everyone had a piece of the puzzle she was missing. "Perhaps you should ride with me."

He nodded and climbed in. Aaron joined them, sharing the opposite squab with the earl.

With a crack of the coachman's whip, the carriage jolted forward.

Her foot rapped an impatient staccato against the floorboards. "Why is the incident at the Peony property of surprise only to me?"

Westfield explained. "The tenant you know as Mrs. Vanessa Pennington is, in truth, Miss Vanessa Chilcott. Bond suspected Miss Chilcott of intending to use her business relationship with you to create a financial liability on your part."

Eliza felt oddly still inside, her thoughts strangely quiet. She wondered if it was shock she felt or simply resignation. The nature of the Chilcott brood was well-known to her, but she'd thought herself beyond their avarice since her mother's passing.

"Such as a fire on the property," she said without inflection. "If I was neglectful as a landlord or deliberately failed to address a safety issue in the building, she might have a claim then."

"Precisely. Bond believed you might pay a handsome settlement to keep your gender and evidence of your holdings out of the courts."

A cold fury moved through her. "But such a

quiet transaction would no longer be likely to occur once I marry. Hence the need for her to act before the vows are spoken."

As they neared Peony Way, they found the street blocked off by wagons set perpendicular to the flow of traffic. Thick, black smoke mushroomed into the air and burned her airways. Eliza withdrew a kerchief from her reticule and held it against the lower half of her face.

They alighted from the carriage at the makeshift barrier and traversed the rest of the distance on foot, pushing their way through crowds of onlookers who fought tenaciously to retain their vantages. Westfield led the way while Aaron brought up the rear, both men attempting to cushion her from the crush but being only moderately successful.

When they neared the charred storefront, they found their way impeded by members of the fire brigade working on behalf of Eliza's insurance company to minimize the damage. She explained who she was, her eyes on the building's façade. Allowed to pass through, she searched the sea of people clogging the immediate area and spotted Jasper's tall frame.

"There." She pointed.

Westfield caught her elbow and shepherded her closer. When they were only a few feet away, the crowd parted and a cleared path appeared, revealing Jasper standing by Mrs. Penning—*Miss Chilcott*. The woman's gown and apron were both singed and covered in ash. Her blond hair was darkened by soot, as was her face, which had a swelling bruise around her left eye. The resemblance to Eliza's stepfather was so obvious, it would be impossible to miss if one was paying attention, which Eliza hadn't been when they'd met. A morning spent with Jasper in the close confines of his carriage, followed by his entrance into the Pennington shop so swiftly on the heels of her own had kept her too preoccupied to pay any mind to the other woman.

It was a testament to Vanessa Chilcott's beauty that she was still riveting in her disheveled condition. Westfield faltered slightly when she turned toward them, his breath leaving his lungs in an audible rush.

"Eliza." Jasper did not appear to be overly surprised to see her. "Why did I know you wouldn't heed caution and stay home?"

"I go where you go." She examined him for signs of injury. He was dirty with ash and soot, as if he'd been in the building as well, but he didn't appear to be hurt.

She turned her attention to the woman standing beside him. "Miss Chilcott."

Vanessa Chilcott's blue eyes were red-rimmed and somewhat vacant. She replied in a painfully hoarse voice. "Miss Martin."

"What happened here?"

Jasper had begun to reply when a fireman approached.

"The fire is contained," the man said. "We found the body and a can of paraffin oil, just as Mrs. Pennington described."

"Body?" Eliza felt ill. "Dear God . . . Someone was caught in the fire?"

Jasper nodded. "Miss Chilcott went up to her

flat to retrieve a special order and caught Terrance Reynolds in the act of setting the place ablaze. They fought, and she brained him with a poker. She barely made it out before the fire engulfed the space. I attempted to retrieve him . . . but it was too late."

"Mr. Reynolds?" Eliza repeated.

Her man of affairs had been excruciatingly thorough in his vetting of prospective tenants. By God, he'd discovered Jasper's ownership of the property Westfield wagered against Montague, despite the intricate nature of the inquiry and formidable time constraints. He would not have missed discovering that Mrs. Pennington was actually Vanessa Chilcott. Why had he withheld the information? What reason would he have to allow a Chilcott to rent space from her?

She looked at Vanessa. "You were his insurance. He hid your identity from me to use at his convenience. What role do you play in this subterfuge?"

"None." Vanessa's chin lifted. "I am more ignorant of this matter than you are."

"What relation are you to my stepfather?"

"I am your stepsister."

Staggered by the day's revelations and the understanding that the employee she'd trusted so keenly had betrayed her, Eliza swayed on her feet. Jasper caught her close.

She clung to him. "I saw him only hours ago. He came with information about you. Information intended to make me doubt the wisdom of marrying you."

He stiffened. "What information?"

"Your participation in the wager between West-field and Montague over land in Essex. He suggested you offered for me as a way to prevent Montague from laying claim to my money, which would afford him the opportunity to reclaim his marker."

"And you were not swayed by this?"

"No. Which left him no option, I suppose, aside from this last-minute attempt to delay the ceremony." She looked up, finding Jasper watching her with a dark, fierce gaze. "But it would only delay the inevitable. Surely, he knew that. What was his aim? I had no intention of releasing him from his position. His circumstances would not have altered."

"We'll uncover his secrets, love." He sheltered her in his embrace, anchoring her as no one else in her life ever had. "I promise you that. Every last one of them."

Chapter 16

With Westfield at his side, Jasper escorted Eliza and Vanessa Chilcott into the Melville residence. Disheveled and reeking of smoke, the four of them were incongruous in a household prepared for the celebration of a wedding. They stood shoulder to shoulder in the foyer, hard-faced and bemused.

Lady Collingsworth hurried from the ballroom where the ceremony was to take place and came to an abrupt halt a few feet away. "Dear God," she muttered. "The parson awaits you, but it's clear I should reschedule."

"No," Eliza said, astonishing Jasper. "If he can wait an hour, I can be ready."

Recovering, Jasper said, "I can be repaired within an hour as well."

Blinking rapidly, Lady Collingsworth took in Miss Chilcott's appearance.

"Regina," Eliza said briskly, "this is Miss Vanessa

Chilcott, my stepsister. Vanessa, this is the dowager Countess of Collingsworth."

"My lady," Vanessa whispered, curtseying.

Admiration and pride filled Jasper. He could think of no other woman who would wade through the morass of the day's events with such aplomb. Eliza could have left Miss Chilcott to her own devices after learning the truth of her identity. Instead, she had asked one question of the woman— "Why?"—to which Miss Chilcott replied, "I want to be self-sufficient and independent. Who better to learn from than you? And how else to manage it, but to shed the Chilcott name that has defined my life thus far?"

Eliza had offered to take the woman in for now, since Miss Chilcott's residence and all her possessions had been lost in the fire. At the very least, it kept the woman close while they delved into her circumstances. They would address other considerations tomorrow.

"Miss Chilcott will need a bath and a room," Eliza said. "If you could see to that, Regina, I would be deeply grateful."

"Of course." Lady Collingsworth looked at Jasper. "You have visitors, Mr. Bond. In the parlor."

Jasper met Eliza's querying gaze by extending his arm. *I go where you go,* she'd said, and despite everything, she wished to be married to him with as much haste as he felt. He treasured her for that and countless other things.

Westfield set off to join the handful of other guests in the ballroom. Jasper and Eliza moved into the formal parlor. There were five people in the room. The Crouch twins, Lynd, Anthony Bell, and Mrs. Francesca Maybourne.

Surveying the group with raised brows, Jasper wondered why the lot of them was in attendance. He was about to ask that very question, when Eliza spoke.

"Good afternoon, Mrs. Reynolds," she said softly. "After today's events, I was not expecting to see you again."

"I went to the jeweler," Lynd explained, "but Bell was nowhere to be found, which raised my suspicions."

Eliza continued listening to the recounting of the second half of the Reynolds's plot with a heavy heart. While she was deeply grateful for the plan's failure, she was painfully conscious that the hazard would not have existed if Jasper wasn't determined to destroy Montague. How much of his energy was focused on that endeavor? Would she ever have all of him? Or was the largest piece of his heart given to the woman from his past whom Montague had destroyed?

And yet she had to take heart. He'd come to marry her and sent Lynd after Montague in his stead.

"Sometimes," Jasper said quietly, "what looks too good to be true is precisely that."

Lynd nodded. "It was wise of you to send the Crouches with me. Together we watched the street for close to an hour and we noted one hackney that was a fixture the entire time. Patrick walked by it and—aided by his tremendous height—was able to see Mrs. Reynolds waiting inside with a pistol in her lap. I sent Peter to fetch Bell so he could confirm the story she gave us. Bell didn't know her, but apparently she knew enough about him, you, and Montague to create the perfect lure to draw you out. We brought her here to see what you thought of it all, having no notion her identity was false or that Miss Martin would know who she truly was."

Eliza eyed Anne Reynolds with something akin to hatred, an emotion she'd never truly felt before. "Were you going to shoot Mr. Bond? Was it your intention to kill him?"

The brunette lowered the sodden kerchief she'd been sobbing into since learning of her husband's demise and glared daggers at Jasper. "That isn't his name. I have no notion what his given name truly is, but I can tell you his surname is Gresham. He is the son of Diana Gresham, who was a whore for Lord Montague until her death from a wasting disease."

Jasper became so still it frightened Eliza. "Moderation would be wise," he warned with dangerous softness.

"I know everything about you, Mr. Gresham," Anne spat. "I told Mr. Reynolds to share what he knew with Miss Martin. After all, she's the one who hired my brother-in-law to investigate your connection to Lord Gresham in County Wexford. 'Tell her he isn't what he says he is,' I told him, but he insisted Miss Martin had only to believe you wanted her money to set you aside. He also feared rousing her concern if she was to learn he never recalled Tobias from Ireland. 'She might wonder what other orders I've disobeyed,' he said. He should have listened to me."

The explosive tension in the room was palpable. Eliza rushed to fill the void before Anne could ignite the situation further. "You wrote the threatening letters Lord Melville received." It was not a question. "Why? What purpose did this all serve?"

Anne's chin lifted and she looked away. "As if I would say anything further. I have done nothing wrong."

"What of the incident at the Royal Academy?" Jasper asked with ice in his tone.

"Dear God. You cannot think we had anything to do with that! We are not murderers. I've had enough of this." She stood. "You have no right to detain me."

"I'll be taking you in to Bow Street," Bell said, rocking back on his heels. He was a short and slender man, almost delicate looking. "We'll see if the magistrate agrees with you. 'Til then, sit down."

"That's an expensive cape you wear," Jasper noted. "And sizable emeralds at your ears and throat. Either you came into your marriage with money, or Miss Martin paid your husband exceedingly well."

Unaccustomed to noting such things, Eliza reevaluated the woman's attire. Anne Reynolds's ensemble did indeed seem far finer than Eliza's own accoutrements. She looked at Jasper. "How? I manage my own funds . . . keep my own ledgers . . ."

"You do not deal directly with your tenants. Who collects the rents?"

"Mr. Reynolds."

"Right," Lynd said. "Is it possible what you believe you are charging and collecting isn't what the tenants are actually paying to Reynolds?"

Eliza paled. "I suppose it's possible, if he was clever enough about it." Which she knew he could have been. She looked at Anne, who was also wan, if defiant. "If he raised the rents over time without my knowledge, or charged for miscellaneous items of which I wasn't aware. We should ask Miss Chilcott and my other tenants. Dear God . . . they are all as much victims as I am."

"That's likely why Reynolds wanted Bond dead," Bell said. "Once you had a husband to assist you, the embezzlement might've been discovered or Reynolds' duties reduced. I'm sorry I didn't believe you when you hired me, Miss Martin. Let that be a lesson to me in the future."

Jasper remained deadly quiet and expressionless.

"This was to be my last Season," Eliza said softly. "I intended to retire to the country with Melville, at which point a greater portion of my affairs would have been left in Mr. Reynolds's hands. He and his wife were so close to achieving their aims that my sudden decision to marry Mr. Bond must have made them desperate."

"If you marry him," Anne said coldly, "you deserve what comes to you. At least Mr. Reynolds was concerned about building your wealth. Gresham, I am certain, intends to squander it."

Eliza pushed to her feet, unable to bear any more. "I shall leave this matter to you, Mr. Bell. I'm confident you will apprise me of the necessary information."

The Runner gave a curt nod. "Of course."

"Mr. Bond," Eliza murmured, which caused Anne to laugh. "Would you accompany me, please?"

"In a moment," he said without inflection. "I'll find you."

Eliza made her egress on wooden legs, wondering if she would, indeed, be found, or if Jasper would now be lost to her. Perhaps he'd never truly been hers to begin with. For all their promises to be truthful to one another, it seemed they'd kept more secrets than they'd shared.

Jasper reached the top of the staircase and turned to the right, following the directions to Eliza's room that Lady Collingsworth had given him. If the dowager countess thought it was inappropriate for him to ask for them, she gave no outward indication. Instead, she told him the parson was having a fine time with both the champagne and Lord Westfield's witty discourse, and he'd agreed to stay as long as they wanted him to.

Inhaling deeply, Jasper lifted his hand to knock on Eliza's boudoir door. As he waited for her to answer, he struggled against the feeling of being made of glass; he felt as if he might break at any moment. Perhaps it was the endless string of unexpected revelations that had him so unsettled. Or perhaps he was simply experiencing a bridegroom's expected nervousness. He thought it might be terror over the prospect of losing something irreplaceable, but he didn't have any frame of reference to be certain.

The door opened, and Eliza stood there. She was in a dressing gown, and her eyes and nose were red. He remembered when they'd first met, he'd thought her pretty enough but no raving beauty. He couldn't comprehend that determination now. He was certain she was the loveliest woman he'd ever seen.

Stepping back, she made room for him to enter, then she shut the door quietly behind him.

Her rooms were decorated in the same hues of cream and burgundy as his own. He noticed that immediately, and took an odd sort of comfort in the similarity. He shouldn't forget how alike they were in the most fundamental of ways. If only they could strip away their exteriors and bare that affinity . . .

"I should have told you—"

They spoke and ended in unison. Startled to have said the same thing at once, they stared at one another. He waited for her to speak first. After the day's revelations, she deserved the opportunity to give him a tongue-lashing.

Her hands tightened the belt at her waist. "I hired Tobias Reynolds in the beginning, when I knew nothing about you. You said the connection between you and Lord Gresham would withstand greater scrutiny, and I told myself I was only confirming the claim before someone else had a mind to. But I recalled Mr. Reynolds from the task before he reported anything. I wanted you to be the one to tell me whatever you felt I should know, in your own good time."

Jasper nodded and linked his fingers behind his back. "I should have told you about my mother. I knew I would have to, but I thought we had time—"

"We do." She stepped closer. "All the time you need."

"The time is now, Eliza. You should know me before you wed me. I couldn't bear for you to turn away from me after you're mine."

"I cannot turn away. I love you."

His eyes closed on a shuddering breath. "Eliza—"

"I don't want you to say anything," she interrupted quickly, "until after we are man and wife. I need to marry you with my heart, not my mind. I need to trust in my own instincts, over my reason, so I can make the changes necessary to be what you require, to be whole. I need you to know I accept you just the way you are, without reservation or doubt, so you can—God willing—someday grow to love me, too."

Eliza was defying all of her routines, setting aside habits of a lifetime, deliberately making one concession after another . . . *for him*. She was determined to leave herself open to trusting him, even when everything suggested she shouldn't.

"I love you," she said again.

He looked at her. She'd taken a seat upon one of the settees with her hands clasped demurely in her lap. Insanely, that aroused him—the vision of her so controlled, when he knew how wild she could be in his arms. It was the way she revealed her deeper self when they were intimate, even more than the physical pleasure, that drove his sexual craving for her.

"I am undone," he said hoarsely. "You rule me completely. I would do anything to possess you."

Eliza's hand lifted to her throat, her fingers wrapping around the graceful column. He crossed the room to her and caught that alabaster hand. Jasper pressed a kiss to the back of it, then moved to the tips of her fingers. He licked the end of the one that would bear his ring by the close of the day, and she shivered. Her lashes lowered and her lips parted on soft panting breaths.

Opening his mouth, he sucked the slender digit inside, swirling his tongue around it until a whimper escaped her.

The sound of surrender freed him from any restraint.

He reached down and opened the placket of his breeches with his free hand. His cock fell heavily into his palm, so thick and hard he fisted himself to stave off his hunger.

"Jasper."

His mouth slid free of her trembling fingers. "I need you."

Eliza fumbled with the belt at her waist. Jasper sank to the floor on his knees and pushed up her chemise, his hands rough with impatience. He caught her hips and tugged her down to his lap, her legs straddling his. The cleft of her sex pressed against the silky length of him.

He caught her nape in his hand, forcing her to look straight into his eyes. "I need to be in you."

"Yes." She grew slick with welcome due to the heat of his rut. She loved him like this, uncontrolled and lustful.

He shifted her, urging her up and then over him, the thick crest of his penis gliding along her slit and nudging her clitoris. She moaned and caught his shoulders, tense with impatience and greedy for pleasure.

When he notched himself at her clenching opening, she trembled. With a groan, he thrust, pushing his thickly veined cock deep into her.

"Eliza." His arms tightened around her, crushing the air from her lungs and immobilizing her against him.

She clawed at his back, writhing. The heat of his skin burned through the linen and velvet of his garments.

"Please," she begged, quivering around him. *"Please."*

Jasper gripped her hips, lifting and dropping her. Working her onto his rigid length. Pumping her up and down. Grinding and screwing deep.

Eliza sobbed with the pleasure. "Yes!"

"I will addict you to this," he promised in a dark, dangerously rough voice. "Addict you to me. Soon, you'll seek me out in public, unable to wait another moment. You will lift your skirts and beg for my mouth on you, my tongue in you. In the extremity of your lust, you won't care where we are. You will crave the taste of me. You will sink to your knees and service me with your mouth, sucking my cock until I spill into you, thick and hot and mad with hunger."

She wrapped her arms around his shoulders, eyes closing as he surged repeatedly inside her. The feeling was incredible. She would never have enough of it. The stroking of the furled underside of his crown rubbed deliciously, finding her most sensitive nerve endings and setting them afire.

He slid inside her, deeply, filling her with the heat and hardness of him. Filling her with pleasure that made her arch wildly. His possession was indescribably erotic. As addicting as he threatened.

He withdrew, and she felt empty. He returned, and she bit her lip to hold back cries that would betray their actions to a multitude of guests.

But Jasper would abide no restraint. "Let me hear you," he coaxed. "Let me hear how much you want this."

His free hand cupped her thigh, opening her wider so that he could thrust deeper. Swiveling his hips, he worked her into a frenzy with ruthless skill, making her insensate with lust and hungry for more. Always more. As much as he gave her, it wasn't enough.

Eliza gasped and dug her nails into the flexing muscles of his back. The horrors of the day created a sharp urgency. "Finish me."

"Too soon," he ground out, sweat dripping down his temple.

"We have forever to go slower. Don't make me wait now."

He crushed her to him. "I love you. Eliza . . . love you."

She climaxed with a force that left her shaking. Jasper followed swiftly, his hips ramming upward with ferocious speed. She felt his climax building, felt the tensing of his muscles and the frantic heaving of his powerful chest. When he came, it was violent, his thick penis jerking inside her with every molten spurt of his seed. Her name fell brokenly from his lips until she kissed him, swallowing the sounds of his pleasure with unconditional love in her heart.

They were married an hour later. Aside from the parson, who was flushed and happy with drink, it was a somber wedding. If the stamp of Jasper's passion was evident in Eliza's appearance, no one said anything to her, and she was certain Regina would have.

Jasper's hair was still damp when he said his vows. He'd sent the Crouches back to his home to retrieve fresh clothes, then bathed in a guest bedroom to save time.

Fewer than a dozen people witnessed the short ceremony. The celebration afterward was equally abridged, since everyone had been present for hours by the time the vows were said.

Eliza wore a new cream-hued satin gown with fine lace sleeves and bodice. It was cut and fashioned in the latest style, the first of many that would assist her transformation. She intended to enhance what beauty God had given her, using every weapon in her feminine arsenal to please her husband and deepen his love for her.

When the time came to retire, Jasper was relieved. Eliza led him to her suite of rooms with his hand in hers.

"I have something for you," he said, when they were alone.

"Oh." She bit her lower lip. "I did not think of a wedding gift for you."

"You're all the gift I need." He reached into the inner pocket of his coat and withdrew a lady's signet ring.

He held his hand out for hers, slipping the golden circlet onto the ring finger of her right hand. "It was my mother's."

Eliza looked up at him with luminous eyes. "Thank you."

He nodded and shrugged out of his coat. "Would you care for a drink?" he asked solicitously. Having taken her body so peremptorily earlier, he intended to savor her now.

"No. I want you."

Satisfaction surged through him. His chest expanded on a deep inhale. His blood thickened and flowed hotly. "Have you no reservations? No questions?"

"Why are you still talking?" She presented her back to him.

"Will you always surprise me?" He approached her and reached for the first button of her gown.

"Haven't we had enough unpleasantness for one day? Tomorrow is soon enough to address the rest."

He pressed his lips to her shoulder, grateful for her.

Her head turned, and her gaze met his. "If you'd gone to the jeweler's today instead of Lynd . . ."

"Eliza . . ."

She pivoted into his arms, catching his mouth with her own in a fervent, awkward kiss. He caught her close, lifting her feet from the floor. Her slender arms wrapped around his neck, her fingers pushed into his hair in the way that never failed to inflame him.

"I want you naked," she breathed, making his cock hard. "I want to touch you everywhere, and your clothing makes that impractical."

"We cannot have impracticality in our bedroom," he said, biting back a smile. Setting her down on the edge of the mattress, Jasper stepped back. He attacked the buttons of his waistcoat.

Eliza's tongue traced the curve of her bottom lip. "Take your time."

"You like to watch."

"I like to watch *you*," she amended. "You are everything I find beautiful, and sexual, and desirable."

He had no idea what to say to that, how to tell her what her candor meant to him. He could only slow the process of undressing, maintaining eye contact with her, allowing her to see how much he loved her. When the last stitch was shed, he straightened and waited for her to tell him what to do next. He'd taken what he needed earlier, and she'd given it to him without hesitation. Only the second time in her life that she'd had a man inside her and he'd been too overwrought to show her the gentleness she deserved. Now, it was his turn to give her what she needed.

"I'm overdressed," she said, toeing off her slippers. Her slim legs dangled off the end of the bed.

"What would you like me to do about that?"

"Undress me. But much more quickly than you bared yourself."

Jasper set his hands at her waist and helped her off the mattress. He resumed his task of unfastening her buttons, working quickly. The wedding gown was set aside with reverence, but the sheer chemise and pantalettes were left to puddle on the floor. Enamored with her softly freckled skin, he wrapped himself around her, his arms tucked under hers and his knees bent to accommodate her shorter stature. With one hand cupping a breast and the other tangling with the dark red curls between her legs, he owned her passion completely.

She purred with pleasure, her head falling back against his shoulder. "I love your hands on me. They are so big and strong, callused and warm."

"A tradesman's hands." He traced the delicately pink shell of her ear with his tongue.

"The only hands that will ever touch me this way."

Scissoring his fingers, he parted the lips of her

sex, exposing the hood shielding her clitoris. "Will I find you wet?"

She began to pant as he rolled her nipple between his fingers. Her stance widened in invitation for a deeper caress. "Yes . . . You linger in me from earlier."

The thought of her drenched in his semen swelled his already heavy erection. He pushed his cock between her thighs, growling at the slickness that coated him.

"Let me," he coaxed, urging her to fold forward over the edge of the bed.

There was a slight tension in her lithe frame. Then she relaxed and lay facedown, presenting the lush curve of her beautiful buttocks. He cupped them, squeezing their fullness.

Reaching between her legs, he urged her to pull one leg up and onto the mattress, her thigh perpendicular to her body, opening her completely. He cupped her there, too, possessively. "I love you."

She rested her cheek on the counterpane and closed her eyes. "Say it again."

He took himself in hand, notching his cockhead into the tiny entrance to her silken cunt. "I love you."

With a slow roll of his hips, he pushed the fat crown into the fist-tight glove of her. Her fingers dug into the velvet and her low moan stirred his blood.

"My wife," he breathed, pushing inexorably deeper.

Eliza arched her back like a cat, which caused

the tiny little muscles inside her to squeeze him. The pleasure of those rippling embraces, the sensation of being lured deeper into her . . . A deep groan escaped him. Hunching over her, Jasper worked his cock into her with quick shallow judders, sliding through quivering tissues until he hit the end of her, refusing to risk either of them climaxing until they were completely connected.

Her breath hitched.

"So deep . . ." she slurred.

He withdrew a few inches, then thrust, going even deeper. She hugged him at the root, clasping his throbbing cock in liquid heat. Catching her by the shoulder, he held her in place and rode her with long, leisurely thrusts. His bollocks smacked against her damp cleft in a steady, erotic rhythm. Eliza whimpered with every weighty tap against her clitoris, her nails leaving visible trails in the counterpane, the curls around her face growing damp with perspiration.

When the pressure to blow grew dangerously high, Jasper would pause at the deepest point of her and grind, whispering soothing words as she climaxed around him. Sweat soaked his hair and matted his chest, a visible sign of the restraint required to remain rock hard and full to bursting to please her.

Time passed, and Jasper lost track of it, as he always did when he was with Eliza. He knew only that she came so many times her fingers no longer had the strength to clutch the counterpane, and the cries she made as the pleasure hit were weak-as-a-kitten mewls.

It was her hoarse-voiced "I love you" that finished him.

With his cheek pressed against her glorious hair and his arms wrapped beneath her, he filled her with hot, wrenching pulses of the lust that sprang from a deeper source. From a well of hope and love inside him he hadn't known was there until she made him whole.

Chapter 17

Eliza was perusing the morning's papers at the breakfast table when Vanessa Chilcott appeared. Her stepsister was dressed in the housekeeper's clothes—a high-neck shirt that was slightly too snug around the breasts and a skirt that was a tad too long—but she carried herself with unassailable dignity.

"Good morning," Eliza greeted her, before returning to reading the reports of the fire the day prior.

"Good morning, Miss Martin."

It took a few moments for Eliza to realize the other woman was rooted to one spot. Frowning, she peeked over the top of the page. She gestured toward the console against the wall where plates and covered platters waited. "The food is there. Please help yourself to whatever you like."

As if all she'd needed was permission, Vanessa nodded and moved to serve herself. When she was finished and settled at the table, she said, "Congratulations on your wedding yesterday."

Eliza bit her lower lip and set the paper down. "Should I have asked you to attend? I was unsure after the events at the store and the discovery of our . . . relation to one another, whether I should or not."

Vanessa blinked. She stared at Eliza in the manner most people did when they comprehended how little she knew about etiquette.

"Good morning, ladies," Jasper said as he entered the room. His stride was easy and inherently sensual, with a touch of leisure as if time was no concern. "My wife is blessed with an extraordinarily pragmatic nature, Miss Chilcott. She rarely means offense when she observes—or does not observe, as the case may be—certain social mores."

Nodding, Vanessa watched as Jasper walked the length of the room to where Eliza sat at the far end. There was blatant appreciation in the blonde's eyes, a knowing understanding of what type of man he was—ruthlessly deliberate and dangerously sexual. Eliza imagined it would be impossible for any red-blooded woman to be immune to him. After all, as oblivious as she'd personally been toward men, she hadn't failed to want him either.

"I took no offense," Vanessa assured. "I'm grateful to have had a roof over my head last night."

Eliza shrugged. "It was the most reasonable course of action to have you stay here. You lost more than I did in the fire."

Jasper set one hand on the table and the other on the back of Eliza's chair. Bending, he kissed her temple and whispered, "I had need of you this morning, madam. In the future, you should order a tray brought to our rooms."

Her breath caught. Jasper had displayed a marked insatiability throughout the night, waking her repeatedly to take her again and again. On her back. Sprawled on her stomach. Arranged on her side. With her heels in the air or her thighs between his. Deep and shallow, hard and soft, pounding possessions and slow, endless glides . . . His repertoire of sensual delights was vast, and she suspected he'd shown her only a smidgeon of what he was capable of.

As he straightened, she turned her head, impulsively pressing her lips to his. He stiffened in surprise, then gave an encouraging hum, remaining still as she kissed him sweetly. When she withdrew, Jasper's smile curled her toes. He traced the bridge of her nose with his fingertip, then he stepped away to fetch his own plate.

Bolstered by his presence and verbal support, Eliza took a deep breath and turned her focus to her stepsister. Vanessa's attention was firmly on her food, her eyes downcast as if to say she couldn't possibly be aware of the scandalous behavior taking place at the other end of the long room.

Vanessa cleared her throat. "Whether or not it was reasonable to provide lodging to a tenant who lied on her application is debatable, I think. I doubt many would have done so."

"But you are not simply a tenant," Eliza pointed out. "You are my stepsister."

A wry smile twisted Vanessa's lips. "Which is

more of a detriment than an endorsement, is it not?"

Jasper pulled out the chair at the foot of the table, which was directly to Eliza's right, and sat.

Eliza nodded, seeing no point in being untruthful.

"Unfalteringly candid," Vanessa said. "My father quite enjoyed that about you, Miss Martin. He said it was freeing. It inspired him to be a better man."

"I don't mean to be rude, but he never mentioned you."

One blond brow rose. "When did you give him the opportunity?"

Eliza opened her mouth, then shut it again.

"Exactly." Vanessa carefully sliced into her black pudding with her knife. "I don't blame you. You are astute, and you knew straightaway that he pursued your mother for the fortune left by your father. It's all true what they say about us Chilcotts."

Nonplussed, Eliza glanced at Jasper, whose face was austere and gave away none of his thoughts.

"See this?" Vanessa set down her utensils and held out her hand. She pointed to a reddish birthmark that rested over the back of her wrist. "My grandmother once told me you could spot the rotten fruit in our family tree because we all bear this 'bruise.' "

"I see," Eliza said.

"What you do not see, however, is that even bruised fruit sometimes has salvageable parts. In my father's case, it was his heart. He courted your mother for her money; he married her because he loved her."

Eliza's hands linked together on the table. "If he'd truly cared for her, he would have been a positive influence."

"That sounds reasonable," Vanessa agreed. "But love is not reasonable. Love is wanting to see the other person as happy as possible as often as possible. Leastwise that's how my father viewed love. As you know, it wasn't an easy task keeping Lady Georgina happy. If he cared for her not at all, he could have had her committed. Or he could have taken her to the country and left her there. Or the Continent. Perhaps she might have taken a liking to America—"

"I understand what you're saying."

Jasper reached over and set one hand atop both of Eliza's.

"I think you should know," Vanessa continued, "*you* were a positive influence on my father, who in turn extolled the virtues of respectable living to me. He's the one who convinced me I could make an honest living."

Eliza was at a loss as to how to handle the conversation. What could she say that wasn't already known to Vanessa? "I'm sorry my difficulties with Mr. Reynolds spilled over into your life."

Vanessa shrugged. "I blame my surname for Mr. Reynolds's actions against my shop, not you. I believe he rented the space to me with the intention of extorting from me whatever money he thought I intended to extort from you. When I caught him igniting the paraffin, he said, 'Don't worry. I can still ensure you see a profit from your plans.' That was when I hit him with the poker."

"Dear God."

"I must have seemed like the kindest of fates to him, falling so neatly into his lap through no effort on his part. A Chilcott to use as another means to garner more of your money."

Jasper looked at Eliza. "By distracting you with the fire and removing me with a bullet, Reynolds likely hoped his services would seem even more valuable. In the process, he would have discredited Mr. Bell and cast suspicion on Montague, ensuring those avenues no longer seemed viable to you."

"He had no way of knowing," she murmured, loving him all the more, "that you would forsake a chance to thwart Montague in favor of me."

He squeezed her hand.

Eliza glanced at Vanessa. "What will you do now?"

"I've spent much of my life making decisions based upon my surname. Even when taking a new direction, I did so by comparing it to the known alternative, which is still allowing the name to define me. No more. The store was a lovely dream, but I'm not certain it was *my* dream."

"I should like for you to stay here in the interim," Eliza said, startling herself.

"Another Martin inviting another Chilcott to live under her roof?"

"The parallel did not even occur to me." She'd made the decision impulsively and from the heart.

Jasper offered an encouraging smile.

"When you're finished," she said to him, "I would like to speak to you privately."

"Of course."

Robbins appeared in the open dining room doorway, bearing a calling card. He crossed the length of the room and set the silver salver in the space between Eliza and Jasper. "The Earl of Westfield has come to call."

"Send him in," Jasper said.

A moment later, Westfield entered the room, looking windblown and dashing for it.

"Good morning," he called out to the room at large, but his eyes were on Vanessa. "How fortunate. I haven't yet eaten."

"You're late, my lord," Jasper drawled.

"I cannot remember the last time I was out of bed at this hour. Only for you would I be conscious."

"Perhaps you should consider retiring to bed earlier, my lord," Vanessa said.

"What fun is there in that, Miss Chilcott?"

Vanessa kept her gaze on her plate. "That would be dependent upon who else is in the bed."

Jasper glanced at Eliza. His dark eyes were laughing. "My wife and I must adjourn, but please, enjoy yourself."

Westfield smiled. "I intend to."

"I wonder if I should warn Miss Chilcott about Westfield," Jasper said, as he and Eliza ascended the steps to her rooms.

"And here I was wondering if Westfield needed a similar warning." She smiled and there was an openness to the gesture that nearly caused Jasper to miss a step. "However, I think they are well-matched. Neither will gain much advantage with the other, I suspect. Although it's clear Westfield is hoping otherwise."

"He has an eye for beautiful women."

She looked aside at him. "Just so long as you do not."

"I cannot agree to that, I'm afraid. You see, there is a beautiful woman who shares my life, and I could never agree not to have an eye for her."

They entered her boudoir, and Jasper expected they would retire to the bedroom. They were newly wedded, after all. But Eliza sat on one of the sitting-room settees and arranged her striped skirts as if settling in for a not inconsiderable length of time. Her assertive nose was lifted high and her jaw was set.

Recognizing the signs of determination, Jasper shrugged out of his coat. "I'm impressed with how the conversation between you and Miss Chilcott progressed."

"I understand what she means in regards to allowing exterior forces to define us. For so long, I allowed my frustration with my mother to define me and my choices." She took a deep breath and said, "Even when it came to marrying you."

He took a seat beside her. "Whatever concerns you had about repeating your mother's mistakes were bravely managed. You would not be wearing my ring otherwise."

Eliza watched him lift her hand to his lips and press a kiss to her ruby and diamond wedding ring. "But you see, as determined as I was not to marry because of my mother, when I reversed my position it was also because of her. I became so determined that she wouldn't be the reason I refused you, that she became the reason I accepted you."

Unsure of where the conversation was going and certain he didn't like hearing she'd wed him for any other reason than loving him, Jasper retained his light hold on her hand. "What are you saying?"

"Mr. Reynolds attempted to sway me against you, and even when he relayed information meant to incite doubt and concern, I dismissed my own disquiet because not marrying you had taken on the meaning of giving my mother a victory." Her fingers tightened on his. "Do you understand?"

"I think I do. Do you still have those concerns and doubts?" He rubbed his chest with his free hand, fighting the restriction he'd begun to feel.

She smiled. "No."

Jasper had to focus on relaxing his jaw. "Did you ever believe, for even a moment, that I wanted to marry you solely to prevent Montague from attaining your fortune? Did you believe I might utilize your fortune to ensure he could not climb out of the hole he dug for himself?"

"I want you to take whatever amount is required to achieve your aims," she said quietly. "Use whatever you need."

He stared at her, speechless.

"What nearly happened yesterday," she went on, "with Anne Reynolds and the failed ambush . . . It was your past defining you. I couldn't give myself fully to our marriage until I released myself from my mother's influence. The same applies to you."

Jasper stood in a rush. "My mother came to London for the Season. She was a diamond of the first water. She had her pick of husbands."

"But she fell prey to the late Earl of Montague?"

Her gentle tone nearly undid him. He'd never shared his mother's tale with anyone. Lynd knew it only because he'd borne witness to it.

"Yes." Jasper shoved a hand through his hair. "Unlike the young lady we heard in the Cranmores' garden the other night, my mother went willingly to Montague's bed."

"Jane Rothschild," she supplied.

"But like Jane Rothschild, my mother became pregnant." He began to pace. "When Montague refused to offer for her, she had to tell her brother. Lord Gresham's response was to disown her."

"Her own sibling . . . Is that why you don't bear his name?"

"I changed it legally. He left her in the city when he retired to Ireland, Eliza. She had nowhere to turn."

"I cannot imagine." Her voice was barely a whisper. "Being so helpless."

He spoke more harshly than he intended. "And yet you freely offer me the means by which you are independent?"

She met his gaze unflinchingly. "You're angry with me for offering my support?"

"No. Damnation. I'm angry at Montague for placing money between us!" He reached the wall and pivoted. "My mother turned to him. Begged him. He made her his mistress, then boasted to one and all that he'd reduced the Season's brightest star to being his whore. When his luck in the gambling hells ran out and his debts mounted, someone offered to take a night with my mother as payment."

"Oh, Jasper," she breathed. "Where were you in all of this?"

"I was in the schoolroom during the day, and locked in my bedchamber at night. Some of the men Montague sent to her brought gifts and tokens of esteem. They remembered how promising her future had been and took pity on her. She pawned them all and used the money to fund my education . . . and her growing dependence on opium."

Jasper didn't look at Eliza as he spoke, knowing if he saw pity in her eyes he wouldn't be able to continue.

"As Montague's financial situation declined," he went on, "so did the quality of my mother's lodging, the men who came to her, and the gifts they brought her. She wasn't willing to allow my education to suffer, so she began to earn money the only way she could . . . through whatever acts and degradation were required."

His voice hardened. "Meanwhile, I learned all I could from my tutors, so that one day I could ruin Montague the way he ruined my mother. I was furious when he passed on before I was ready."

There was a length of silence, during which all he heard was Eliza's elevated breathing. Finally, she said, "What happened to your mother is unconscionable, Jasper. A cruelty so vile I could never have imagined it possible. And his son is cut of the same cloth."

She stood and came to him, catching him around the waist mid-stride and forcing him to accept the comfort she offered. He stood stiffly for a long moment, breathing hard, his mind filled with scenes from a past he wished desperately to forget. Then the scent of her perfume penetrated through the fog of memories and brought him back to the present. Back to the wife he'd never expected to have, yet could no longer imagine living without.

He pressed his cheek to her crown. "I know what you sacrifice with your offer. As consumed as I've been by vengeance, I could easily squander everything you and your father have built. You know this, but you love me enough to put my needs first."

"I do love you." Her arms banded tightly around him. "I want you to be happy."

"And I love you. I understood when I sent Lynd to deal with Mrs. Reynolds's assignment that what I wanted most was to spend time with you. I also realized Montague could rob me of that, if I allowed him to." He leaned back to look at her. "If I allowed him to define me and my actions."

She swallowed. "What will you do?"

"I intend to ask Westfield to return the deed to Montague, and I will wash my hands of him. That's why Westfield is here this morning. You see, my mother wins if I enjoy a life of happiness with a beautiful wife and rambunctious, extremely bright children. The victory would be hers."

Her hands cupped his face, her blue eyes shining with unshed tears and a love that humbled him. She was about to speak when a knock came at the door.

"Don't move," Jasper admonished.

Eliza's dimple flashed, and he almost told whoever was bothering them to return in a few hours. Or days . . .

He pulled the door open.

Robbins stood in the gallery. "Forgive me, Mr. Bond. There is a Runner here to see you and Mrs. Bond. A Mr. Bell."

"Right. Thank you. We'll be down in a moment."

Jasper collected his coat. Eliza accepted his arm when he was ready and they descended to the ground floor. As they passed the parlor, Westfield could be heard speaking with Miss Chilcott. He sounded affronted.

They met with Mr. Bell in Eliza's study.

The Runner declined to take a seat and looked grim. "Yesterday, Mrs. Reynolds mentioned the Earl of Montague multiple times."

Jasper kept his expression neutral, but shot a quick look at Eliza, who nodded.

"Right," Bell said. "I've no notion—yet—of how his lordship is connected to yesterday's events, but I thought it might be relevant to tell you he was murdered an hour ago."

Eliza lost the color in her cheeks, but said nothing. Jasper, too, needed a moment to absorb the news. He was surprised, then relieved to realize he felt no regret or anger, as he'd felt when his father died. Montague's escape into death robbed him of nothing. Everything he needed was standing right beside him.

"How?" Jasper asked finally.

"Miss Jane Rothschild did the deed," the Runner relayed. "Shot his lordship in the heart with her father's pistol."

Epilogue

Eliza stood in the middle of her uncle's study and wondered how she would find a slender journal amid the multitude of books.

"Are you quite certain it's not in your bed-chamber?" she asked.

Melville's wild head of hair appeared on the other side of a high table. His face was seen shortly after, his cheeks red and eyes bright. "I'm certain I looked for it there."

"Can we not purchase a new journal for your use on the island?"

"I require the information in the journal," he said. "Not simply blank pages on which to write."

"Are we ready?"

Eliza jumped at the sound of Jasper's voice, startled as ever by how silently he moved. He stood directly beside her. "Not quite. We're still searching for his lordship's journal."

"In the barren desert of my heart,

*you bloom with radiance
and fill the air with heaven's scent."*

Jasper's brows rose as Lady Collingsworth entered the room while reading from a thin-spined book.

"I'm delighted, Burgess," Regina said, with a telltale blush. "Who knew you were a poet?"

Eliza was of the mind that her uncle was less than proficient in poetry, by any estimation, but she'd learned that the sentiment behind a gift or gesture was the most important aspect. Practicality came a distant second.

"Now may we set off?" Jasper held out his hand to Eliza. "I, for one, would prefer not to miss the ship carrying our luggage."

"I'm ready," Regina said, closing the journal and holding it out to Melville. When he accepted it, she took his arm.

"It will sound better when I read it to you," his lordship whispered, leading Regina out to the waiting carriage.

Setting her hand in Jasper's, Eliza wondered if the vibrating excitement reverberating through her was obvious on the exterior. He squeezed her fingers and smiled. "I can feel how anxious you are."

"Not anxious. Eager." She followed him back out to the foyer, where Robbins held her pelisse and bonnet. "I love the ocean and temperate weather. I cannot wait to be surrounded by both."

"There's nothing like falling asleep to the sound of crashing waves," he murmured. "I intend to lay a blanket on the sand and ravish you in the moonlight."

"Jasper." Eliza was scandalized . . . and intrigued. "Outdoors?"

"In sunlight, and in rain. On the beach, and beneath the trees. Also indoors, in every room in the house."

Her smile was wry as he helped her up into their carriage. Melville and Regina were in a separate equipage behind them. Although the two claimed to be no more than friends, it was clear there was a connection between them. Eliza had initially been surprised to learn of their affection, until Regina explained that Melville had courted her long ago. In the end, he felt it would be best for her to marry a man who spent the majority of his time connected to the rest of the world, and Regina had assumed Melville simply didn't love her. Eliza and Jasper's delayed wedding provided the time and opportunity for the two sweethearts to reconnect. So far, their renewed relationship seemed highly promising.

"I don't see how you expect to schedule all these hours of sexual congress," Eliza said, as the carriage lurched into motion, "while attempting to make a success of a sugarcane plantation."

"Is that a challenge, madam?"

"Could be . . ."

"There is a guesthouse. Melville and Lady Collingsworth will be no deterrent. With unhindered access to you, the possibilities are endless."

Eliza smiled. "Melville intends to cultivate a variety of seeds while he's with us, taking advantage of the warmer weather."

The light in Jasper's dark eyes was wicked. "I suspect it will be Lady Collingsworth he will be cultivating and tending."

"You have a lascivious mind."

"I do," he purred. "But my claim is bolstered by the indefinable magic of the tropics that stirs a man's blood."

"Ah." She nodded sagely. "Now your true intentions are revealed."

He leaned back into the squab and watched her with slumberous eyes. "Didn't I tell you the first day we met that seduction was my method of choice with you?"

"Yes. I'd forgotten." She hadn't, but in the weeks since they wed, she learned that teasing him led to delicious results.

"Shall I remind you?"

She licked her lower lip. "You are welcome to make the attempt."

He moved quickly, grabbing her by the waist and dragging her over him. "Wifely satisfaction is a point of pride with me, Mrs. Bond."

"I fear you may be too handsome for the task."

"Oh?" Jasper grabbed fistfuls of her skirts. "Considering the shortness of the distance to the docks, that's likely a boon."

"In addition," she went on, her voice growing husky, "it's impossible to disguise the air about you which distinguishes you."

"Pray tell me what that is." He reached into the opening of her pantalettes and parted the lips of her sex. He found her slick and hot for him.

"You are a predator. A dangerous man."

"Dangerously aroused," he agreed. "And madly in love."

She reached for the placket of his breeches and pressed her lips to his. "And mine."

"Always."

Don't miss the book that inspired *Bared to You*. Read *Seven Years to Sin*, available now!

"And this," the captain said, turning slightly to gesture at the gentleman, "is Mr. Alistair Caulfield, owner of this fine vessel and brilliant violinist, as you 'eard."

Jess swore her heart ceased beating for a moment. Certainly, she stopped breathing. Caulfield faced her and sketched a perfectly executed, elegant bow. Yet his head never lowered and his gaze never left hers.

Dear God . . .

What were the odds that they would cross paths this way?

There was very little of the young man Jess had once known left in the man who faced her. Alistair Caulfield was no longer pretty. The planes of his face had sharpened, etching his features into a thoroughly masculine countenance. Darkly winged brows and thick lashes framed those infamous eyes

of rich, deep blue. In the fading light of the setting
sun and the flickering flames of the turpentine
lamps, his coal-black hair gleamed with health and
vitality. Previously his beauty had been striking,
but now he was larger. More worldly and mature.
Undeniably formidable.

Breathtakingly male.

"Lady Tarley," he greeted her, straightening. "It
is a great pleasure to see you again."

His voice was lower and deeper in pitch than
she remembered. It had a soft, rumbling quality.
Almost a purr. He walked with equal feline grace,
his step light and surefooted despite his powerful
build. His gaze was focused and intense, assessing.
Challenging. As before, it seemed he looked right
into the very heart of her and dared her to deny
that he could.

She sucked in a shaky breath and met him
halfway, offering her hand. "Mr. Caulfield. It has
been some time since we last met."

"Years."

His look was so intimate she couldn't help
thinking of that night in the Pennington woods. A
rush of heat swept up her arm from where their
skin connected.

He went on. "Please accept my condolences on
your recent loss. Tarley was a good man. I admired
him and liked him quite well."

"Your thoughts are appreciated," she managed
in spite of a suddenly dry mouth. "I offer the same
to you. I was deeply sorry to hear that your brother
had passed."

His jaw tightened and he released her, sliding

his hand away so that his fingertips stroked over the center of her palm. "Two of them," he replied grimly.

Jess caught her hand back and rubbed it discreetly against her thigh, to no avail. The tingle left by his touch was inerasable.

"Shall we?" the captain said, tilting his head toward the table.

Caulfield took a seat on the bench directly across from her. She was discomfited at first, but he seemed to forget her the moment the food was brought in. To ensure a steady flow of conversation, she took pains to direct the discussion to topics addressing the ship and seafaring, and the men easily followed. No doubt they were relieved not to have to focus on her life of limited scope, which was of little interest to men. What followed was a rather fantastic hour of food and conversation the likes of which she'd never been exposed to before. Gentlemen did not often discuss matters of business around her.

It quickly became clear that Alistair Caulfield was enjoying laudable financial success. He didn't comment on it personally, but he participated in the discussion about the trade, making it clear he was very involved in the minutiae of his business endeavors. He was also expertly dressed. His coat was made with a gray-green velvet she thought quite lovely, and the stylishly short cut of the shoulders emphasized how fit he was.

"Do you make the trip to Jamaica often, Captain?" Jess asked.

"Not as often as some of Mr. Caulfield's other

ships do." He set his elbows on the table and toyed with his beard. "London is where we berth most often. The others dock in Liverpool or Bristol."

"How many ships are there?"

The captain looked at Caulfield. " 'Ow many are there now? Five?"

"Six," Caulfield said, looking directly at Jess.

She met his gaze with difficulty. She couldn't explain why she felt as she did, but it was almost as if the intimacies she had witnessed that night in the woods had been between Caulfield and herself, not another woman. Something profound had transpired in the moment they'd first become aware of each other in the darkness. A connecting thread had been sewn between them, and she had no notion how to sever it. She knew things about the man she should not know, and there was no way for her to return to blissful ignorance . . .

Read on for a sneak peek of *The Stranger I Married*, on sale now!

Prologue

London, 1815

"**D**o you truly intend to steal your best friend's mistress?"

Gerard Faulkner, the sixth Marquess of Grayson, kept his eyes on the woman in question, and smiled. Those who knew him well also knew that look, and its wicked portent. "I certainly do."

"Dastardly," Bartley muttered. "Too low even for you, Gray. Is it not sufficient to cuckold Sinclair? You know how Markham feels about Pel. He's lost his head over her."

Gray studied Lady Pelham with a connoisseur's eye. There was no incertitude about her suitability for his needs. Beautiful and scandalous, he could not have designed a wife more suited to irritating his mother if he'd tried. Pel, as she was affectionately referred to, was of medium height, but stunningly curved, and built for a man's pleasure. The auburn-haired widow of the late Earl of Pelham had a brazen sultriness that was addicting, or so rumor said. Her former lover, Lord Pearson, had gone into a long decline after she ended their affair.

Gerard had no difficulty seeing how a man could mourn the loss of her attentions. Under the blazing lights of the massive chandeliers, Isabel Pelham glittered like a precious jewel, expensive and worth every shilling.

He watched as she smiled up at Markham with a wide curving of her lips, lips which were considered too full for conventional beauty, but just the right plumpness to rim a man's cock. All around the room, covetous male eyes watched her, hoping for the day when she might turn those sherry-colored eyes upon them, and perhaps select one of them as her next lover. To Gerard, their longing was pitiable. The woman was extremely selective, and retained her lovers for years. She'd had Markham on a leash for nearly two now, and showed no signs of losing interest.

But that interest did not extend to matrimony.

On the few occasions when the viscount had begged for her hand, she refused him, declaring she had no interest in marrying a second time. Gray, on the other hand, had no doubts whatsoever that he could change her mind about that.

"Calm yourself, Bartley," he murmured. "Things will work out. Trust me."

"No one can trust you."

"You can trust me to give you five hundred pounds

if you drag Markham away from Pel and into the card room."

"Well, then." Bartley straightened his spine and his waistcoat, neither action capable of hiding his widening middle. "I am at your service."

Grinning, Gerard bowed slightly to his greedy acquaintance who took off to the right, while he made his way to the left. He strolled without haste around the fringes of the ballroom, making his way toward the pivotal object of his plan. The journey was slow going, his way blocked by one mother-and-debutante pairing after another. Most bachelor peers similarly hounded would grimace with annoyance, but Gerard was known as much for his overabundance of charm, as he was for his penchant for mischief. So he flirted outrageously, kissed hands freely, and left every female in his wake certain he would be calling on her with a formal offer of marriage.

Casting the occasional glance toward Markham, he noted the exact moment Bartley lured him away, and then crossed the distance with purposeful strides, taking Pel's gloved hand to his lips before the usual throng of avid admirers could encircle her.

As he lifted his head, he caught her eyes laughing at him. "Why, Lord Grayson. A woman cannot help but be flattered by such a single-minded approach."

"Lovely Isabel, your beauty drew me like a moth to a flame." He tucked her hand around his forearm, and led her away for a walk around the dance floor.

"Needed a respite from the ambitious mothers, I assume?" she asked in her throaty voice. "I'm afraid even my association will not be enough to make you less appealing. You are simply too delicious for words. You shall be the death of one of these poor girls."

Gerard breathed a deep sigh of satisfaction, an action which inundated his senses with her lush scent of some exotic flower. They would rub along famously, he knew. He had come to know her well in the years she had been with Markham, and he had always liked her immensely. "I agree. None of these women will do."

Pel gave a delicate shrug of her bare shoulders, her pale skin set off beautifully by her dark blue gown and sapphire necklace. "You are young yet, Grayson. Once you are my age, perhaps you will have settled down enough to not completely torment your bride with your appetites."

"Or I can marry a mature woman, and save myself the effort of altering my habits."

Arching a perfectly shaped brow, she said, "This conversation is leading somewhere, is it not, my lord?"

"I want you, Pel," he said softly. "Desperately. Only an affair will not suffice. Marriage, however, will take care of it nicely."

Soft, husky laughter drifted in the air between them. "Oh, Gray. I do adore your humor, you know. It is hard to find men so deliciously un-abashed in their wickedness."

"And it is lamentably hard to find a creature as blatantly sexual as you, my dear Isabel. I'm afraid you are quite unique, and therefore irreplaceable for my needs."

She shot him a sidelong glance. "I was under the impression you were keeping that actress, the pretty one who cannot remember her lines."

Gerard smiled. "Yes, that's true. All of it." Anne could not act to save her life. Her talents lay in other, more carnal activities.

"And honestly, Gray. You are too young for me. I am six and twenty, you know. And you are . . ." She raked him with a narrowed glance. "Well, you *are* delectable, but—"

"I am two and twenty, and could ride you well, Pel, never doubt it. However, you misunderstand. I have a mistress. Two, in fact, and you have Markham—"

"Yes, and I am not quite finished with him."

"Keep him, I have no objections."

"I'm relieved to have your approval," she said dryly, and then she laughed again, a sound Gray had always enjoyed. "You are quite mad."

"Over you, Pel, definitely. Have been from the first."

"But you've no wish to bed me."

He looked at her with pure male appreciation, taking in the ripe swell of her breasts above the low bodice. "Now, I did not say that. You are a beautiful woman, and I am an amorous man. However, since we are to be bound together, *when* we decide to fall into bed with one another is moot, yes? We shall have a lifetime to make that leap, *if* we decide it would be mutually enjoyable."

"Are you in your cups?" she asked, frowning.

"No, Isabel."

Pel stopped, forcing him to stop with her. She stared up at him, and then shook her head. "If you are serious—"

"There you are!" called a voice behind them.

Gerard bit back a curse at the sound of Markham's voice, but he faced his friend with a careless smile. Isabel's countenance was equally innocent. She truly was flawless.

"I must thank you for keeping the vultures at a distance, Gray," Markham said jovially, his handsome face lit with pleasure at the sight of his paramour. "I was momentarily distracted by something that proved not to be worth my time."

Relinquishing Pel's hand with a flourish, Gerard said, "What are friends for?"

GREAT BOOKS, GREAT SAVINGS!

When You Visit Our Website:
www.kensingtonbooks.com

You Can Save Money Off The Retail Price
Of Any Book You Purchase!

- **All Your Favorite Kensington Authors**
- **New Releases & Timeless Classics**
- **Overnight Shipping Available**
- **eBooks Available For Many Titles**
- **All Major Credit Cards Accepted**

Visit Us Today To Start Saving!
www.kensingtonbooks.com